# FARIEH

## A NOVEL

# BILL SAMPSON

Flint Hills Publishing

For Dru

# Part I
## Summer & Fall

# Lunch with Helen Lochlear

What did you think of the British Summer Institute?"
As direct as ever, Professor Helen Lochlear was asking her strongest student about the month-long program that had brought Farieh Bukhari and other Kansas University undergraduates to England and Scotland in May. Helen had created the BSI. She had led it for several decades, and it had become the premier summer-abroad offering at KU.

"I loved every minute of it," said Farieh as she pressed cheeks with her mentor, "especially Scotland. I had never been there before."

Lunch was at Galvin at Windows, their window table allowing a look across the dark green treetops into Hyde Park. Farieh asked the maître d' for a Chablis as she sat down, then returned to Helen Lochlear, who would leave for Wales with her husband as soon as they had finished. "I know you and Paul are leaving this afternoon; you are so kind to make this time available for me."

"There are few people I would rather see for lunch today, Farieh. What are we going to talk about?"

"First, I want to thank you for the British Summer Institute. All I've said so far is how much I liked Scotland. I did—of course! But the entire month was wonderful. Summer in Edinburgh was like a medieval fair with its stone buildings and walkways and bridges, and the banners and flags at the castle. We could walk home after a late dinner and there was still light in the sky. Leaving it was hard. But the rest of Scotland was just as magical. I had never seen country like the Highlands. And Skye—so *much* to see on such a small island. Where did you ever find that pub?!"

"Years of careful research!" smiled Helen. That was her

"problem" with Farieh, a problem she shared with several of her colleagues. She could not help but smile when she was with this young whirlwind from Iran.

Yet Farieh was as appealing curled up quietly into the corner of the couch in Helen's office, reflecting upon an author or a poem or a kind gesture from a fellow student, as she was flogging her honors seminar through a discussion of Middle Eastern politics, which she had managed to superimpose upon the announced topic of women writers. Had she played cricket or rugby, Cecil Rhodes himself would have chosen her for his scholarship to Oxford, despite her gender.

Helen had had outstanding students before, hundreds of them over the course of her decades of teaching at KU. But she had never had anyone like Farieh. The young woman from Tehran showed intellect, energy, curiosity, decisiveness, and an offhand eloquence—in several languages—as though she were a seasoned runway model showing dresses. And a runway model is what she looked like: 5'9" tall, slender, with thick auburn hair, the carriage of a princess, and the face of a movie icon, all packaged in jeans and boots and a Beak 'em Hawks T-shirt, which was what she had showed up in for lunch! Who could not smile?

"You're welcome, of course," said Helen. "I was glad you could join us. And your fellow students liked you, as well. I don't know what prompted you to balance spoons on your nose at the pub in Skye, but it was the highlight of the evening!

"Still, I can see you have more on your mind than Scotland. What else?"

"Richie Armstrong. I'd like to talk with you about Richie."

"Of course," said Helen, "Richie. How is he? Did he stay in Lawrence with the basketball team?"

Farieh's weak, "I don't know," disappeared into her napkin. Because she had communicated with Richie so infrequently that month, and hardly at all when she did, she knew next to nothing about how the young man who had pursued her so eagerly spring semester was spending his time this summer. "It would be trite to say I have been conflicted about him. I realized as I was walking to join you for lunch that I have spent almost no time thinking about him since I left Kansas. I was eager to leave, and I was eager to accompany you and the others through London and Scotland. Now, I'm eager to see my sister in Oxford and to fly on to Tehran to see my parents. I rarely think of Richie; and when I do think about him he doesn't seem to fit in any of this. Does that make me a bad person?"

"It makes you a young person," replied Helen. "For years your parents and your sisters have been the most important people in your life. You haven't seen your parents for a year; you haven't seen your sister for longer than that. Why shouldn't your attention go to them?

"But you said you have rarely thought about Richie since you left Kansas. That's more than a month. In the context of how often you saw each other last spring, that seems significant. Is it?"

Helen asked about the soup. Lentil did not excite either of them, so they ordered salads. It was Farieh's turn.

"Richie is the most athletic person I have ever known. He is very handsome in that way. And he is kind. I think he would do anything for me. But he is so young! He seemed uncomfortable with the idea of our going out anywhere together—to a movie, for example, or a concert, or even downtown to see a band. So we spent a lot of time walking. I would always have ten things to talk about to his one. And when I had finished talking about something, like the author we were studying or what my sister was doing in England or events in Europe or Iran or China, he often had nothing to say back to me. So, I would have to choose another topic. There were many quiet moments; there were many moments when I felt like his older sister.

"We spent a lot of time together last spring, but it never felt like dating. I have no idea what dating Richie Armstrong would be like. I think he would like a boy-girl relationship. Yet emotionally, and I'm not trying to be harsh here, he comes across as a middle schooler. I see him as much a mascot as a boyfriend.

"I was not looking for a boyfriend last year. But once Richie came along, with the remarkable visibility he enjoyed as a basketball player, nobody else was looking for me, either!

"This coming year, if someone is interested, I'd like to be open to that."

As Farieh reached for the next bite of her salad Helen tried to reconcile "mascot" with the student she had met last spring. On one of their many walks down Jayhawk Boulevard, Farieh had impulsively dragged Richie up the stairs of Wescoe Hall and into the building so she could introduce him. Helen had heard about him from two sources. Farieh had described him as "tall" and "handsome" and "sweet." Captain Miles Breckenridge, the Commander of the Navy ROTC unit at KU and Richie's first-semester honors seminar instructor, had spoken with Helen about him at a faculty meeting after reading his leadership essay. Richie had selected Horatio Nelson as his model; and Breckenridge thought his paper—"Is There A Place For 'The Nelson Touch' In 21st-Century Combat?"—was brilliant. Helen agreed Richie was handsome. He was certainly tall. Observant and articulate as well, he was far more engaging that afternoon than she had anticipated. She had really liked him.

Farieh may have felt like Richie's older sister, but she was young herself. And Helen knew from much experience that young women could move quickly from one attachment to the next. How much they thought about it, how much angst they experienced as they were moving on, was a function not just of the intensity of the relationship but also of the young woman's confidence. If the faculty had been asked to submit a short list of KU's most confident undergraduate women, Farieh would have appeared on everyone's. Her question about being a bad person had seemed obligatory; the "mascot" comment confirmed the relationship had never been a deep one.

Helen picked up her glass of wine and spoke over the top of it. "It seems to me you have made a decision about Richie, Farieh. You sound a bit uncomfortable with that decision, but only a bit. Am I right?"

"Yes," said Farieh. "But shouldn't I feel stronger about it? There must be *hundreds* of KU women who would gladly trade places with me. Am I being unbelievably selfish?"

"I don't think selfishness has anything to do with it. You either have feelings for Richie or you don't. If you don't, and not thinking about him for a month and not talking with him when you had the chance to do so are persuasive that you don't, then your decision to move on makes sense."

Farieh played back Helen Lochlear's last comments. They were what the lunch was about; they were what she had come for. "Dessert?" she asked.

# Freshman Year

The young woman staring out of the Chiltern car as it pulled away from Paddington Station had much to talk with her sister about. It would be no exaggeration to say she had taken KU by storm. Her testing out of her entire undergraduate math degree, and doing so in a bravura, 90-minute, chalkboard recital that left the professors applauding her work, had been a dazzling start to her first semester in Lawrence. Add in her first-in-class performances in her chemistry and engineering courses and that would have been enough for most freshman.

But Farieh's honors seminar had been led by Helen Lochlear, perhaps KU's finest teacher of English Literature and certainly its most popular. Helen had fanned a desire to read and write about fiction that burned hot Farieh's entire first year. That Professor Lochlear knew everyone had allowed Farieh to meet the university's finest teachers and its finest undergraduate students in a string of lectures, art exhibits, receptions, and dinners. Once among them, Farieh's curiosity, her grounding in economics and history and science and the arts, her reservoir of energy, and her green eyes made her the focal point.

A Muslim, Farieh was covered whenever she left her room in Miller Scholarship Hall. Her favorite color was yellow—bright yellow. As she often wore head scarves in that color, a yellow scarf became a kind of calling card. Her teachers and her peers knew her because they spent so much time with her. But Farieh was curious about everything, she was outgoing, and she made friends up and down Jayhawk Boulevard. That she liked contemporary clothing made her all the more approachable, especially among KU's women students. She would show up one day in sneakers, torn jeans, and a KU sweatshirt and the next in Celine boots, a St. John skirt, and a Ralph Lauren jacket. And always the head scarf.

By the start of her second semester, Farieh had attracted the attention of the school's best freshman basketball player, Richie Armstrong. Once Richie started following along after her, even the male students knew Farieh.

Richie was not just a KU basketball player. He was smart—also in the honors program, he was courteous, and he could be sensitive to her and her feelings, as he proved one night in a remarkable dinner at 715. But they were worlds apart in their experience. Richie was an only child from Salina, Kansas. His father had left when he was young, and Richie had been raised by his mom and his grandfather. A gifted athlete and successful in more sports than basketball, he was busy with his teams.

Farieh grew up with two sisters as smart as she was in a household led by two brilliant parents. Her father became a senior officer at the National Bank of Iran and a member of Iran's business elite, and he was no stranger to those who ran the government. Her mother taught in Iran's leading university until the work, and the joy, of having a daughter prompted her to stay home. There was a second daughter, and then a third—Farieh.

Richie traveled frequently during junior high and high school, usually with his grandfather, almost always to sports events—tryouts and games, track meets and camps. He might be in Hays one weekend, in Wichita the next, and in Overland Park the next.

Farieh and her sisters were part of a large extended family with grandparents and aunts and uncles and cousins whom they saw frequently for holidays and birthdays. She and her sisters traveled frequently, too, usually with their parents. As they got to be teens there were trips in the summers to Istanbul and Dubai and Vienna and Paris. In the winter they would go to their mountain house for skiing. Farieh's father's work took him to Great Britain as an economic attaché while Farieh was in middle school, and the entire family accompanied him to London for two years.

Richie spoke English. Farieh spoke Farsi at home and in school, English with her friends, and French when she traveled abroad with her family. She could read and write in all three languages, she spoke English with barely an accent, and she spoke French as though raised on the Left Bank.

Richie was well prepared for KU when he graduated from high school. At the same age, Farieh and her sisters were ready for graduate school. Where an American residence might have flat-screen TVs, Farieh's home in Tehran had chalk boards. Growing up with affectionate but demanding parents and relishing their sibling rivalry, Farieh and her sisters made huge strides in STEM. Farieh had chosen the University of Kansas for petroleum engineering. She would have been admitted at Texas or LSU or anywhere else. But she felt the culture in Lawrence would be more welcoming to a woman student from Iran.

As her train approached Oxford Station, Farieh finished her tally of the pros and cons of her freshman year. She had been welcomed by the faculty, and by the honors program in particular. She had experienced no difficulty with her choice of teachers, her choice of friends, what she wore—including her head scarf, and what she ate—an odd combination of favorite foods from Iran, fruit, and French fries. Beyond that, she liked the campus, which for her was compact and pretty. Nunemaker, the home of the honors program at the west edge of the main campus, and Gray-Little, just down the hill to the east, had been her longest walks; but even Nunemaker was barely 12 minutes. Most of the time she was back and forth to Wescoe, where Helen Lochlear's office was located and where Helen taught all but her honors seminar. Wescoe was not even five minutes away from her scholarship hall. Downtown Lawrence was ten minutes the other direction, its main street a visual throwback to the 19th century, its merchants as friendly as the KU faculty. Her dinner with Richie at 715 came into focus as she thought about the downtown's old buildings. That night, Richie *had* talked. And when Farieh walked out onto the sidewalk that evening, she felt she had been attended to affectionately by him and by the entire restaurant.

*Yes,* she thought to herself, *Kansas has been a good choice.*

Richie Armstrong brushed past her consciousness as she stepped down onto the platform. She had become fond of him by the end of their spring semester. But she had left Lawrence for England and Scotland without any sense of longing for him. Once the British Summer Institute took off she had thought of him hardly at all. Her times with Professor Lochlear in Lawrence had always clarified school things for Farieh. Today's lunch had clarified her and Richie.

Zahra was also on the platform—100 feet away at the station end. When Farieh saw her sister, she shouted her name and ran to meet her.

# Oxford

You know about the protests?"

The sentence was not so much a question as her older sister's checking in with her, making sure she had kept up with events in Iran during her first year of school in the United States.

"Yes," Farieh replied, returning her tea cup to the table far too casually for her older sister. Farieh was just as casual as she wiped her lips with the boldly-patterned napkin from Rajasthan. They were not in India but at her sister's favorite Oxford cafe, Vaults & Gardens—inside, looking out on a weather-perfect English summer morning.

"*What* do you know, Farieh joon?" Her sister used the affectionate form because she loved Farieh. Still, Zahra was skeptical her younger sister had paid much attention to the events that were rocking their homeland and had triggered social media eruptions in Tehran and Mashhad. Farieh had made no mention of it in the several days since she had trained up from London, and Zahra felt the whiff of skepticism might prompt a conversation about the protests. She was wrong. Farieh placed the napkin on the table, pushed back her chair, and left for the loo. When she returned, she directed the conversation to print summer dresses— she wanted one—not to protests, and they left the café soon after.

Their shopping completed and Farieh excited about her new frock, Zahra decided to try again. The weather had held, so Zahra booked the rooftop restaurant at the Ashmolean. As her friend Jennifer was working the phone that afternoon she had secured a table at roof's edge. Their view across the top of the museum took in low stone buildings and high gables, with chimneys poking up into a sky trading the tinge of the afternoon robin's egg for the more serious blues of the oncoming evening. A very cold champagne was opening up as Zahra opened the conversation. "I want to go back to the protests, Farieh. At lunch, you said you were aware of them. Are you? Did you know *Sara* was arrested?" Sara was Zahra's best friend at the University of Tehran, where Zahra had studied mathematics before enrolling at Oxford for graduate school. "She was returned to her parents that same night; but she was shaken by the experience, and humiliated by the way the Security Police treated her.

"That must have been terrible," said Farieh evenly as she reached for her champagne.

"It *was* terrible!" That Zahra had again failed to draw a reaction from her sister was incidental; her own emotions would sustain several conversations. "Sara and I managed a single telephone call about it, and Sara was a mess. Her humiliation was nothing compared with her anger: at the authorities for cracking down so hard, at the Security Police policy for their rough handling of her at the time of her arrest and the strip search by matrons at the station, and at her parents—who could not understand why she was parading down Valiasr Avenue with dozens of uncovered young women to begin with!

"Did *nothing* like this happen to you at Kansas? It is all I can do to cross the street here before I encounter some band or other that wants to grind a name off a building or admit every refugee from Europe or go to Moscow and personally arrest Vladimir Putin!"

Intending to say something lighthearted but entirely forgetting her audience, Farieh responded. "We have basketball at Kansas, Zahra. If there is a protest in the spring in Lawrence it has to do with the team's seeding in the NCAA Tournament!" Zahra's expression, which had changed from impassioned to opaque, told Farieh her attempt at humor had failed. "I apologize, sister. That was a poor joke.

"No. I have not encountered anything like this. My school

year was wonderful, and my month with the British Summer Institute before I came here was a joy. But your concern for what is happening at home, and for Sara, has my attention. And I agree we should talk about it."

They did. The three hours of dinner were not nearly enough so they bent the 30 minutes for the walk home to the same purpose, as well as the several hours that followed their return to Zahra's apartment. When Farieh went to bed in the early hours of the next morning she was too tired to feel different. But she was far better informed. And her sensitivities to the summer's rapidly-moving political currents, at least those in Oxford and in Iran, were now on alert.

They had another day and a half before Farieh had to leave for Heathrow and then home to her parents. They spent the full day, the next day, on bicycles—Zahra's idea. Farieh's older sister had become an Anglophile during her time in Oxford, and it was obvious her sister felt she could coax Farieh in that direction as well. Why she chose an unstable conveyance that went either too slow (uphill) or too fast (down) was a mystery. But their route was in the countryside outside the City of Dreaming Spires, and that helped. It was a "loop" actually, the Swinford Toll Bridge—Christ Church Memorial Gardens Loop, and its first leg took them out of the city to the bridge. Farieh had read several of the Ken Follett novels of medieval England and she immediately recognized the large stones of the bridge's foundation piers. Smaller stones were laid up into the Georgian arches that supported the roadbed. Like its earlier-built brothers and sisters all over the kingdom, Swinford Bridge replaced an inadequate ferry—in its case, one dating to 1299. John Wesley nearly died there in 1764 when his horse slipped on the causeway; the bridge was completed five years later. It was now a quaint stretch of the commute to Oxford whose toll booth frustrated the trucks and cars and motorcycles who crossed it. But the sisters didn't mind; their bicycles crossed for free, and they were not late for work.

There was little conversation on their route. Both wore helmets and they mostly rode single file. But it was luxurious exercise, and there was certainly time for thinking. It would be too strong to say Farieh's conversation with her sister about the political situation in Iran had made her apprehensive about her visit to her parents, now only days away. But that next stop in her summer travels had taken on a different shade at least. Not dark; certainly not dark. "Hazy" was a better term. Farieh was excited to see her parents. There was still bright light in the background. She would ask her sister about them when they got back to Zahra's place.

As the pedaling became more familiar Farieh came to like the time out of doors and the quirky place names like Elsfield kicker. They finished back in the city, leaned their yellow bikes against the High Street wall of Brasenose College, and walked to Zahra's apartment to clean up for dinner.

"What do Mom and Dad say about the protests?" It was Farieh who spoke into the brief silence created by the departure of their server at The Folly. They were outside again, this time on a terrace overlooking the river, and their wine had not arrived. Erin, their server, had just gone after it.

"What a difference a day makes!" remarked Zahra. "Yesterday I could barely find a pulse in you for the protests; today, it's the first topic out of the box."

"I know," said her sister in a gentle laugh. "You brought me a long way last night."

"They prefer to say nothing about it," said her sister, picking up the menu. "That's how I read them." Zahra had been home at the beginning of June while Farieh was in Scotland, and she had just returned from Tehran. "Mom clucks, Dad clears his throat, then one of them either tries to change the subject or, that failing, shares whatever regime-favoring comment was last started around by one of their friends.

"We spent no time on it when I first got there. I was tired from the flight the first evening, I slept in the next morning, and Mom had her sisters and our cousins over that next afternoon and evening—hardly the forum for gender politics. But the protests were all over the news and the media, and they were impossible to ignore, at least for me. So I brought it up the second day, first to Mom over breakfast. She professed to be surprised by my choice of topic and just stared at me for a few seconds. Then she said something like, 'I don't know what to make of these women. So much privilege, and to respond to it like this!'

"To hear our mother even *say* the word 'privilege' struck me as comical. For her to use it to condemn young women my age who, as the protests continued, were being arrested and *detained*, then released with real warnings—that was too much for me. But when I responded and tried to make those points Mom stopped listening. She muttered 'disrespectful' and 'dangerous,' then got up from the table in the middle of my sentence to heat more water for the tea. It may have been the first rude gesture I ever saw her make—to anyone."

"Wow!" Farieh's response was quick and sharp but muted, too, and barely audible over the river. "What about Dad?"

"He was so serious. I had to work at it to keep from laughing sometimes," responded Zahra. "But he doesn't get it any more than Mom does. He spoke of the women in the protests as though they were children at some kind of picnic, walking on egg shells, obliged to be careful not to break them. The Security Police use *riot gear* and *clubs*! And the crowds are really *angry*. These young women are a hair's breadth from physical violence and they go out every day anyway. My *God* they are brave!"

Farieh had been with her sister for days now, and it only just occurred to her that Zahra was not wearing a head scarf. That was no surprise to Farieh; Zahra had not worn a head scarf when she had visited her last summer, either. But it prompted a question. "Did you wear a head scarf in Tehran?"

Zahra had been looking at Farieh across the small table. She looked past her now, over the railing to the water moving slowly beneath them. A moment later she turned back. "Yes. I am embarrassed to say so, but yes. I was at our home so much of the time it wasn't an issue. The few times we went out I was always with Mom and Dad; and I knew it would kill them for me to be uncovered, especially when we met their friends, which we did all the time. I rationalized my visit was for me to see them, not throw myself into Iranian politics. I—I chickened out."

Farieh responded immediately, in real sympathy and to boost her sister's spirits: "I would have done the same thing, sister."

Erin was back. They ordered, then spent the rest of the evening searching for happier topics, hoping the difficult feelings—Zahra's first-hand and Farieh's vicarious—would be eased by the trout and the Montrachet and the soft sounds of the water. But they weren't. They passed on the port, walked back to Zahra's apartment, and went to bed.

But they were kids again their last morning. Croissants and pain au chocolat from the patisserie around the corner leavened their conversation, the flaky remnants of the pastries strewn like dropped commas across the small kitchen table and the counters as well. Café au lait, with the milk poured directly from the sauce pan, alternately burned their lips or cooled in Zahra's bright mugs. And the crepes—Zahra's specialty—were attacked before they left the griddle. Their laughter, chased away by their brooding over events outside the apartment, had found its way back inside and the sisters had welcomed it, falling out of their chairs at one point only to spy familiar weapons and finish with a full-on pillow fight.

It was Zahra who noticed the time and shooed Farieh to her room to shower and pack. And then the Uber came. And then they were hugging on the stoop as though Farieh were flying not to Tehran but to Venus. Farieh watched her sister through the back window of the car as it pulled away from the curb, willing herself not to blink. But she failed. And in the moment lost her sister disappeared into the warren of red brick buildings.

# Mehri
## Leaving Heathrow

Emirates called the flight at precisely 8:55 p.m. Farieh was glad for the window seat in business class even though she did not expect to be awake long after dinner. She could at least look at the sprawl of Heathrow on takeoff, at a once-bucolic countryside that had surrendered to the developers, and at the green of Tehran when they arrived the next morning. She stowed her bag and her purse, sat at the edge of her seat, flipped open the lid beneath the window and tested the meal tray to be sure it worked smoothly, then adjusted her pillow. Next, she took off her sneakers and replaced them with the slippers she had removed from the drawstring pouch on the console. She would get the eye mask and loungewear later. Then she pulled out her phone and scrolled through the messages she had received while napping in the lounge. She was conscious of none of these things. Her thoughts had raced to Iran before she had left the jet bridge to step onto the giant aircraft, and she was still there when the steward appeared and asked whether she would like anything to drink before the cabin was secured for departure. She wasn't thirsty; she asked for water anyway.

Fastening her seat belt forced her back to the reality of getting an A380 into the air, which had always struck Farieh like getting an ocean liner away from the dock—methodical, deliberate, ponderous. The great bird whose winglets moved up and down so much it might have been flapping was at last airborne; and as the plane reached and leveled at 35,000 feet Farieh's thoughts again reached away toward Iran, and to her friend now only seven hours away.

Though Farieh and her two sisters had fought like Amazons growing up, she loved them. But Mehri had been her best friend from as early as she could remember. They had lived in the same apartment building, one floor removed. They wore the same clothes, they rode the same bikes, they liked the same music and the same food. They had spent their first week getting to know each other. They spent the next month completing one another's sentences, giggling endlessly as they did so.

"Wait! Wait! Wait!"

That's how they started. Farieh had reached the ground floor of their apartment building and was just walking out the door to go to the park when Mehri, who had come down a different elevator, yelled after her. Farieh turned around and saw a girl her age running toward her. They were the same height and were dressed the same. But Mehri's curly hair was piling out from beneath her hijab and her energy, which would astound Farieh from then on, spilled out as well, filling the entryway. Mehri rushed up to Farieh and barely stopped before pushing her right through the opening to the outside.

"I'm Mehri!" She said it like she had spotted a fire in the lobby. "We live on 19. I don't have any brothers or sisters. I like to go to the park, and to the fruit sellers, and to the bread bakers. I like peaches the best, but plums are okay. I'm six. I'll be in first grade next fall. Who are you?!"

Farieh did not know what to say but she knew not to share her thought: *Is this what children who grow up without siblings are like?!* After that, she knew if she did not say something Mehri would loose another avalanche of words. "I'm Farieh," she said. "We live on 20." Then, since Mehri had brought up her family, she added: "I have two sisters, both of them older." Just saying those words reminded Farieh that her sisters *were* older, and had their own friends, and that she really had no one of her own outside the many-branched structure of her family. Aunts and uncles, and a grandmother—her "Mamani," and cousins galore. But nobody just for her.

The face framed by all the curly hair was excited. But it was also hopeful—so hopeful Farieh could feel it. When Farieh added, "I like peaches the best too," the tension in the new girl's face went away. In its place was a different look. There was a smile, and a warmth Farieh knew from her grandmother. Farieh had never seen a smile like that in someone her own age.

And then Mehri was excited again. "Let's get some!" she said, grabbing Farieh by the arm and pulling her through the doorway into a perfect summer day. Both knew the way to the fruit seller. Both had gone there alone before. "Don't worry, Mamanjan," Farieh's mother would say to her own mother, "you will be able to watch her the whole way from our window." Farieh and Mehri would wear out that route over the next six years, talking past every milepost, the destination as bright before them as the star of their friendship.

# The Fruit Seller

A peach, please," said Mehri.

"A peach, please," said Farieh as if to be agreeable, although she really wanted one. They were big—yellow and red on the outside and the most marvelous orange on the inside. And they tasted like candy, like honey had been drizzled over the top of the pulp. The girls went there every day for a week. They had just enough money to buy one each and enough time to carry them reverently out of the shop to the nearby park, where they would see who could wait the longest to bite into her prize. Mehri could never wait; Farieh always won.

There were parks all over Tehran. The one across the street from the fruit seller was full of flowers and exercise equipment. Mehri and Farieh never used the exercise equipment. They were six; it never occurred to them. But they loved the flowers, which were carefully tended and replaced regularly and, for holidays, arranged so the blossoms became images of famous people. Mehri and Farieh did not recognize the politicians and the clerics. But frequently a popular actor or a musician would emerge out of the sweep of colors to surprise and delight them.

On the first day of the second week, they had a serious conversation about whether to return to the fruit seller. The problem was the peaches. "They're perfect," said Mehri. "They're always perfect. No bruises, no cuts, just yellow and red on the outside and candy on the inside."

"What's wrong with perfect?" Farieh was truly puzzled. It wasn't like the older boys in her family, her cousins, who just thought they were perfect and were intolerable because of it. Farieh loved their walks to the fruit seller, and she loved the perfect peaches. For Farieh, the perfection made them dependable. She could count on them. She had been disappointed by only a few things in her young life. But she thought she knew what disappointment was, and she was glad not to worry about adding peaches to the list.

But Mehri would not be deterred. "They're boring," she continued. "We'll go to the bread baker's this week." And so, they did.

The fruit seller and the bread baker could have been the same person. Each was middle-aged; each was pleased to see the girls when they came into the shop, usually mid-morning; each was a good listener; each knew the two young customers had only enough money for one item. But the bread baker was a woman, and that made a difference. For Farieh, going to the bread baker was like visiting her favorite aunt.

They tried the Lavash that first day, but it was too familiar to be interesting. They moved on to Barbari their next visit, a yeast-leavened flatbread thicker than Lavash, furrowed end to end, then topped with sesame and nigella seeds. The glazed crust turns golden brown in the oven and takes on a pretzel-like texture. But the bread is soft and warm beneath the nutty crust. They had had Barbari before, at family meals. But having an entire piece for themselves was luxurious. On very special days the bread baker would give them small paper cups filled with jam or feta to spread on the Barbari. To Farieh's surprise, Mehri would survey the pieces in the case like she was picking out a new birthday dress before settling for the one that was the most "perfectly" golden-brown!

There was not much summer left when Farieh met Mehri. Farieh was shopping for school clothes with her mother when she realized it was over. As it became clear to Farieh's mother and sisters that Farieh had an important new friend, her mother would ask about Mehri frequently, always in a tone signaling both her approval and her sincere interest in knowing about the curly-headed girl from the 19th floor. Farieh's sisters would listen to the conversations initiated by their mother, but they never had questions of their own. The second time that happened, and as her two older sisters left the kitchen and went off on their own without saying anything, Farieh thought to herself, *I like peaches the best too.*

# School

A friend can be impetuous. She can be restless and hard to engage in a conversation. She can get excited and be hard to hold in a conversation. She can also be moody, or self-absorbed, or scattered as she thinks about too many things at one time. But Iranian parents have no need to obsess over their school children's safety like their counterparts in the United States. Grade-schoolers in Tehran walk themselves to school all the time. And when you walk with your friend to school, walk home with her for lunch, return with her for school's afternoon session, and walk her home at the end of the school day, all of the things that might interfere with a friendship tend to sort themselves out. Farieh and Mehri had limitless time to talk, and none of their idiosyncrasies was weird enough to get in the way for long.

There was a competition in first grade to see which student could read the most books. Farieh won; Mehri placed second.

In third grade the competition was in arithmetic. Despite the enormous head start provided Farieh by her parents, Mehri won. Farieh placed second.

Along the way both sets of parents discovered they had gained another daughter. The girls had been first to propose the families meet. These early meetings were traditional: tea, a table of snacks, a bordered conversation about the girls and their school and about Farieh's sisters and about themselves. The parents liked each other well enough, but they never became close friends and the meetings fell off. For the two girls, though, there were other meetings. Farieh's family, in particular, was large and it met regularly in mehmooni, casual, drop-in gatherings to which Farieh soon enough invited Mehri. A mehmooni involved hours of eating and talking as well as music and dancing. Occasionally numbering 100 and stuffing the apartment of the elder who was hosting, the mehmooni of Farieh's family could go into the late evening.

If there was a sure-fire conversation starter for the next week's walks to school and back it was the previous weekend's mehmooni. "Could you believe Aunt Noora?!" Farieh would say. "Who knew she had a dozen boyfriends before she met Azad?!"

"I know!" answered Mehri. "Do you suppose *he* knows?"

"I can't even imagine," Farieh would reply. "He is so easy-going, and he dotes on her."

"And what about your *sister*?!"

"What *about* my sister?!" challenged Farieh.

"Oops!" Mehri was already giggling. "Probably wasn't supposed to mention that. Sorry!"

"Not mention *what*, Mehri?! This isn't fair. You've *got* to tell me!"

"There isn't anything. Really. But you are *such* an easy target for gossip about your sisters it's hard not to tease you about them!"

When they ran out of tales from the mehmooni, real and make-believe, they would move to music, or celebrities, or TV. When even these vast sources ran dry they would walk into a park and sit down on a bench and watch. They watched the trees and the shrubs and the flowers. They watched the birds and listened to them. Mehri was sure she saw a hedgehog one morning. Unable to contain her excitement, she jumped down from their bench and started hopping until Farieh assured her it was a squirrel. But they would also watch the people.

There were rarely young people in the parks during the time Mehri and Farieh were there. The regulars were middle-aged or older, often men, often walking with a cane or walking slowly without one. What Mehri and Farieh watched for, for they were young girls, were quirks. Did the man wear a funny hat? Did he continually push his hair away from his forehead? Did he seem to be talking to himself? If so, Mehri would imagine the monologue as a series of questions, Farieh would make up the answers, and they would laugh until their sides hurt.

Were his clothes too heavy? What colors did he wear, if he wore anything but grays and browns, and why? Did he have a girlfriend? A dog? Which had more hair? More laughter!

Where were his shoes made? Berlin? London? Madrid? If he carried a newspaper or a book they would guess which bench he would sit on to read it. Though the options seemed endless they could still get bored. And when they got bored they would try the swings, or the monkey bars. And when they had lost all interest in the park they were ready to talk again.

A brisk pace would get them home from school in 10 minutes. They never arrived that soon, and their mothers never gave a thought to their being late. Supper was served three hours after school was out. They were always home in time to help with it, and that was soon enough.

# Trouble

The moment that introduced everyone to the young woman Mehri was becoming came in sixth grade. Mehri had observed her math teacher spending increasing time with one of the students, the one who had the most expensive calculator, and she became wary. At the beginning, Mehri would simply raise her hand and ask the teacher to help her and the girls around her. But the teacher was always too busy to stay. He would return to his desk, spend a minute or two looking out over the entire class, then sneak open the book to his left, which Mehri knew was a popular novel, and lose himself in it.

The first math test came in October, six weeks into the school year. Mehri, who had been ready for this level of mathematics years ago, was not concerned about the test. But she and Farieh, who was as little concerned as Mehri, had classmates who were stressed that morning. Doing well in math was important.

What got Mehri's attention at the outset was the teacher's standing over the girl, whom she now knew was the teacher's niece, and talking quietly with her as the others took the exam in silence. That was disturbing enough. When the girl got up and followed the teacher to the teacher's desk and took a seat next to it, Mehri put her pencil down and watched every movement.

The girl was clearly looking for answers to the problems; the teacher, alternately pointing to the test paper and speaking quietly to his niece, was as clearly giving them.

Mehri stood up and walked to the teacher. Before he had even raised his head at the interruption, she was speaking to him in a stage voice loud enough to be heard at the back of the classroom. "You can't do that," she declared. "That's cheating!"

The teacher may have been casual about Mehri's approach, but his reaction to what she said was assured. He stood up and gestured to his niece to return to her desk. Cowering, the girl did so. Then the teacher addressed the class, directing everyone to stop work on the test and pass their test papers forward. All but Mehri complied; Mehri was still standing across the desk from him.

It was when he came around the desk and took Mehri by the elbow and headed toward the door of the classroom that Farieh blew out of her seat and rushed to the door and threw her arms across the opening, blocking the exit. Though Farieh was very tall for a sixth grader and stood nearly eye-to-eye with the teacher, her anger obscured her proximity. "You can't DO that!" she shouted. "You WERE cheating! EVERYONE saw you!"

Using his other hand for Farieh, the teacher forced both girls out of the classroom and into the hallway. The principal's office was not far.

This was the only day in six years the girls made it home from school in 10 minutes. They had been suspended *for two weeks*! They said nothing the entire distance. They took the same elevator, Mehri getting off the floor ahead of Farieh. They were now so angry they were shaking.

When Mehri stormed through the door of the apartment her mother looked at her only child as she might have looked at a ghost. But the ghost was upset, and she needed to vent the fury that had been building, and she took at least another 10 minutes to do so. When she had finished talking and screaming and crying and jumping up out of the kitchen chair and sitting back down again for the last time, Mehri looked like the solitary warrior in James Fraser's *The End of the Trail*.

It is a rare parent of a sixth grader who has just been suspended from school who can push back the urge to find out how the child might have precipitated the event and just listen to the child. Mehri loved her mother, but her mother was not one of those exceptional parents. For Mehri, the resulting exchange felt much more like cross-examination than solace and she soon ran from the kitchen to her room.

Farieh's experience was different. Farieh's mother was not only rare but exceptional. When Farieh had finished her own ranting and the sobbing that broke it into loud, jagged parts, her mother slid her chair next to Farieh's and put her arms around her daughter and said nothing. They sat like that for a long time. Finally, Farieh dried her eyes on her mother's apron, stood slowly, said, "I love you," and walked to her room.

Farieh's father was exceptional, as well. He heard of the suspension from his wife, not from his youngest daughter. She had called him at work. He spoke about it with Farieh that evening, but only to say in a whisper as he held his sobbing daughter in his arms, "I am so sorry, little one. Cry as much as you wish, but know this will be all right."

Farieh's father had worked for Bank Melli, the National Bank of Iran, since graduating from Tehran University. He had many traits that were valuable to the bank. He was personable and a good listener and easy to work with; he was always on-time, usually a bit early; he completed assignments when they were due and would regularly ask for extra work. That he was just over six feet tall and handsome, as well as outgoing, made him popular. When the bank recognized he was also supremely well-read and could carry on a conversation with every level of supervision and every level of society and could speak English like an Englishman, he was identified as someone to watch. What moved him from the watch list into international banking, the bank's most important unit, was his mind. He completed the most complex assignments straightaway, delivering summaries that were easy to read and analyses that often went beyond what the senior bankers had been thinking when they made the assignments. And so he was promoted—to Executive Vice President of International Banking. His promotion meant his daughters would attend a private school, but not until next year. He would say nothing about it until the time came next summer.

There were many levels of approval for so senior a position in Iran's largest bank. Because the financing obligations for his unit extended past Iran's borders, especially to Iran's political allies and to her proxies like Hezbollah, and because he was now one of the bankers most responsible for these obligations, the critical level of approval was Iran's Revolutionary Guard Corps, commonly known as the IRGC or "the Guard." Farieh's father knew about this vetting like a member of Skull and Bones would know about his initiation into Yale's oldest secret society. He never spoke about it in public. But he knew who he was, and he knew where his support lay.

Farieh's father made inquiries first. Discretely, he asked about the principal at his daughter's school; he asked about her teacher; he asked about the teacher's niece. When he had the information he called the principal and arranged to meet him at his office at the bank. Farieh and Mehri had been suspended on a Monday; the meeting took place on Wednesday at 2:00 p.m. Neither Farieh's mother nor Farieh, nor Mehri nor Mehri's parents, ever knew it had happened or that Farieh's father had been a part of it.

Farieh's father arrived at the bank that morning looking like he always looked when working: an understated single-breasted suit, this time charcoal, black tie shoes, a patterned tie, and a white shirt. To the very careful observer, bespoke clothing top to bottom. The principal was escorted to the 14th floor, where International Banking had its spaces. They met in the lobby. Farieh's father introduced himself—Farzan Bukhari, then walked him to his office with a minimum of chitchat. Farzan closed the door and invited his guest to sit with him at the low table and offered him tea, which the principal accepted. Farzan poured but had none for himself.

"I have only a few questions," said the father to begin the conversation. "Is the teacher's niece a student in his class?"

"Yes," said the principal. His answer was as smooth as he could make it given the precision of the question and the immensity of the office, which was as big as one of his classrooms. Tall windows allowed the principal to look out across the northern residences of Tehran to the Alborz Mountains. "That is quite common in our public schools."

"I understand the teacher spends a great deal of class time with the niece, to the exclusion of the other students. Do you know anything about that?"

The principal's reply was again unruffled. "Our teachers are given considerable leeway in their classrooms so they can provide attention to the students who need it the most."

Farzan was almost finished. "There was a test given just before the two girls were suspended . . ."

The host had barely begun his question when the principal sat up straighter and spoke into the middle of it, his voice louder this time and fraying at the edges. "Yes!" He took a hurried breath. "The first student interrupted the test and, unfortunately, was most disrespectful in doing so. When the teacher attempted to exert control over the outburst the second student rushed forward as though to assault him! Like the first girl, the second girl was screaming at the teacher. The teacher had no choice but to stop the test—a great inconvenience to the rest of the class—and escort the girls to my office and report the incident. It cannot surprise anyone they were suspended. But the school recognized the girls had excellent records until that unfortunate moment. We treated the girls respectfully, and their suspension was far less severe than it might have been." He took another breath. "Do you have any other questions?"

Farzan did. Having dismissed the principal as a toad, Farzan found it easy to sit through his self-righteous precis of the events. "It has been reported that the teacher actually stood next to his niece during the opening minutes of the test, talking with her, then invited her to the front of the classroom so they could sit side-by-side. Do you know anything about that?"

The principal sputtered for several moment before replying,

"Absolutely not! I interviewed the teacher myself; there was no report of that."

Farieh and her mother had ultimately spoken at length about Farieh's confrontation with the teacher, and her mother had asked whether she reported all she saw and said and did to the principal. "Yes!" she had insisted. "He kept cutting me off and telling us we were being disrespectful, but I went on anyway. He had to know the entire story. But when I said I told the teacher 'You WERE cheating!' and when I said I blocked the door, he threw his hands up and shouted 'Enough!' and called for help. Two assistant principals, both women, came and forced our arms behind us and pushed us out of his office."

Farzan was proud of Farieh. She had handled an awkward situation promptly and directly and with admirable regard for her less-advantaged classmates. In confronting the teacher she had held up well. But when the principal had dismissed her and Mehri into the custody of the assistants, who were large, sullen women, she had been humiliated. And when the assistants frog marched the two girls into an empty classroom both Mehri and Farieh had started to cry.

Farzan cleared his throat and looked across at the principal. "It is also reported that the teacher and the student spoke to one another as they sat together at the teacher's desk. The student would ask a question and gesture to the test paper; the teacher would point at the test paper and give an answer. Do you know anything about that?"

The principal reacted suddenly and loudly. "That is an outrageous suggestion, Mr. Bukhari! This school prides itself on the character of its faculty and its students. We have no room for dishonesty, and none for innuendo." He jumped up. "With respect, sir, our meeting is at an end!"

Farzan stood up carefully so he would not spill the principal's tea, which was barely 18 inches across the table. Once upright, he did not extend his hand or make any other gesture toward his guest. He only moved to the office door and opened it, then looked straight ahead as the principal rushed past him.

"What an arrogant ass!"

The principal had returned to his office at the girls' school and was sitting with the math teacher. The office door was closed, yet he was speaking in the low tones he might have used in the theatre.

"How did you leave it with him?" The question came from the teacher, who was the principal's younger brother.

"There was nothing to leave!" He answered immediately, his voice more animated. "This jumped-up banker with the fancy tie wasn't asking my opinion about anything. This was just meddling. But I showed him. I made it clear there was no cheating in this school and that was the end of it. I told him off and got up and left."

"Will that be the end of it?"

"Yes," said the principal. "We will have to be more circumspect with our niece," he went on, returning to the low tones with which he had started, "but that will be the end of it."

"Good," said the teacher. "Thank you, my brother."

"You're welcome, of course. Have some more tea."

The telephone calls came to the girls' mothers on Thursday morning. Mehri and Farieh were at the bread baker's. When they came home they were told the suspension had been withdrawn and the school would welcome them back. As the next day was Friday and school was closed, they waited until Monday.

It was a jubilant return. The girls had barely stepped onto the playground before they were mobbed by their classmates and by students from the other grades, as well. The well-wishing that continued in the hallways throughout the morning made them late for math. But when they entered the classroom, they were met not by their teacher but by someone new, a woman just graduated from university, young and excited to be there. Also missing was the teacher's niece.

Mehri and Farieh took their seats across the aisle from one another. "Wow!" said Mehri in the voice she used to avoid attention. "THIS is different. What about the principal?"

Farieh did not know. Leila did, and she leaned forward from behind Mehri and spoke in a whisper. "A car came yesterday at noon. Two young men got out—they were dreamy!—and came into the school and watched him pack his things. Then they escorted him to his own car and followed him as he drove out of the parking lot."

It was Farieh's turn. "What about the two assistant principals—the two women?"

"Gone, too," said Leila. "Nobody saw them leave. But their offices were dark yesterday afternoon right after the principal left, and they are dark again today."

# Moving

It was early June. Farieh and Mehri stood in the park at the base of the laurel. They were sobbing at first, then they were catching breaths, then whimpering, then sobbing again, pausing occasionally to wipe their eyes on their sleeves. Always they were touching, hugging or holding hands, looking at each other or unable to do so. Mehri had called that morning to say they had to talk. Knowing something was wrong, Farieh proposed they meet in the lobby of their apartment building and go to the park, the one only a block away. They had been outside in the park ever since, never moving from the tree.

It was an hour before Mehri even named the city that would be her new home. Her father had been promoted; he was beaming at breakfast, so pleased with the recognition. They would move to Isfahan, he had told them, "a beautiful city to the south famous for its business, its Persian and Islamic heritage, and its tiled mosques." But it was five hours by car from Tehran, a world away for girls who did not yet drive. And even at their age—they had both turned 12 that summer—they knew Isfahan was different than Tehran. Every city in Iran that was not the capital was different: not as modern, not as liberal, not as safe. Their recognition of that made the gloom settling around them even darker.

They decided to go to the fruit seller. The colors were bright there, more likely to cheer them up than the browns at the bread baker's. But even the ripest peaches and apricots, even the sweet lemons in their electric yellow, even the darkest plums could not pull them out of their depression. Each bought a peach. They were so discouraged they ate them immediately on leaving the shop rather than going to the park first like they always did to see who could wait the longest.

They finished their peaches and carried the pits for blocks before returning to the park nearest their apartment building, circling it several times before entering, dropping the pits in the green bin for compost as they walked by. Then they sat on the nearest bench and stared at the passersby. Even that failed to cheer them.

Mehri stood up first. "We leave for Isfahan in two days. We will come back tomorrow; it will be better then." Farieh stood up beside her friend, took her hand, and walked her into their apartment building, where they took the elevator to 19. Mehri stepped through as the doors opened.

"Goodbye, Mehri," said Farieh, still holding Mehri's hand from inside the car. "I will see you tomorrow, right?"

Unable to say anything in response, Mehri dropped her head to her chest and walked slowly to her family's apartment.

They were so upset the next day they did not even leave the lobby. When they got into the elevator and pushed the button to return to 19, Farieh hugged her friend as tightly as she could. "I will come tomorrow to say a final goodbye," she began. "When do you leave?"

"Don't come," said Mehri, pushing back from her friend but still holding her at arms' length. "If I see you I will never get in the elevator with my parents. But I will come back next summer! And we will still be best friends! And I will love you every day until then."

As the doors opened behind her Mehri leaned in and kissed Farieh on both cheeks. Then she ran out of the elevator and down the hallway, never looking back.

# Mountain Passes

Farieh followed the two-lane road as it climbed out of the maple and the hackberry and the walnut, then stretched for the alpine meadow that lay just beneath the higher ranks of pine and juniper. Rocks of every hue circled a small lake before hiking past the scree of small stones that had fallen from the steeper slopes and had lain there maybe 10 minutes, maybe 10,000 years. Growing larger as they continued past the last of the wildflowers, the rocks finally melded with the muscular slabs of the mountain proper, the great flat irons that lifted Farieh's gaze almost straight up toward a summer sun striving to sear a cool, blue sky. Farieh had driven to the spot from her parents' house in Tehran, now thousands of feet below her. When she had reached it, she pulled her mom's Jaguar F-Type convertible into the parking area, let it roll to a stop, hit the "OFF" button, and levered herself up past the steering wheel so she could slide out over the car door rather than open it. While she rarely drove, her mother had always had convertibles, and Farieh had mastered the exit calisthenics when she was 12. Upright, she removed her head scarf and tossed it to the passenger's seat.

The path around the lake measured 1,000 steps, a comfortable nine minutes or a brisk seven. In no hurry today, she picked up several small stones as she moved closer to the water and threw them across it. But she was standing too upright to skip them, and the stones sank as soon as they cut the surface, just like her mood. *More later*, she thought to herself.

She had last been here nearly a year ago, in the week before she left for Kansas, wanting the solitude of the place so she could work out how she felt about going so far away on her own. She had not been anxious then. Eagerness accompanied her everywhere, invading every conversation, forcing repeated apologies to her parents and her friends alike. Those feelings had been so much easier than the ones she carried now. A year ago she had danced around the lake. Today she had trouble even walking. Farieh exhaled and put her left foot forward.

*What happened to Mother?* she asked herself. *How can one of the smartest women in Iran have so completely lost touch with an entire generation of women? We love Iran. But we would love her more if we were allowed even a breath of freedom. How can not wearing a head scarf be worth arrest? Or days in prison? Or worse?!*

She slowed, stopped at the water's edge halfway around the path, and reached down for another small stone. This time she leaned over almost parallel to the ground and the flat stone obliged her effort by jumping once, twice, three times before settling beneath the surface. Smiling despite her mood, Farieh picked up another stone and skipped it out into the center of the pond.

*And what about Father? The tutor of our mathematics and the teacher of our culture? Who insisted we be patient with one another, and look for the merit in every point of view? What happens to the point of view of the protest when the Guard doesn't approve? Can it really become valueless?! The Guard is not even a shill for the regime. The Guard says nothing; it only enforces— arrests and imprisons. What point of view can one find in wrist ties and blindfolds? And in the suppression of newspapers? And in the shutting down of the internet?*

She had reached the place where she had started. Far more tired than her 1,000 steps should require, she found a large rock, sat on it, and stared at a surface that returned the blue to the sky as faithfully as it had received it. The blue looked familiar. Mehri had eyes that blue.

Mehri had moved from Tehran to Isfahan, a commerce center since the time of the Silk Road. But they had stayed in touch through middle school and the beginning of high school even though their daily calls became texts. Both were busy in high school, and soon they were communicating less often, recently only on birthdays and holidays. But Farieh's affection for her friend did not depend on the frequency of their messages; besides, she could keep up with her in other ways. A force of nature among her contemporaries, Mehri was a goad to her teachers and to all other adults. Farieh could read about her in the papers. Mehri made headlines for her scholarship and her leadership and even more often for her challenging whichever school traditions had struck her as foolish. She was no athlete. But she got as much ink for her sit-ins as the star football players did for their goals.

Mehri had visited Farieh in the month before their senior year of high school. They had come here often, circling the lake when they were not sitting with their toes in the water, saying nothing and everything. Farieh's father wanted her to study petroleum engineering; he believed it was the most important area of study for their country's economic future. She would do that. But she wanted more of an education than fluid mechanics and reservoir management. She wanted to go to the United States. She wanted to drink tea and read novels and stay up all night talking about them with her classmates.

As advanced as Farieh in mathematics, Mehri wanted to be an astronomer. They had come here in the cool of that summer's evenings as well. Lying beside the water's edge, the sky untouched by the lights of Tehran, Mehri could name the stars above them and find them again on the surface of the lake. It was Mehri who showed her the ones in its center sparkled brighter than those close to shore.

Mehri had stayed nearly three weeks. They came here again on Mehri's last day but the finality of it was too much for them. Unable to find a subject that would sustain more than a moment's conversation, they managed one circuit of the lake, then drove down the mountain in silence.

The head scarf protests in Tehran had continued and the reactions by the government had seemed to relax. For months now, so many young women went uncovered the local police had nearly stopped the daily harassment. Arrests had become something that "used to happen." But enforcement could still pop up in the capital: a leading e-commerce business was raided after its largely female staff was seen on social media without the hijab.

The cities outside Tehran were different: lax cafes and restaurants were regularly shuttered. In one of these cities a woman caught without a head scarf was sentenced to a month of washing and preparing corpses for burial.

Farieh's drive in from the airport had been a welcome burst of color and chaos, and she had smiled repeatedly at how little attention the motorists paid to trifles such as speed limits. Many of the thousands of motorbikes and scooters were driven by women, their hair blowing loose behind them, some of them even baring tattoos.

Farieh had behaved conservatively. She was rarely out, and when she was she wore a head scarf. She felt the same fealty toward her parents her sister had spoken of in England. But she was also concerned about college. If she were arrested her chances of leaving Tehran on time were poor; and an arrest for any reason might compromise the visa that was critical to her return to the United States. She wore a head scarf; she was safe.

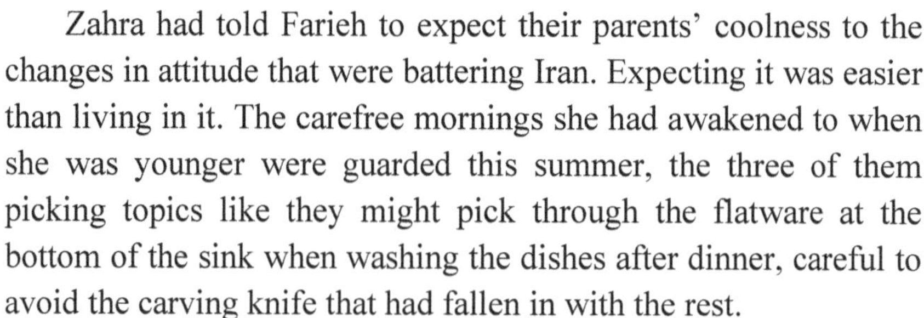

Zahra had told Farieh to expect their parents' coolness to the changes in attitude that were battering Iran. Expecting it was easier than living in it. The carefree mornings she had awakened to when she was younger were guarded this summer, the three of them picking topics like they might pick through the flatware at the bottom of the sink when washing the dishes after dinner, careful to avoid the carving knife that had fallen in with the rest.

On the flight from London, Farieh had thought about Mehri until she fell asleep, and she had thought about her daily since arriving at her parents' home. On the second morning she had sent a chatty text that covered her first year at Kansas and proposed they get together. Farieh would be glad to drive to Isfahan; would Mehri mind her spending the night? Just sending it had been exciting. The trip gave her something to look forward to.

Farieh's parents had been seven in February of 1979 when the Ayatollah Khomeini and his followers overthrew the Shah. Over the next 10 years, as the revolution had settled in and had worked past its early, violent phase, they had lived with their own middle-class parents and gone to public schools. But their intelligence marked them early.

They were admitted to the University of Tehran in the fall of 1989, just after the Ayatollah's death that June. They started college the following year and graduated in 1994. Apolitical, they were the unknowing beneficiaries of President Hashemi Rafsanjani's expansion of higher education, which he saw as a key to Iran's economic development. The number of newspapers and journals trebled over the time they were in school. Unaware of the censorship that underlays their publication, Farieh's parents saw only a growing diversity of thought and expression.

In the early years of their marriage, when their freedom to discover one another was buttressed by the freedoms springing up all around Tehran, they spent the early hours after work walking the markets and the parks and the cultural centers that were growing up like spring flowers after a winter's drought. While they had never been unhappy, not as children in their parents' homes and not as students, they were euphoric then.

There was no gap in their relationship, no hole to be filled. But had there been one, their first child would have filled it. Overwhelmed by it all, Farieh's mother quit her job to stay home with the first person she had known who could make her smile all the time. Two more daughters increased a joy that was already immeasurable.

Farieh's father rotated steadily through the bank's divisions. Work then was challenging but never consuming. He was home in the evening and on weekends. He had time for his family—playing with the girls when they were toddlers, reading to them every night before bed. He would take them on walks. He talked with them about all the things they could see—the trees and the flowers, the birds and the weather—then added things they could not see. He talked about family and about friends, about the young and the old, about the poor and the rich, about the freedom of good health and the restraint of illness. The family did not travel as much when the girls were young. His assignment to England as Iran's financial attaché, for example, would not come until Farieh was a teenager. Until the dramatic financial advance that accompanied his promotion to Executive Vice President, until he was able to take the girls to France and Turkey and Dubai, his stories would have to do. He told magical stories.

Dinner was the most special time. It could take hours, the food leading the way. There was an occasional recipe. More often the dishes were curated from memories shared by careful women who believed the evening meal was critical to the success of their families. Farieh's family was successful, and their dinner-table conversations were the proof of that. Everyone talked, everyone interrupted, everyone laughed. If there was important homework, if there was a friend waiting, even if there was a lecture or a concert, getting up from the table was the hardest part.

Change came with the family's move to London, where Farieh's father took a position critical not only to the bank but also to the government. He was rarely home; he was even more rarely home for dinner. His family understood that. Still, the table was now set for four. When they moved back to Iran her father was just as busy, and just as rarely home at night. Dinner, the family's anchor, had slipped in England, and it would not hold them again.

Like teens everywhere, Farieh made her way through high school spending most of her time with friends. Her father spent an increasing amount of time on the affairs and the financing of the Iran Revolutionary Guards Corps. Hashemi-Rafsanjani had used the period of reconstruction following the Iran-Iraq war to turn the IRGC into an economic powerhouse. Satellite companies sprang up beneath the Guard's umbrella. More significant, the engineering arm of the IRGC expanded into construction, transportation, and the oil and gas sectors. By the time of his return from England, keeping track of the Guards and of the Quds Force, whose budget was classified and directly controlled by the Supreme Leader, had become a full-time assignment.

Perhaps unanticipated by the Ayatollah Khomeini when he seized power in 1979, Iranian society had become nearly as stratified by the time of Farieh's graduation from high school as it had been under the Shah. Iran's economic center was no more democratic than its political base. There were the Guard, the mullahs, and the Supreme Leader.

Her father's business attention to the IRGC inevitably limited his social life. Casual gatherings with neighbors and family were replaced by obligatory gatherings with his clients and their friends. In the early days after their return from England, Farieh's mother attended the neighborhood and family affairs on her own. Yet things changed there too. Cautioned by her husband about disclosing anything meaningful to their neighbors, or to their brothers and sisters, Farieh's mother disclosed less and less. Soon it was uncomfortable for her even to participate in the conversations, for she never had anything to offer.

By the time Farieh and her sisters were the most active in high school, the scope of her parents' social life had centered on the Guard. The Guard were the ultimate insiders, their elitism infectious. The girls were too busy to notice.

Farieh had lived and traveled on her own—to Kansas in the

United States, and to England. She had been gone a year and had returned to Tehran as a young woman. She saw herself as more observant; she thought her parents had changed while she was gone. They had changed years ago.

Farieh skipped one last stone toward the center of the lake and turned toward her mom's convertible. Farieh had driven into the mountains to get away from her parents and to talk with herself; she wanted to explore whether there was any future for her in Iran once she finished school. She had reached no conclusions. She approached the Jaguar, sat on the door, and lifted her legs over it to settle into the driver's seat.

As Farieh took the wheel in her hands she looked across the lake. She thought again of the text she had sent to Mehri several days ago, and how concerned she had become over not hearing from her. There was not enough wind to rouse the smallest leaf, yet the lake surface became so choppy there was soon spray as the white caps broke against the rocks on the shore. Farieh wondered whether she was dreaming this change in her perception; Mehri's appearance between the lake and her mother's car confirmed it.

Mehri was standing in a stone courtyard, smiling—laughing really, surrounded by older women in chadors. Their faces were lined from years of work, but they were pleasant in their expressions. Mehri had been wearing a head scarf. When she stopped laughing she reached up and ripped it off and stood bare-headed in front of the women, staring back at them. One by one the older faces disappeared from within the hoods of the chadors—quickly, as though thumbed off a cell phone display. Charcoal images replaced the real ones, looking out from where the real faces had been. The new images reminded Farieh of the Aurors in the Harry Potter novels. These images were rounder, and they were less forbidding, but only slightly.

# Kaveh

Mehri was past tired. She had not slept last night, and it was 2:30 in the morning as she moved along the exterior wall of the abandoned apartment building in the industrial city of Kaveh, clinging to concrete blocks still damp from yesterday's shower. She had fled to Kaveh from Isfahan after being accosted by street thugs on the second day of the protest she had led against the regime's treatment of women. Mehri had participated in other "head scarf protests," and she had praised the day when the government had grown tired of confronting so many young women and had relaxed their patrols. But the conservatives had regained the whip hand, especially in the cities and towns outside Tehran, and Mehri felt it was now her turn to rally the women of her city. She and her friends had been exultant that first evening. They had gathered in their favorite restaurant, laughing and crying and singing, proud to have taken a stand against the mullahs who had so completely lost contact with the youth of the country. Mehri had been the first to remove her head scarf that afternoon, waiting until she had reached the center of Naqsh-e Jahan Square; and she was the first to be photographed without it.

When she returned to Naqsh-e Jahan Square the next afternoon, driving most of the way with Layla and Shirin in Layla's Toyota, she wore no head scarf. She had left it in her apartment; she would no longer be seen wearing it. They parked the Camry maybe a half mile from the UNESCO World Heritage Site that dominated the center of the city and walked the rest of the way. Her bold visage preceded her into the square and lasted perhaps a minute, until she was spat on by several women in traditional dress who had walked up to her to do so. Mehri was staggered less by their saliva than by the hatred that flashed from their eyes. But she gathered herself and walked farther into the Square. When she met the half dozen men—no more than boys, really—screaming at her, she steeled herself again and tried to move forward. But they shoved her, and she lost her balance, and when she fell their screams grew louder and the kicking started. Layla and Shirin were still covered. When they rushed to help Mehri the enraged men parted to let them through; and when they had helped Mehri to her feet her friends turned and ran with her in the direction they had come.

They were almost to the edge of the square when Layla saw the first of the placards that carried Mehri's head shot. They were large—two feet wide by 30 inches high; the photograph had been taken the previous day after she had removed her scarf. Just beneath the image, in bold red letters, was the message: PRISON! or DEATH! As she rushed Mehri ahead of her through the Qeysarie Gate, Layla looked over her shoulder. Mehri's face was everywhere.

Layla drove them to her apartment with a calm that came more from shock than prudence. Her parking facility was below ground—a blessing—and they ran to the elevator as soon as the car stopped moving. At the fifth floor they ran again, down the hall to Layla's door. Shirin and Mehri hovered over her as she fumbled with the key, then burst through the door behind her when it finally opened.

When Layla reached toward a light switch Shirin whispered, "No! A candle, only a candle." Layla found one, placed it on the coffee table, and lighted it. Long moments passed while the three friends stood and looked down at the flame, saying nothing. But Shirin was hungry as well as cautious, and when she moved to a refrigerator she knew almost as well as its owner both Layla and Mehri followed her. They could close the door to the kitchen, and that allowed them to turn on the light.

"My God, Mehri," exclaimed Shirin. "I was so scared I did not even ask you if you are hurt! How *are* you?!"

Mehri was not sure. She was sore from the several kicks that had landed on her buttocks and the backs of her thighs before her friends had reached her and helped her stand up again, but only sore—not in pain. What upset her was the reaction of the women in the square. The virulence of their emotion had taken her by surprise; she did not understand how women her mother's age could react that way to someone who looked like their own daughters! And she was angry. Layla had told her about the placards during their drive to the apartment. Only Iran's Revolutionary Guard could have reacted that quickly to their demonstration the day before—obtained her photograph, printed the placards, organized the young men, transported them to the Naqsh-e Jahan, and brought them to the desired level of malice by the time she arrived. Why would an elite combat unit formed decades ago to protect the new government against reprisals from a holdover armed force be mustered and wielded against the nation's young *women*?! Mehri did not know. What she did know was that her life was in danger, and she needed to get out of Isfahan—tonight.

She turned to her other friend. "You have already saved me once today, Layla. Dare I ask you to save me again?"

"*How* can I save you? Just tell me; I'll do it—anything you want!"

"You have to take me to a place where the Guard would not expect me to go. Not Tehran; not anyplace 'nice' a young woman student might run to; for sure not the airport."

"All right," said Layla. But her fear for her friend had stoppered any thought of where that might be. "Where do you want to go?!"

Mehri answered: "Kaveh."

Layla and Shirin said nothing at first. Kaveh was not a real place for either of them. They had never been there; they had never thought about going to Iran's oldest industrial center. But Layla remembered her geography, and she responded. "That's almost five hours!"

"Yes," said Mehri. "All the more reason for the Guard not to expect it. Pardon me for being so practical, Layla, but do you have a full tank of gas?"

"Yes," said Layla. "I filled the tank this morning. But I can't get there and back on a tank of gas—it's too far."

"I know," said Mehri, "But you can drop me off in Kaveh and drive on to Tehran and spend the next several days with Shirin's family." Mehri turned to Shirin. "Don't they still live in Tehran?"

"Yes—yes, they do," stammered Shirin. "Actually, I'm sure my mother would be relieved to see me in the midst of all this."

"Then that's the plan," said Mehri. "If we leave in 30 minutes we'll make Kaveh by the middle of the morning. You can drop me off and drive on to Tehran and get there by daybreak. Shirin can call her parents—they won't know she's already in town. You can spend the day in Tehran, then go to Shirin's parents' home in time for dinner."

"That will work well enough for us," said Layla. "But you will be in Kaveh by *yourself*! What are *you* going to do?"

"I have a friend there," replied Mehri. "Farhad. I knew him at the University of Tehran; he was an engineering student. Within the group I ran with he was by far the most radical. I don't remember who he went to work for after he graduated—some oil and gas company; but I remember he moved to Kaveh. He may not care a fig about my head scarf. But he will hide me until it is safe, or until it is clear I have to leave the country."

"Are you really this quiet inside, Mehri?" It was Shirin who asked the question. Of the three, she was barely holding herself together; and she didn't have her face on placards and on electronic news feeds all over the country.

When Mehri lifted her head, she was looking at the refrigerator, so she turned it to face her friends. "The quiet lives next to the terror, Shirin. I have both to keep me company." Then she held up her cell phone and looked at the time. "It's nearly 9:30," she said. "Let's leave at 10:00. Layla, may I borrow a backpack and some other things?"

They pulled out of the parking facility into light traffic—Isfahan was drowsy but not yet asleep. Layla lived close to the highway and they were on it in minutes, heading north toward the capital, making excellent time. The road to Tehran, a main artery of the nation's road network, was like the highway in every other developed nation an hour after nightfall: it had truck traffic and little else. Shirin had taken the back seat, and for the first 30 minutes she had frantically ducked down behind the front seats with each new set of oncoming headlights. Finally exasperated, Layla told her to lie down and go to sleep.

Over the next three hours, Layla and Mehri covered familiar ground—their homes, their parents, their siblings, and their schools, even old boyfriends. When 2:00 a.m. arrived well ahead of their looking for it, Kaveh's outskirts jumped out of the night into the high beams of their headlights. Layla took the next exit and turned toward the first group of warehouse and apartment buildings, which boasted broken glass when they had any glass at all. More than a few structures stood stripped of everything but their reinforced concrete skeletons. One skeleton, at least seven stories high, loomed over the rest. Mehri told Layla to stop there. "This is perfect," she said. "I can text Farhad when I get out of the car to let him know I'm here, go to the top, sleep a few hours, and meet him just before daybreak." She reached into the back seat, careful not to wake the still-sleeping Shirin, grabbed her backpack, and pulled it to her.

Though Layla had turned off the car's lights, randomly-sited street lamps lit its interior well enough for them to see. They leaned into one another across the console and hugged for a long time before Mehri gently pushed back from her friend. Still holding her across the console, Mehri leaned across again to kiss her. "Goodbye, Layla," she said. "I love you." And then she was out the door and walking rapidly to the tallest of the skeletons, head down, her cell phone already in her hand. Layla watched Mehri disappear around a column as thick as the Toyota was wide, checked on Shirin, and drove back to the highway. Three hours to Tehran.

# The Guard

Hashem had been sleeping.

Part of the nationwide search protocol established by Iran's Mobile Telecommunications Company at the request of the Iran Revolutionary Guard Corps Commander in Isfahan, the ping was loud enough to wake Hashem and call his attention to the very large screen just up from his forehead, which was still resting on his desk. In the screen's center left, at a point represented as roughly 100 kilometers southwest of Tehran, the beams from a simplified beacon were radiating outward at one-second intervals, pinging each time. Hashem sat up instantly. His right hand on the mouse, he moved the cursor to the panel at the top of the screen and the word "Locator." When he clicked on it the area around the beacon expanded and then expanded again, just as Google Maps had programmed it to do. In seconds "Kaveh" appeared across the top of the screen, followed by geographic details of the city. Large areas appeared first, dotted with an occasional park and other green spaces. The city's major streets were laid on next. After that came the feeder streets, the subdivisions, and the industrial parks. The beacon was located in an industrial park in the city's southwest corner.

Hashem moved the cursor to the right and clicked on "Locator/Details." This time the screen brought up a street grid in the industrial park, honed in on a specific block, and placed the pulsating beacon in the middle of it. It appeared to Hashem that a single building occupied the entire block. Sure enough, when he moved the cursor directly over the beacon and clicked again, a single address appeared at the bottom of the screen:

## *17 Amir al-Saad, Kaveh*

Hashem picked up his phone so rapidly he dropped it into his lap. Trying again more slowly, he held it in front of his face with his left hand and dialed precisely with his right. The numbers he was dialing came from the piece of paper that was sitting on the desk where his head had been resting a moment ago, and he said each out loud as he dialed it. It was 3:00 a.m. The Revolutionary Guard Corps Commander in Isfahan was still on duty, and it was the Guard Commander who answered.

"Hashem! Salaam-Alaykom. How are you doing so early this morning?"

Kamran Shariq was 29, astonishingly young for his position. Originally assigned to Quds Force, the IRGC's "expeditionary unit," and posted to Beirut, Kamran's success with the intelligence operations entrusted to him had quickly separated him from his contemporaries. It wasn't just that he was smart or could work past midnight. Kamran had a gift for relationships. His conversations with the most highly-placed officers and civilian authorities were remembered by his seniors for their deference, their skillful questions, and their warmth. In one of the most difficult cities in the Middle East he was a young man going places. But his conversations with Beirut's street vendors and pickpockets were even more successful. To them he was insightful and energetic to be sure. But that is not what distinguished him from the other Guard officers, who were too often arrogant, too seldom interested in anything but the transfer of data in the least amount of time. Kamran asked about the data, as well. But Kamran had time. He would also ask about a child who was struggling in school, or a spouse who was ill, or a brother who had been jailed. And these conversations might lead to a tutor, or a doctor, or an early release. The pickpockets and the street vendors remembered, and the intelligence repaid to the charismatic Guard officer was stunning.

Kamran's four years in Beirut were rewarded by early

selection to the IRGC University of Command and Staff, where he had again distinguished himself, especially in the courses dealing with irregular military science and intelligence. His teachers recommended that he be transferred out of Quds to the Basij, the Guard's morality and anti-riot police arm. The transfer sent him home, to Isfahan, where he became the Deputy Commander. Two years later he was the Commander.

A young Guard captain in Tehran, Hashem had never met the rock-star officer at the other end of the line whose name was first on his call list. But Kamran remembered him. He had spoken with him several times before and each conversation had begun with the welcoming tones of this one.

"My Commander," Hashem went on, "it is so good to hear your voice this morning. We have found the student who provoked the riot in Isfahan! She sent a text message, and it pinged, and we have located her phone to Kaveh, and she is in an industrial area, and we have the address, and…"

Kamran interrupted. "Hashem, my brother! You have brought wonderful news. But let's slow down just a bit so I can follow you. Is that okay?"

"Of course, my Commander. Please forgive me. The woman is in an industrial park in southwest Kaveh—a tall building, probably long-abandoned."

Kamran interrupted again. "Do you have the address?"

Hashem read it to him.

Kamran continued. "You said you intercepted a text message?"

"Yes," replied Hashem, "that's correct."

"Do you have the number of the recipient of the text—the person our young woman was reaching out to?"

"Not yet!" said, Hashem, almost breathless this time. "But as soon we finish our call I *will* have it. I called you first, of course."

"Of course," said Kamran. "Thank you."

A short pause followed while one man composed himself and

the other continued to think. Kamran spoke next, "Do you agree there are three more hours until daybreak?"

"Yes," said Hashem, puzzled at the change of direction, "at least three hours."

"All right," said the young Commander. "Here is what you will do, but *only* this. You will locate the recipient of her text and—before 5:00 a.m.—you will have them arrested. Once arrested, you will make sure they do not see or speak with anyone until you and I speak again. This is a tall order, Hashem, and I realize that. But you are highly capable, and I know you can accomplish it. Am I right?"

"Yes, my Commander. I will accomplish it. Thank you for your trust in me!"

"You are welcome, Hashem." Kamran wished God's blessing on his devoted subordinate and hung up.

His next call was to his colleague in Kaveh, the IRGC Commander there. "Azar, my brother! Salaam-Alaykom. And I apologize for calling you at such an early hour."

"Salaam. Think nothing of it—I am sure it is important. Tell me."

"We have located the young woman who instigated the riot in Isfahan. She is in Kaveh—in an industrial park: 17 Amir al-Saad."

"I know it," replied Bahar. "There is not much park left there, or industry!"

"All the better," laughed Kamran.

"It sounds like you already have a plan, brother. How can I assist you?"

Kamran realized the woman could have ended up anywhere or disappeared. That she had stopped in Kaveh was a blessing, for Bahar counted among his assets the most accomplished counter-terrorist operative within the IRGC. "I would like to employ Siavesh. As he is part of your team, I am calling to ask your permission to use him and your help in deploying him immediately—this very moment. Again, I apologize for such an early intrusion on your day."

Azar smiled at Kamran's unfailing courtesy. He had become aware of him when Kamran was deep-selected for university, he had met him soon after his posting to Isfahan, and he had worked with him. Notwithstanding an approach to people Azar knew was as much studied as instinctual, Kamran was easy to like. Azar did like him, and his results were impossible to ignore. "Why so quickly?" he asked.

"We found her because she used her phone to text someone. But the person may be in the area, she may have asked for help, and the most effective time for a pickup would be just before dawn. That's barely three hours. We would like to find her before that."

The young woman called "Mehri" was not from his city, but Azar knew her. Times past, when the head scarf protests first appeared, she was a mere participant. But she had been a force. Her ability to confront a security patrol, find the watch commander, engage him in a debate—often televised, and shred him with her logic and the power of her personality was an embarrassment to Guard officers throughout the country. The threat she now posed to the state as the leader of a renewed protest in Isfahan grew each time her uncovered image flashed across the internet.

There were protests all over Iran. What was happening in Isfahan was a bagatelle in comparison with the daily disruption in Tehran. Mehri was not the only leader. She was not the only young leader. There were hundreds of young women who, in the eyes of the Guard, seemed to live to cause trouble. Until now, the protests would ebb, then surge, then again become quiet. There was no national movement to sustain them and build them. None yet. The movement wanted only the right person—the woman, preferably young, who was brilliant and charismatic and articulate and photogenic.

The Guard kept track of the candidates. Each had a file; each a photograph. Periodically they were ranked. In the last year one had emerged as the consistent Number 1: Mehri. From the Guard's perspective, she was exactly the wrong leader at exactly the wrong time.

Azar knew Kamran had planned carefully for Mehri's appearance in Isfahan on the second day of the protest. He had positioned mature female operatives at each of the entrances to Naqsh-e Jahan Square, confident she would encounter them. They would be the first to confront her. He had reserved his arresting officers for later, in the square's center, where he had his media crew. The young men she had encountered were not his operatives. That they had lost their tempers was understandable, but their physical reactions were unfortunate. When the woman's friends rescued her from the men who were kicking her and rushed her back out of the square to an unknown location, that was beyond unfortunate. The steps taken since to mitigate the threat were known to Azar, including the national telephone surveillance that had apparently found her. But the threat was still there, and he knew Kamran felt personally responsible for her being at large.

"If I call Siavesh and refer him to you it will take too long. I will call him now, while you are on hold, then join him to our conversation. I will tell him this is a matter of the greatest importance, that he must act immediately, and that he must take his lead from you in exactly the way he would take it from me. Please wait a moment."

The rest of the conversation went as Bahar had said. Siavesh, too, was awake. He understood the assignment, dressed while he was listening to it, and was on his way to his car in two minutes, agreeing to telephone Kamran again as soon as he had picked up his assistant.

When Siavesh had signed off, Kamran exhaled audibly before speaking to his colleague from Kaveh. "Azar, my brother. I had feared what just happened would be impossible to arrange. You made it possible. Thank you. If God wills it, I will one day have the chance to repay you. But for now, I must go."

"I understand," said Azar. "We will talk again soon."

# A Silent Scream

Siavesh had worked with the same assistant long enough to know where to find him. His work notwithstanding, he was traditional; he would be in his apartment, sound asleep. But Reza was a light sleeper, Siavesh's call had him wide awake, and he was already at the curb when Siavesh pulled his black Peugeot 508 Sport alongside him. Reza got in without a word, and as the Peugeot surged ahead Siavesh spoke into the windshield: "They found the girl."

Reza knew who "the girl" was; he and Siavesh had talked about her since the first day of the protest, well before the Guard had sent its APB following her disappearance the evening of the second day. It was now the third day—early morning. "Where?" asked the assistant.

"The industrial park on the south side," said Siavesh. "I have already programmed the address." Reza looked at the car's center screen and the GPS readout. They would be there in seven minutes.

"What are our instructions?"

"First, we find her," replied Siavesh. "It will be more than an hour since she sent her text message. I believe she will try to hide in the building, probably on the top floor. When fugitives want to hide in a strange building they always go to the top. We will move toward the top, but we will sweep each floor on the way up."

"That will take hours," said Reza.

"No, not hours," Siavesh continued. "The building is naked. There is nothing left but the concrete skeleton. We will use our flashlights. We can cover a floor in two or three minutes; we will be on top in 20."

Siavesh slowed the eager Peugeot as he approached Amir al-Saad, lowered his headlights to dim, and turned carefully onto the debris-strewn roadway. No. 17 was two blocks ahead on their left side. As Siavesh moved into the next intersection he killed his lights altogether, turned right, and let the car drift toward Building No. 4, whose delivery dock had not seen a visitor for years.

Stopped now, they sat in the dark while Siavesh changed his shoes and whispered his plans to enter the target building and find the girl. They would go to separate corners of the ground floor; each would climb the staircase at the corner. At each level up they would slowly walk across the slab to the other corner, crossing each other's path as they did so, then take the opposite staircase to the next level. They would repeat this until they reached the seventh floor. Once there at the top of the staircase, Reza would stay put. Siavesh would canvass the entire floor himself, flush the girl, and bring her to Reva.

"When you get to the top floor you must wait, and you must be quiet. Don't become impatient. This may take two minutes, or it may take 20. But if you make a noise you will cause trouble. Do you understand?"

Reza nodded, but he had a question. "What if the girl has gotten loose and is running away from you? What am I to do then?"

Siavesh's laugh was as derisive as it was immediate: "You should give her a round of applause, no?" Having drawn the embarrassment he wanted from his assistant over the foolish questions and their implicit lack of confidence in his superior, Siavesh went on, his voice a hiss but no louder than before: "*Tackle* her! Do *whatever it takes* to keep her on the seventh floor! She must *not* get away from us! Do you understand *that*?!"

Reza nodded again, but this time deeply, like a supplicant. He had no other questions. They opened the doors carefully, wincing at the click of their opening. Relieved to close them to almost no noise at all, they made their way across the street and down the block to No. 17.

Siavesh wore Clohoo leather boots in the shape of high-top basketball shoes. His concession was not to foreign fashion but to effectiveness: they were quiet. On this assignment, high in the night air on a concrete floor with nothing but the light from a thin moon, Siavesh had to be noiseless. The Clohoos would help.

They moved through the first six floors as rapidly as Siavesh had predicted; there was almost nothing left on any of them, and certainly no people. Reza stopped at the top of the stairwell on seven, turned his flashlight off, and waited, pulling up his jacket to mask the sound of his breathing. Moving alternately left then right in taut semicircles, Siavesh worked his way down one side of the seventh floor, column by column, until he reached the next corner—one side of the building removed from Reza. The beam of his flashlight told him there was nothing between him and Reza but columns and open air. Then he returned to his stairwell and moved out in the other direction. When he cleared the column at the next corner he continued toward the final corner, where Reza waited in his stairwell.

The column ahead of him at the last corner was larger than the others, purpose-built as a kind of shelter. The thick wooden door built to enclose the interior had splintered and was stuck open at least a foot clear of the column. Inside, a narrow concrete closet ran left to right to what appeared to be a pile of trash pushed up against the far end. But the end was not an end. There was a hole in the concrete just shy of the end—half a meter high, which opened into a parallel closet in the center of the column. Exploring the seventh floor with the light from her cell phone, Mehri had found it, had pushed the trash aside to climb into it, and had replaced as much of the trash as she could before allowing herself to fall asleep. That was nearly two hours ago. She had awakened to the tramp of Reza's footfalls on his staircase, which was just outside her column.

Siavesh had turned his flashlight off before he looked past the open door into the small space. The sky obliged him with just enough light to see the trash piled at the back. Also visible, but barely, was the black straight-edge of the hole's opening at the top of the trash. Assuming the girl was on the other side of the hole he backed away from the column, making no more sound than he had made approaching it. Then he moved to Reza, his left hand gesturing for quiet as his right hand gestured they move farther back into the stairwell. Once there, Siavesh continued to gesture for what he wanted: Reza was to turn on his flashlight and go back down the stairs to the sixth floor. He would walk normally, making noise with his boots as he did so, and continue all the way to the ground floor. Once there he would walk into the middle of Amir al-Saad and continue down the street toward their car, waving his flashlight left and right. If nothing happened, he would continue until he reached the car.

Mehri had heard someone walk up the stairs to her floor; the distinct gait had awakened her. But it was not clear what had happened after that. As her head cleared in her pitch-black chamber she was relieved her breathing was so close to normal, but she had to deal with the beating of her heart. She took deep breaths; that helped. And she listened. For what seemed minutes she heard nothing. Then she heard the sound of the same person descending the stairs, and turning a corner, and descending a few more stairs—until she could hear nothing more.

A sliver of light revealed her exit. When she had crawled to it she pulled away the pieces of trash as though they were Jenga blocks. Once she had cleared the trash she crouched through the opening, stood, slid along the interior until she reached the door, and slowly moved past it onto the seventh floor. She took her time with this final passage out of the column, grateful for the protection she had received there, and turned right toward the stairwell.

She had taken three steps when a latex-gloved hand closed

over her mouth and another settled on her right shoulder.

"Don't scream." She understood the soft command of the voice next to her ear but took a sharp breath in order to do just the opposite. It was then the right side of her body caught fire—from the shoulder where the hand had rested, down her side to her hips, all the way out to her fingertips. She had never experienced such pain, and she collapsed under its weight.

The voice returned, barely surfacing through lapping waves of agony: "I will make the pain stop, but you have to promise not to scream. Will you do that? Nod your head up and down if you do." It was all Mehri could do to move her head; but she moved it a fraction, and that was enough. The pain went away.

Before she could form another thought the same latex fingers that had closed her mouth were forcing her to open it. They pushed an object that felt like a small lemon between her teeth, then closed her mouth over it. Next came strong adhesive tape, which held her mouth closed over the lemon. Whoever attacked her must have had four arms, because her own arms were pulled behind her and bound with something narrow and sharp—plastic, probably; maybe a zip-tie by the sound of it—at the same time everything else was happening. Whoever was a man, and he was now kneeling in front of her. "Let me help you up," he said. Mehri desperately wanted to stand, and without his help she would not have been able to do so.

The man facing her was no taller than she was. He might have been 30 years old with dark hair and a thin beard, carefully trimmed, beneath thin lips and a hawk nose. He was dressed entirely in black: light-weight, loose-fitting pants; a light-weight hoodie, probably nylon; and black leather shoes with no soles—an adult's version of the booties her sister bought for her toddler. He was not powerfully built; if anything, he was slender. But he was alert, his eyes steady in the moon's light. And if he was the person who had disabled her through pressure on her brachial plexus he knew anatomy like a surgeon, and had more grip strength than power lifters twice his size. Mehri was terrified.

"I am Siavesh," he said. "I recognize you cannot speak back to me." He was almost apologetic. "I have to get you out of this building, and to do that I need to have you walk with me. Will you do that?" Had Mehri been able to make a sound she would have laughed. But she knew there was only one answer, and she made it—nodding her head up and then down.

As they began to walk along the edge of the seventh floor, Mehri wondered who this man was and why he had given her his name. She was thinking about the name, and his description, and how she might use them later when she noticed they were walking away from the nearest stairwell—the one just outside her hiding place. And then the hand that had steadied her in her walking was gone. And then she was outside the building, alone and in space, falling past the sixth floor and the fifth into the still-black night.

They found her lying on her back, her legs at an odd angle from her pelvis. The cell phone whose text message would end two lives that day was two meters from her outstretched right hand; her left arm lay splintered beneath her. Siavesh stepped away from the body to retrieve her cell phone. Reza knelt, removed the adhesive tape, and pulled the lemon from her mouth. Her face was intact, her eyes were open. Reza had never heard a sound as he had walked down Amir al-Saad with his flashlight, but Mehri looked like she was screaming.

# Breakfast at Home

Farieh watched her father as he stood up. If to be older was to be less flexible in one's thinking, then her father was older than she remembered him. If to be older was to misplace one's sense of humor, then her father was older still. And if to be older was to refuse even to listen to a perspective that opposed the government, then her father was old indeed. He did not push his chair back; he did not look at her as he walked out of the kitchen and into the living room, where his paper awaited him. He just went there and sat in his chair and began reading. The large newsprint pages cut him off from Farieh so effectively he might as well have left the house.

Farieh's mother had stayed at the table and Farieh turned to her with her question: "When did father become so old?"

Farieh's mother did not take the question well. She removed her napkin from her lap and placed it in the center of the small plate that had held the cucumber slice and the few grapes and walnuts and the slice of cheese she had taken for herself. She had finished her tea. She looked across at her youngest daughter and spoke in tones warmer than the expression on her face.

"Your father is not old. He is as energetic and as bright as he ever was. But he has little patience for young people who show such little respect for our faith and our traditions. He has no more patience for a daughter who would not only apologize for them but would hold them up as praiseworthy."

Farieh had promised herself she would listen carefully to her mother and would respond softly and with great care. She broke her promise immediately. Responding rapidly and in a voice that swelled from emphatic to shrill, she flung her words at her mother. "Is it not common for young people to question their faith? To challenge it? Has that not *happened* in our country, and all over the world, since the beginning of time? If the Guard were not so intolerant, so repressive, many of the young people you see on the streets today would grow *through* this. But when they are arrested and imprisoned and even *beaten* for nothing more than removing a head scarf, it is harder for them to grow through this; and it is *impossible* for them to respect either the Guard or the government it works for.

"What is so disappointing about father is his unwillingness even to *listen* to me talk about the points of view of the protestors. He is so wrapped up in the Guard and its support of the government, so blind to its violence against young people, that there is no place for conversation. Where did *this* come from?

"What happened to the man who taught us to be alert to the *feelings* of others? To regard those feelings as a part of *reality*? And to ignore them at our peril? When the young people of Iran are beaten, do they not bleed? Yet Father does not care. Why must I respect *that*?"

Farieh's mother had done what Farieh had promised to do. She had listened with great care, and when she responded she did so softly. "Your father is an honorable man who believes in our faith and who knows right from wrong." Even delivered softly it was a rebuke. And when she had finished it Farieh's mother got up from the table and followed her husband into the living room. Farieh watched them. As her mother approached her husband, Farieh's father put his paper down and placed it on the table next to his chair. He stood up, and the two of them left the house. Farieh knew they would walk for an hour or more.

She shook her head as she stood up, placed her own dish in the sink, poured more tea, and walked into the living room. She did not ordinarily read the paper, but she had little else to do.

The article was just inside the front page. The headline read:

# EMBARRASSED BY ROLE IN PROTESTS
# STUDENT JUMPS TO HER DEATH

There was a photograph just beneath the headline. It showed a young woman whose body had been broken by a fall from a great height but whose face was nearly intact. There was blood coming from her ear, and she looked like she had been screaming.

Farieh's screaming back at the photograph tore through the silence of the house and ebbed only as she ran out of breath.

She dropped the paper onto the carpet and ran upstairs to the bathroom where she threw up her breakfast and everything left over from the night before. She shook so violently at one point she thought she might pass out. She would have welcomed that. But if anything her consciousness became more acute, and it was joined by a powerful sense of dread. She stood up, washed her face, and ran to her room.

It had been 20 minutes since her parents had left the house. In fewer than 20 minutes more Farieh was gone as well. She had stuffed her clothes and her other things into her two suitcases, she had taken the keys to her mother's convertible, and she had cleared their carport and their neighborhood. She would be at the airport in 35 minutes. She would use her phone; she would advance her flights back to the United States by a week. If she were lucky, the flight to Dubai would be boarding by the time she got to the gate.

She had worn a head scarf; she would not be foolish. But she was driving very fast. When instinct made her look in the rear-view mirror to check for police vehicles, she did not recognize the face looking back at her.

# Jamie

The flight from New York City arrived at MCI on time. She had been with The British Summer Institute group when she left Kansas City for England and had paid little attention to the new terminal. This time, even with a mood as dark as the thunderclouds building to the southwest, Farieh noticed the bright new building with its unisex toilets, its wide concourses, its myriad food sellers, and its art. The art was everywhere, especially overhead: bright, contemporary, complementing the high and light-filled spaces, welcoming.

Farieh knew the new terminal was doing its best but she didn't feel welcome. The only things she felt were what she had carried with her to Imam Khomeini International Airport as she fled the suffocation of her parents' home in Tehran—a hole in her heart where her friend had been, and shame. She could not understand how the rulers of her country could send the Revolutionary Guard after its young women. She could not understand how her parents could defend them. She could not accept that Mehri was dead.

She walked into the bathroom. When the mirror reminded her she was still wearing a head scarf she ripped it off and jammed it into the bin for "food waste." Farieh didn't care.

She thumbed across to the app and booked a car to Lawrence before she pulled her bags to the ride-share location. Her Uber Black arrived two minutes after she did. Farieh plugged in her ear buds, found her play list, leaned into the back seat, and closed her eyes.

It was nearly 6:00 p.m. when the Uber stopped at the end of the sidewalk running from the porch of Miller Scholarship Hall to Lilac Lane. The driver got out quickly to open the tailgate and pull out Farieh's two very large roller bags. Nodding to the front of the scholarship hall and using raised eyebrows to ask whether she wanted the bags taken to the door—she did—he carried them across the curb and down the several steps, rolled them along the sidewalk until they bumped up against the porch, then lifted them into a place between the columns. Farieh thanked him, but more brusquely than she had intended, and opened the front door from her side just as Jamie, who would be her roommate again this year, was opening it from hers.

Jamie might have been the only person in the United States Farieh wanted to see right then, and the two young women screamed at each other as they hugged in the entryway. They hugged a long time. Farieh was still clinging to her roommate as Jamie gently pushed out of their embrace and looked back at her. Farieh's face was darker now from days in the sun in England and Iran. As Jamie once again took her roommate in her arms she noticed Farieh was not wearing a head scarf. "Hey. Hey there," Jamie said quietly. "We need to get you something to eat, and we need to talk. Leave your bags in the living room—they'll be fine, there's hardly anybody here yet. Let's go to the Oread."

The Oread wasn't exactly "on" campus, but it was as close as a hotel could get. North of the Union where Jayhawk Boulevard tees into 12th Street, the Oread commands views in all directions—from its rooms, from the condos on its upper floors, and from The Nest, its rooftop bar. Farieh and Jamie walked. Once they got past Danforth Chapel it was barely five minutes—straight north on Jayhawk Boulevard.

They asked for menus as they made their way to the bar's stone terrace on the south side. Farieh had not been there before, but the chicken wrap looked good, and so did the fries that went with it. She surprised Jamie by ordering a glass of the Sauvignon Blanc. They ordered a bottle when the food arrived, and that bought them another hour; the second bottle bought an hour more. There were several glasses left when Farieh finished telling Jamie about her time in England and Scotland with the British Summer Institute, her time with her sister in Oxford, and her abbreviated time with her parents in Iran.

Mehri was harder. Farieh made it through their childhood friendship and Mehri's early activism with occasional breaks for a last piece of fruit or another sip of wine. It was the transition to the Iran Farieh had just left that led to longer pauses. Jamie listened to her roommate's voice and to the silence. If the silence carried a beat too long, Jamie would ask a question, softly, nudging Farieh back toward her story. The silence that followed Farieh's reading her father's newspaper was a long one. And when Farieh had finished telling Jamie about Mehri, the last glass was gone.

Nearly two days had passed since Farieh had boarded the flight from Tehran to the UAE. Her fatigue alone would have made the walk back to Miller a challenge; the wine made it harder. They had to stop twice: once at the statue of Moses across from the Union, all three of them blinded by the burning bush; once at Danforth, where Farieh wondered out loud whether she or any of her sisters would ever marry and, if so, whether "the Guard" would attend. Jamie had known nothing about the Guard until that evening, when Farieh had told her about Mehri. She did not understand why they would be invited to the weddings.

The half block left to Miller was the hardest. Barely able to get Farieh through the front door, Jamie only glanced at the two roller bags in the living room before pushing her up the stairs, down the hall, and through the door. Inside their room, Farieh managed only a few more feet before collapsing onto her bed. She was asleep in seconds.

Jamie had never worried about her roommate before. Staring down at a face that had challenged everything their freshman year, she wondered how close to broken it had been by the anger and the dread that had flown with her for so many thousands of miles. She removed Farieh's boots, covered her with a blanket from the closet, then lightly kissed her roommate's forehead before turning for the bathroom.

But Jamie did not go to the bathroom; Farieh's conversation about Mehri pushed in as she was halfway down the hall. Jamie turned around, not to her room where Farieh was sleeping but past it and down the stairs to the living room. As Jamie took a seat on the sofa, their evening scrolled in front of her.

They had finished their meal but had not gotten up from the table. Farieh was drifting in and out of the conversation, her eyes closing for longer and longer periods of time. In the midst of such a moment she began a quiet casting back into the hours of her flight to New York City, when she had been locked up with the memory of her friend.

"I know how Mehri died," Farieh had said, her eyelids open but her eyes unseeing behind them. "The papers reported it as a suicide. It wasn't.

"She was pushed out of an industrial building. There was a tiny moment of surprise as she felt the floor disappear beneath her feet. There was another moment before she realized it had not been replaced with anything. And then she was alone—alone like she had never been before, accelerating through an indifferent darkness.

"She fell 100 feet onto an asphalt parking lot. The impact fractured every major bone in her body, including her skull, but left her face intact. The Guard photographer focused on the blood coming from her ear, then spread the ghoulish photograph across the internet.

"She felt the impact like she would have felt being struck by a train traveling 60 miles per hour. But she would have been propelled away from a train. Because the parking lot gave her no place to go, the mass of her body parts kept crashing down against the ones underneath until she had finally spent the entire energy of the fall.

"The pain was bright and hot and everywhere, reminding her of stars in a constellation. In the instant she had left she remembered a constellation contained vast spaces surrounding its stars, cooler spaces; so she chased the spaces in front of her in the hope they would be cooler too.

"As the shock from the massive internal bleeding exploded, tearing through her cells and her organs like a rabid tiger, her eyelids would not open. So she scoured the dark spaces. She cared less about the temperature now than about finding something. She was looking for herself.

"She was too late. The heat and the light had displaced the darkness until there was space left for nothing. Nothing but the pain."

# Steven Mobley

The view to the northwest from the top-floor corner unit in 901 Lofts ran right down Massachusetts Street, from its 9th Street intersection all the way to City Hall and the Kansas River Bridge. To the west you could see across Weaver's Department Store, across the churches and residences, all the way to the freshman women's dorms on the top of the hill. Now a sixth-year senior, Steven Mobley had not started on the northwest corner of the seventh floor; he had had a second-floor unit his junior year and was on the fourth floor his senior year. But he was on top now, and he loved it.

His circumstances had changed as radically as his class schedule. Now he had almost no classes—the product of strategic delays in enrolling combined with a base level of indifference to whether he graduated or not. He had finished his major courses for his Bachelor of Science degree in Business Administration his fourth year; what remained was the rest. At 12 hours a semester he could have completed all of them last year, his fifth year. But Steven had found a job he loved, and the job pushed the classwork out. As a result, he completed but 12 hours his entire 5th year. It was anybody's guess whether he would get the other 12 done this year.

Steven grew up in the Chicago area, in Winnetka. He was successful in high school—tall at 6'4"; blond; a trim 190. He was the starting wide receiver in football, the backup point guard in basketball, and an all-conference center fielder in baseball. He was good looking, he could talk about anything, and he liked hip-hop. The high school girls loved him, even though he was cocky. But most of all, he was smart—as in, "Calculus exam? No problem;

I've got this."

Like so many Chicago kids who did not want to accompany 200 of their closest friends to the University of Illinois or DePaul, Steven applied elsewhere. He sent lengthy applications to several of the Ivies and to Northwestern, the top-ten university right in his backyard. But he needed a safety school; so he drove to Lawrence and took a look at Kansas. He liked it. He liked it that the campus was pretty and built around a hill, he liked the fraternities, he liked the nearly 600 miles that would separate him from his parents, and he liked the basketball. Steven had been admitted to Brown, to Penn, and to Northwestern. But the average of $10,000 those schools made available in annual scholarship money barely dented his projected living expenses. Even at Northwestern, the least expensive of the three, projected four-year costs in Evanston were crowding $400,000. In a cursory conversation his father told him the family could not afford to send him to Brown, or Penn, or Northwestern. So Steven became a Jayhawk.

He enrolled, pledged a fraternity, and was admitted into the School of Business, which meant most of his classes met in Capitol Federal Hall, just east of Allen Fieldhouse. He did well. But at the end of every spring semester he was out of money and on his way back to Chicago, where his dad had once again found him a summer job that took all of his time during the week and that was either dull (the warehouse job his first summer) or terrifying (the construction job after his junior year for a start-up that had never heard of OSHA). Steven returned to Lawrence his senior year with his eye out for something that would break the summer cycle, and he found it.

Steven was a drug dealer. He had started helping out some guys in the house who had let their stash get too low and had run out just ahead of Thursday night—really bad timing. Steven had actually worried about what to charge them; he found out none of them cared. All they wanted was five or six grams, enough to get themselves and their dates stoned that night. Availability was the key, not price.

Next, he learned there was no dependable market for weed in Lawrence, at least none for the guys he knew. They all knew somebody. But on a given weekend night "somebody" was as likely to be stoned himself or out of town as he was available on his cell near midnight with product to buy. Steven wasn't all that into marijuana, and he figured if he'd lay off he could become the dependable somebody people wanted to deal with. He was right.

It wasn't a month before word got out and Steven had more business than he could manage. There were so many calls by Wednesday afternoon that he dropped the classes that met Thursday and Friday. Deliveries were getting to be a major problem. And as his business kept growing he began to run up against his own supply-chain issues. He had exhausted his first source—a high school classmate. He was becoming uncomfortable enough with the classmate's replacement that he dropped a few messages he was looking for someone who could handle his business.

But the business was changing, as well. One of his runners had approached him very early on. "Hey, man." He always sounded like a refugee from a Cheech & Chong movie. "One of the chicks up on sorority row said she didn't smoke and would *really* dig it if we could hook her up with some Adderall. No hassle on the price; just wants it." Steven had considered that carefully and had decided Adderral was a terrific idea. Within months, what started as a side hustle had become more than half the business. Supply chain was again the key concern. But it was already packaged. It was so much easier to transport and deliver. And the profit margins made weed dealing look like his younger's sister's lemonade stand in Winnetka.

Abdul Barakzai knocked on the door of Steven's fourth-floor apartment at 9:00 a.m. on a Sunday. Steven was not fully awake. Saturday was not just a big night for business; Steven had been running the entire day, as well. But he heard the knock, threw a

Beak 'em Hawks T-shirt over gray sweatpants, and made it to the door, which he opened the same way any other KU undergraduate male would open it on a Sunday morning—wide open, with no concern for his own safety or the contents of his apartment. Abdul was so taken with the young man's naiveté he could not help but smile. He introduced himself immediately: "My name is Abdul. Abdul Barakzai. Are you Mr. Mobley?" Abdul's inflection peaked at the first syllable of Steven's last name before dropping at the second.

Abdul had been born in Afghanistan but had come to the United States for college and for graduate school in engineering, both at Iowa State, before starting a branch of the family business in Kansas City. He was nearly as tall as Steven but more slender, with thick, dark hair. Unlike the smooth-cheeked Midwesterner in front of him, Abdul wore a carefully-trimmed beard and mustache. He was dressed in khakis, a blue Polo chambray shirt, and sandals. His middle name might have been "courtesy," for when Steven made no attempt to answer him Abdul added, "I know I have surprised you. May I come in?" Steven pulled the door open even farther and stood out of the way as Abdul walked past him into the living room.

Abdul turned toward Steven with another question: "May I sit down?"

Steven found his voice, gestured to the worn couch in front of the large west window, and said, "Of course." He added, "May I get you something to drink?"

"Yes," said Abdul. "If you have a glass of hot tea I would like that very much."

Steven disappeared to the small apartment's galley kitchen. The last bag of English Breakfast was in a tin just left of the sink. He fished it out, dropped it into a rough-sided mug, added water from the hot-water dispenser, let it steep for 30 seconds, then returned to the living room. Still groggy, as his evening had not ended until close to 4:00 a.m., Steven said nothing while placing the mug on the chipped table in front of his guest. Then he took a seat opposite the couch and stared at Abdul.

"The street says you need a more reliable source for your business." Abdul got that out while moving a very hot mug from the table to a place just in front of his lips. As it was far too hot to drink he returned it to the table.

"What do you know about my business?" Steven voiced the question quietly while continuing to stare at the young man across from him. He guessed Abdul to be about 30, and his guess was a good one. Abdul was five years older than Steven.

"I know your product is good, you keep meticulous track of your orders, and you deliver on time. You started dealing with friends—the fraternity members who lived in the several senior houses off campus. They sang your praises to people outside the fraternity and you were soon so busy you could barely keep up. But you did keep up, and your reputation for timeliness and reliability grew to the point you had to find a new supplier, as well as a runner to make deliveries. That helped, but only for a few weeks. Your new supplier is already cracking under the load of your orders, and you have a mediocre delivery driver. 'Chris' is his name, I believe. Chris likes the work well enough, and he likes the money, but he doesn't understand the concept of 'on time.' If a delivery is due at 7:00 p.m. Chris believes it is acceptable to get it there by 7:30, or even later. You have had several conversations with him about this. You see it as a problem. Chris does not.

"How am I doing?"

Abdul's comments had been so on point, so far beyond anything Steven thought a person might be able to find out, that he just sat there staring while Abdul delivered them. But Abdul's question roused him, and he answered it. "Fucking amazing! Who did you get this from?! I have been fairly direct with Chris. Did you talk to him? You must have!"

"I have not talked with Chris," replied Abdul. "But I do know your supplier, and more people than me know about your business.

That is one of the reasons I have come here this morning. Everybody talks about you.

"Your business has grown and you believe you need to make important internal decisions about it. But there are external elements in play that have the potential to eliminate your business entirely as you currently know it. Please forgive me—I know this sounds presumptuous—but I am here to identity these elements and to help you make the decisions."

Steven's first impression was that Abdul had come to scare him, or even threaten him, and to take his business from him. But the comment about "external elements" did not fit with that scenario. Steven decided to ask about that.

"Exactly what 'external elements' are you talking about?"

"Missouri's Legislature has authorized a ballot initiative that will come up for vote in November. When Missouri's voters go to the polls they will approve it—just like every other electorate that has considered it, and Missouri will begin the lawful sale of marijuana in January. With marijuana available legally from dozens of Kansas City shops, KU students will no longer need your services. Your business will dry up. Maybe not overnight, but it will end. There will be nothing you can do about it.

"We have watched you since you started. We like everything about you. We like your focus on your customers; you strive to make deliveries on time and in precisely the right quantities. We like the way you arrange for payment; you insist on cash at the time of delivery. You have recruited drivers who can and do say 'No!' and refuse delivery if they are not paid. Several of the people on my team have purchased product from you. At least once, having established themselves as a repeat customer, each has told your driver they did not have enough money and has asked for credit until the next time. On every occasion your driver has politely refused to make the delivery. That is excellent.

"You don't run out of product. Or, if you do, my team has not observed it and has not heard about it. That requires careful inventory management.

"You maintain a low profile. Everyone knows your name but few people have ever seen you. My organization believes that is the right way for the business leader to behave.

"What I have come with is news about what's happening in Missouri and a proposal to shift the focus of your business organization from marijuana to something else."

"To what?" asked Steven. "Cocaine?!"

"Precisely."

There was a long moment while Steven considered Abdul's efficient response to his aggressively sarcastic question. As he did so, two things occurred to him: Abdul was almost certainly right about what Missouri's legalization of pot would mean to Steven's marijuana business; and, for reasons Steven did not yet understand, he had just been given as fine a compliment as he had ever received.

He had several questions for Abdul, and he saw no point in beating around the bush.

"I can understand what you're getting at—that I need to transition to a new business. But why should I talk about that with you? What is the nature of *your* business?"

Abdul answered carefully, sharing his birthplace, his father's prominence in Afghanistan, his coming to the United States for school, his coming to Kansas City, and the focus on the college market.

Steven asked another question: "I thought Afghanistan grew opium poppies, not coca. How is it your family is involved in the distribution of cocaine and not heroin?"

"Barter," answered Abdul. "These details are managed by my father. The United States is a college market for the family, and our business is strictly cocaine."

"Okay," said Steven, "cocaine. But that is a very big step for someone like *me*. Why are *you* here? Do you propose to sell me IT services? Or security? Or something else so I can make this transition? Are you some kind of fairy godfather? Or—do you just want to buy my customer list and move me out of the way? Is this a friendly visit, or is it something else?"

This time Abdul could not suppress the laughter. But everything about Steven's guest and his laughter was friendly. "I would like to hire you," said the guest. "I want you to be a part of our organization.

"We have been transitioning away from marijuana for some time now. We hardly sell it anymore. But we sell a lot of cocaine. We operate out of Kansas City and include Lawrence and Manhattan in our territory. We include Columbia, as well, and St. Louis. And Des Moines and Ames and Iowa City. We serve Omaha and Lincoln, Oklahoma City and Tulsa, Norman and Stillwater. We employ many sales representatives and many runners. We have what we call 'product specialists,' the people in our lab in Kansas City who examine and test the incoming material before we package it for the street. We have business specialists— IT techs and accountants and realtors and lawyers. But we have no executive team, and no board of directors. As I said before, this is a family business. There is only one owner—my father, and only one manager—me. I have wanted an assistant for some time, someone I could train and trust but someone who had already demonstrated an aptitude for the work. I believe you are that person. That's why I have come here this morning. As I said a moment ago, I would like to hire you."

Steven's best high school sport was baseball. He was fast, he had a sixth sense for where to field a line drive, and his throw to the plate from center field came off his shoulder like an RPG. His coach had friends who were college coaches and one of them got him a spot in The Cape Cod League, where Steven learned he could handle every facet of the center fielder's position except one. He won the League's gold-glove award. But his batting average of .246 and his OPS of .635 told him everything he needed to know about his future in baseball. Still, he had played enough to know what baseball success looked like. When Abdul finished and told him for the second time he wanted to hire him, Steven felt he'd been called up to The Show.

# House Party

Dusk had yielded to nighttime. There was little light to see by on this cloudy evening and the faint purple from the failing streetlight at the intersection of 12th and Ohio wasn't helping. Farieh had to step onto the walk leading to the two-story frame house on the high side of the street to get a better look at its street number. She was at the right place. That the concrete wasn't cracked meant the property had been updated, more likely by parents who had purchased the house for kids going to school at KU than by an area landlord. Once she crossed the threshold into the noisy foyer it was clear it was the former. New oak floors gleamed beneath modern wall sconces. Through the arched opening was a large room that spanned the structure left to right. It was already accommodating 30 people and could handle 20 more, its space a product of tearing out the wall between the original living and dining rooms. It was October, the night was warm, and the windows she could see were all opened.

She moved into the living room looking to see whether she knew anyone. She didn't, so she kept moving into a sparkling kitchen at the back of the first floor to the left. It was crowded too. The young people who were not standing and drinking were carrying drinks to others, the music seemed much bigger here in the smaller space, and the din that resulted from the movement and the music and the people trying to yell over both was one decibel short of an uproar. Farieh saw the door at the back of the kitchen and pushed past the screen into a back yard that might have been dropped out of the garden section of *Southern Living*. Stone walkways led left and right to trees turning color, to tended flower beds, and to a very large stainless-steel grill. In the center was a fire pit whose raised stone surround supported cushions in crimson and blue. The backyard was nearly empty. Only one person sat at the fire pit, and he was looking down at his phone. Curious, Farieh moved to the fire pit, looked across at him until he finally lifted his head, then sat down.

"Hello," she said, "I'm Farieh. I'm a student here. Jamie invited me." She said Jamie's name as though everyone knew her roommate.

"Steven" was his name. He gave it as he reacted to the mention of Jamie's invitation. His reaction was not sarcastic, as it might have been, but kind, as though he had been interrupted by a close friend. There was caution in his reaction, as well. Steven was older than Farieh—nearly four years older. He needed something—someone, actually. And this stunning young woman with the trace of a Middle Eastern accent who had just materialized in Abdul's backyard struck him as ideal to his purpose. Steven put his phone down and looked across at her.

"I'm guessing you're a senior. Am I close?" Had he been forced to guess, Steven *would* have picked Farieh for a senior. It had little to do with her height, although she was tall—probably 5'9" or 5'10". And it had little to do with her attractiveness, although she was one of the most beautiful women Steven had seen at KU, and he had been there well past four years. It was the way she looked at him when she spoke. She was confident. Able to look at him directly when she spoke to him, her face relaxed, the timbre of her voice even. She wore her poise like a favorite pair of jeans.

It wasn't just her face or her voice or her bearing, it was all of her. There may have been a pinch of sadness at the corner of her eyes. He saw something there; he was not sure what. But what eyes! Shimmering green in the low light of the garden. He felt he had joined a conversation with a seasoned member of the foreign service, but someone who was 22 years old, and gorgeous.

If she recognized the artifice behind his answer Farieh did not react to it. There was no blush, no "Really! How nice of you to think so." In their place only a simple, "Sophomore. Petroleum engineering and English literature." She added, "Are you a student?" Another direct question, still wrapped in a faint accent but warmer this time.

Relaxing, Steven laughed and said, "That, I suppose, would depend on the audience! Some of my teachers last spring had real doubts; but I passed, and I'm enrolled again—I'm one of those sixth-year seniors, so I would say, 'Yes.'"

Farieh did not understand what it was to be a "sixth-year senior" and Steven explained. Her next question was more personal. "Why are you out here by yourself when the house is full of people?"

Growing in the conviction this young woman was exactly what he needed, and impressed by her directness, Steven thought for a moment about answering truthfully: *I have a business to run and it's essential that I keep track of it 24/7.* But the moment escaped and he chose a different response.

"I guess I get bored. You see the same kids you see at The Wheel or The Hawk, drinking too much, yelling instead of talking. I'm not trying to hold myself out as someone who's exceptional at social conversation, but I think I'm better than that."

"What do you like to talk about?"

Steven wondered whether there was something behind the softball question. But the young woman's expression had not changed; she was still relaxed, still focused. So he answered it: "Myself."

Farieh smiled involuntarily and Steven smiled back. She was beautiful in repose, but when she smiled her beauty moved to another level. Reminding himself he needed to be careful, he continued.

"I'm like everyone else in that respect, although maybe a little more honest about it. I don't believe I have a more compelling story than anyone else. But I have one, and I enjoy telling it, and it's important to me whether the person I'm talking with cares about it. If they do, I am glad to keep talking—about me or about anything else. But if they don't care about my story then it's easy for me to look for someone else. Tonight, inside, there may be two people sober enough to care about my story or anyone else's, and I didn't have the good luck to meet either of them when I arrived, so I came out here. I don't see myself as a loner. I'm comfortable being by myself.

There was a small, quiet moment before he sent a question to her: "What do you like to talk about?"

Farieh had looked away, back toward the house, allowing Steven to steal a glance at his phone: nothing new. When her head rotated back to him he was looking right at her.

Farieh had looked away because her attention had drifted far from what he was saying. Steven was tall. His short blond hair was a crew cut in contrast with the guys she saw on campus whose overly-long hair was coifed. He was trim, athletic—she liked that. And he was handsome, his Nordic features dominating his face and surrounding his blue eyes. What she was warming to was not just his conversation. His question should not have caught her by surprise. But it did, and she took a second or two before she started her answer.

"Until now..." Farieh, too, was unsure whether to answer honestly. *Until now,* she thought to herself, *I liked to talk about British novels and the new labs at Gray-Little and my honors advisor and her scones. They were more than a distraction from my thoughts of Iran and my best friend. Former best friend. They were real thoughts about real people and real things. But this garden, this sequestered spring night—they are real too. And tonight I am not interested in talking as much as I am interested in looking at you, and listening to you while I'm doing it.*

As she hesitated, Steven's phone rang.

"Excuse me," he said. "I'm very sorry." He stood and walked

across the grass to the grill. The call was short, not more than a minute; but when he returned to her he apologized again. "I have to leave. I am *much* more sorry about that." As he watched Farieh's expression cloud over he spoke again, wanting to rescue the moment. "I have really enjoyed talking with you. Where do you live? Can I see you again?"

Farieh smiled at his question, which had pushed back the disappointment. "Miller," she said, her voice feeding Steven's. "Miller Scholarship Hall. It's next to the chancellor's house. And, yes, I would like to see you again!" Her hopefulness reached for Steven as he made ready to leave.

"Okay!" he said. "Miller." And then he turned toward a gate in the backyard she had not seen before, walked through it, and was gone.

Steven's call had come from Abdul. Steven had asked him to call, to give him an excuse to leave the party he had been certain would be dull. But the last 20 minutes had not been dull. Just the opposite, they had provided Steven the very person he needed to accompany him to Chicago for the meeting Abdul was planning, the meeting when Steven would meet Abdul's father.

Abdul had spoken often about his father and about the things he was known for. One of them was beautiful women. Knowing his father as well as anyone, Abdul knew he admired men who shared that fixation. The people at the highest ranks of the family business were "players"—men who attracted beautiful women and who enjoyed showing them off. Abdul had suggested to Steven that his bringing such a woman to Chicago would be a strong positive. Here she was.

Farieh and Jamie had uncharacteristically locked the door of their room. When the flowers began to arrive there was no place to put them except the living room, which they soon overwhelmed. There were dozens of spider mums in reds and oranges and yellows, sunflowers by the armloads, dahlias in purples and white and rusts, yellow carnations, a battalion of crimson amaranthus, and six dozen long-stem roses, 36 red and 36 yellow. A sealed card was addressed to "Farieh."

It was five minutes shy of dinner when Farieh and Jamie finally returned to the scholarship hall. The other residents were not in the dining room or the kitchen but were sharing the living room with the flowers, waiting for them. "My God, Farieh," one of them shouted, "Open the card!" She did.

I HOPE YOU LIKE FLOWERS!
PLEASE CALL ME: (224) 970-0001
STEVEN

# Citation X

Their server, Charles, had presented the cake as though on cue from the weather gods, who had pulled back the cloud curtain a moment before to reveal a sun as reluctant to surrender its place in the western sky as Farieh was to surrender her seat at their table. They sat next to the windows on the 30th floor of the Commerce Bank Tower in a space Steven said had once been a famous Kansas City restaurant. Tonight—not yet late—it was still serving food, but only to the two of them.

They had seen each other for weeks now. A walk to class became a walk to the Union for tea; tea on campus became tea on Mass Street downtown; several long walks came next. Appearing only to be making conversation, Steven had asked her what she liked to eat. Her first thought had been of her childhood and breaking the fast of Ramadan, so she told him about the festival meal her mother served at Eid al-Fitr. The main course was tajine, the stew of either lamb or beef along with vegetables and plums and apricots. Farieh and her sisters liked lamb in virtually all forms; and if by itself and not in a stew they liked it as a lamb rack, broiled. Next was manti—dumplings, this time with beef for the contrast. Accompanying all of the courses was bolani—the thin-crusted Afghani bread her mother stuffed with spiced pumpkin. The crowd-stopper was lapis legit, a Dutch cake transformed by its Indonesian colony into a thinly-layered marvel of flour, eggs, butter, cloves, and cardomom. Her mother made the other desserts too. For dessert lovers like Farieh and her sisters, Eid was like birthdays on a plate! But she always made them wait until the end for the lapis legit. Farieh had not yet been able to share Mehri with

Steven, the friend of her childhood, but she had shared the food.

Steven had been a good listener. They had had casual dinners in Lawrence. Tonight, Steven had told her, would be special. He had driven her to Kansas City, and their meal featured lamb. The rack served to her had been a perfect size—three ribs, as well as a perfect temperature—medium. Preceded by an elegant salad made entirely of mint leaves lifting up tiny blueberries and crumbled feta, all of it shining in a light vinaigrette, the lamb was served with julienned carrots and with a couscous so good it reminded her of Tehran. It had been just right—all of it. But the dessert had pushed it right over the top. This was the first course to be served with a cover—in this case, a silver dome; and Farieh was curious. But the flourish with which Charles removed her dome did not begin to match Farieh's excitement when she saw what waited for her on the gleaming white dinner plate beneath: lapis legit— surrounded by brilliant red raspberries in the shape of a heart.

Farieh was standing. At the moment she realized she was upright her thoughts were of Mehri, and the bread baker, and the park in Tehran. Had she been alone she would have cried. But she wasn't alone. She was looking at Steven, and with her next breath she was rushing to a position behind him and throwing her arms around him. Farieh was nearly as strong as she was tall, and Steven realized after a few moments he would have to remove her arms from around his neck or pass out! He gently did so, pushed his chair back, and stood up to join her—holding her at arms-length. "I love it when you're happy! Thank you for being here tonight."

Farieh was looking at the last of the berries when her attention was drawn to the window. A lone jet aircraft glided left to right as it descended through the sunset to Charles Wheeler Airport, the private aviation facility immediately across the Missouri River. "What a perfect evening to fly somewhere," she said as she moved her napkin across her lips. "I wonder whether that plane will stay—or go."

"What would you like it to do?" asked Steven.

"Go, of course! Can't you imagine flying somewhere this evening—having the freedom to get up from the table, even a table like this one, and go to a completely different place? To spend the weekend visiting shops and galleries, and maybe speaking a different language?" She looked across at Steven as she placed her napkin next to her empty plate. "Do people really do things like that? Or is that just in the movies?"

"Why don't we find out?" He pulled his phone out of his jacket pocket, dialed a number from memory, waited only a few seconds, and spoke: "David? Steven. We saw your approach out the window. What about Quebec?" Steven looked up at Farieh, smiling quietly as he waited on the response. Then he returned his attention to his phone. "Okay? Good. We are almost finished; should be there in 15 minutes."

No words came. Farieh could only stare back at him. Steven helped: "You said you always carry your passport, right?"

Farieh sputtered, "Yes."

"All right," Steven continued as though discussing tomorrow's weather report. "That's really all you'll need. David will book Chateau Frontenac—it's winter, not a holiday, and it shouldn't be a problem. I know you have only what you're wearing and your jacket. But it's Friday, and you will be able to find anything you need tomorrow morning, either in the hotel shops or in the shops surrounding the hotel. The waterfront shopping district just down the steps is lovely. And, of course, you will have your own room."

Farieh still said nothing. This was not a fantasy. They were about to leave the dinner, drive to the airport, and fly to Quebec. Steven Mobley, an older KU student, handsome, with obviously-limitless resources, had spent hours planning this dinner and the weekend to follow. All for a woman he had kissed goodnight but once, and that barely. Even her sisters would have voiced some caution. But they were not here. She was here. She was looking west through a dark sky—into Kansas, wondering what it would be like to wake the next morning—in Canada. She would find out.

"We'll have to leave if we're going to be there in 15 minutes," he said. And with that they stood. Steven shook hands with Charles, who gave them their coats, and they walked to the elevator.

It wasn't two miles between the Commerce Bank garage and the airport. After crossing the Buck O'Neil Bridge, Steven's red Tesla Plaid turned left down the slope, left again to the parking lot for the Fixed Base Operator, and stopped in front of the low building. Steven came around to open her door and help her out; then they walked side by side into the FBO lounge and past its lone, young employee who looked up and said "Hi!" before returning to his paperback and his coffee. David and his co-pilot were talking at the other end of the lounge. They had looked casually in Steven's direction when they heard his response to the young man behind the desk. But there was nothing casual about their response to Farieh. Still, they were professionals, and they knew Steven, so they greeted Farieh with a handshake and a level smile. David did almost all of the talking for the pair as they led Steven and Farieh out the back door, across the pavement, and to the foot of the stairs for the Citation. "It's a beautiful Friday night, Steven. Air traffic is light; weather is clear; winds aloft are negligible. We should have you to Jean Lesage in just over two hours."

David extended his hand to Farieh as she approached the bottom of the stairs. "Let me help you, Farieh. This is a narrow ladder." David had flown F-18s in the Navy, and "stairs" would always be "ladders" to him. "Once you get to the top it's a right-hand turn into the cabin. I know you just came from dinner. But if you get hungry, there's food on the table in back and something to drink in the refrigerator under the table." Farieh took his hand, placed her other hand on the railing, and moved smoothly up into the aircraft. Steven came next, followed by the pilots.

She had to duck her head to get through the door, but the cabin height over the aisle was just high enough to let her stand upright, which she did, taking in the interior as she did so. Except for the leather seating, every surface gleamed. The metal brightwork reflected the overhead lights like crystal; the wood grains just beneath the mirrored surfaces of the furniture and the side panels popped in the same, low light. Farieh thought she had walked into a Faberge egg.

Steven spoke quietly into her ear. "Let's sit in the two seats in back; that will even out the load." She walked the several steps to the back, put her jacket on the couch, and turned into the starboard seat, immediately turning to look out the porthole window. Across the main runway were large hangars with an old, swollen, large-body jet parked to the south of them. Farieh turned back to the interior and saw David in his seat in the cockpit forward of the cabin. He was buckling his seatbelt and turning back to them as he did so. "We'll roll in under a minute," he said. "Please buckle your seat belt for the takeoff. Once we hit 10,000 feet you can remove it. The overhead lights will change from soft red to soft green at that point." Farieh complied, as did Steven in the seat across from her. Then she leaned back into one of the most comfortable seats she had ever sat in and closed her eyes as the lithe aircraft began to move.

Farieh had flown first-class on many high-value commercial jet aircraft, right up to the super-luxurious spaces on the UAE flag carrier's A380. But this was her first time in a private jet. As the winds were out of the north and the FBO's apron was at the south of the runway, David had his aircraft into its take-off roll almost immediately. The Citation's lift-off came well before she was ready for it, followed by its even-more-stunning acceleration. And almost before she could rotate her head to look at the ceiling lights they transitioned to green. "Wow!" she thought—out loud as it turned out. "How fast *is* this thing?!" But her *wow* fit more than the Citation X. This whole evening was wow!

Across from her, Steven smiled and answered. "This is the hotrod of the Citation fleet. That's why David likes it. He says it's as close to his experience with military aircraft as he has found in his new career as a charter pilot."

"Does he work for *you*?!" Steven was a college student. But tonight, anything seemed possible.

"No." Steven smiled again. "He works for the father of a friend of mine. Abdul is my friend, and Hassan is his father. Hassan and his companies own several aircraft. I asked Abdul if I could have one tonight, and the Citation seemed the best-suited since there would only be two of us. It's also the fastest. I know Abdul's pilot, David, and I really like him. He's checked out in the entire fleet. But he likes the Ten the best, and I knew there was a good chance we'd draw him if I asked for it. So I did, and it was available, and so was he."

They were already straight and level at Mach 0.93. Fareh's head had been spinning for some time now, but the rush of the Citation added a new dimension to it.

"Do you mind if I close my eyes?" she asked. "I think I'm getting a little dizzy."

"Anything you want. This is your evening." And with that he reached across the aisle, took Farieh's hand, brought it to his mouth, and kissed it. He held it for a long moment, the smell of the dessert she loved so much still faint on her fingertips, then returned it to the armrest on the adjoining seat. Eyes closed, her shoulders relaxed, Farieh was already asleep.

Farieh slept all the way to Quebec, she slept through the landing, and Steven had to jostle her when it was time for them to leave the aircraft. The car was waiting just on the other side of the perimeter fence, and they made it to the old city in only a few minutes. Now restive, Farieh looked out the side and back windows like she had first looked out at London from the back of a black cab years ago. She marveled at the old stone structures and the heavy white cloak they wore in the maritime winter.

Chateau Frontenac faces the Plains of Abraham. The approach to the hotel by foot from Battlefield Park is stunning, especially in winter when the chateau can rise up out of the fog like a glorious relic of the *ancien regime*. Because it was clear tonight, the approach to the hotel by car along the Rue Saint-Louis, past the old buildings and past the small square on the north side, was not so dramatic. But it was still beautiful, especially at midnight.

There were few lights on as they approached the desk at the south end of the lobby. To its right was an elaborate oak key box, now empty of the heavy metal instruments that might have served a Norman keep. Even this late, with but two persons on one side of the desk and one on the other, check-in was a tutorial in European professionalism and discretion. The clerk acknowledged Farieh first, with a warm smile whose only message was "Welcome." His conversation, entirely with Steven and in low tones despite the emptiness of the large space, was focused and brief. There was no mention of the absence of luggage; there was nary a glance past the shoulders of the two young people standing in front of him. They were taking the two rooms that had been reserved for Steven just hours before: one, a Gold Suite for the young woman; the other, a standard king for the young man. Plastic keys made to look like wood were passed to the new guests, the clerk bowed slightly as he said "Good night," and Farieh and Steven made their way to the central elevator bank. Cased all in brass, the middle car took them to the 14th floor. Steven accompanied Farieh to her room, watching her from the center of the hallway as she walked all the way inside and turned on the light.

"I have no expectations of you this evening, Farieh," said Steven. "There is no sexual quid pro quo you have to worry about. Quebec just struck me as fun—something you had probably not experienced before, and it looks like I was right. That's plenty enough for me. Good night."

As Steven turned and walked down the corridor Farieh breathed an ambiguous sigh. She was grateful for Steven's respect for her. Yet the part of her so alive to the night and the place was disappointed he had not tested it.

# Morning: Chateau Frontenac

Having taken a moment for her eyes to adjust to the still-dark room and for her brain to take in its size, Farieh lifted her head deliberately from the embroidered pillow case and rotated it slightly right. She pulled back the duvet and slid her legs over the side of the bed, her feet finding the embroidered slippers where the staff had placed them the afternoon before. Then she leaned forward into a steady motion that brought her upright. Freed from any attachment to the bed, she moved to the closet, found the hotel's terry robe, and stepped into it. More needlework: the back side of the coat of arms ran roughly across her breast and brought her fully awake.

She closed the closet door and turned toward the other two—the bathroom was left and the suite's enormous living room was right. She walked right and began an immediate search for a coffee bar. On top of the elegant side table where a Keurig and its pods might have been sat a small silver tray and the card it was holding: "*Pour le service en chambre, veuillez composer le 8700.*" Farieh saw the phone on a lamp table next to the sofa, walked to it, and dialed the number. The woman's voice answered in French so Farieh responded in kind, ordering a pot of coffee, orange juice, croissants, butter and marmalade, and a bowl of fruit. When she had finished, she returned the handset, moved to a dining room table that would have seated eight, then past it to stand at the tall windows on its far side.

Unlike the bedroom, the heavy curtains flanking the dining room windows had been left open. Farieh was looking east to a sun just barely up, its low rays skipping across the shallow crests on the St. Lawrence until they met the brick buildings and breakwater of the Quartier Petit Champlain just below her. Ashore, they danced through the streets and alleyways of the shopping district telling anyone up that another day had come to Quebec City.

The hushed knock turned her around. Gathering her robe around her, for it had come open as she had stretched before the sunrise, Farieh walked toward her breakfast.

# Do You NoMI?

The routine of the weeks after her return from Quebec was helpful to Farieh's school work. Her engineering classes were stimulating in a narrow sense of the term; many of the concepts were new, especially in thermodynamics. And the work could be challenging, even hard. Yet none of it seemed right for a dorm room or a coffee shop in the late afternoon, heavy wool socks up on the furniture above discarded boots, tea or coffee cooling as conversations did the opposite. Entropy and energy transfer were no match for English novelists.

She saw Steven, though not often. They would walk from Miller to the Union; Farieh would have a tea and Steven a latte. They would talk, but not long. Things were busy, they were busy, and they didn't mind.

Nearly a month had passed when Farieh noticed Steven's eyes twinkling as they stepped off the Miller porch. He had another trip in mind. North again, but not so far north. There was only one big city in Steven's life—the toddlin' town on the western shore of Lake Michigan. Farieh had said "Yes!" before Steve could voice its third syllable.

They had taken the Citation X again. But this time Farieh sat alone in the back, reading. Steven and Abdul were side-by-side in the front seats, and they talked the entire flight. Signature MDW's people were ready for them when the Cessna taxied up to the FBO, and they quickly left the aircraft and got into the black Yukon that was idling only a few yards away. Like his father, Abdul preferred Midway to O'Hare. It was only slightly closer to the Loop; but it was far less congested—for air traffic and freeway traffic both.

The northbound traffic on Cicero was sluggish for a weekday afternoon, but they were eastbound on the interstate soon enough and they were into the city in no time. The big GMC left little room for anyone else at the Park Hyatt, whose entrance on the south side of the Park Tower was compact. Their evening destination—NoMI, the hotel's signature restaurant—pooched out from the east façade at the eighth floor, an intrusion into the air space above the small park that had turned heads when the tower was built in 2000. Today, no one noticed the architectural bleb, but everyone knew the restaurant.

"Dinner is at 8:00," said Abdul as they finished checking in. Each of them would have a room. "Why don't we plan to meet in the bar at 7:30?"

"That works," replied Steven. It was 6:00; that would give him time to scan through his e-mail and return any calls that were important.

Abdul turned to Farieh, who did not seem to mind that Steven had not only answered first but had also begun walking toward the elevator. "That's fine, Abdul," she said. "Really." They took the same car, although to different floors. Farieh got off first on 16. Abdul, Steven, and Abdul's father were all on 18, the highest hotel floor in the 67-story building. They would be there only one night; each had one roller bag; Farieh's was the largest, and the brightest.

Farieh opened the door to a suite and could not help smiling. Neutral tones on the walls and ceiling played well with the nearly-new hardwood floor, the Persian carpets, and the bright abstract oil painting above the couch. She walked straight ahead to the window and found her rooms were also beautifully-sited: the view ran to the east, far past the edge of Lake Michigan.

What Carl Sandburg might have called "the big shoulders" of the John Hancock Building were just left across Michigan Avenue. They had only begun with Sandberg. Farieh liked the heft of the language in the "Chicago Poems," which seemed to go well with the buildings she had seen, especially after they turned north at

McCormick Place. These buildings were a century newer, of course, and their heft was as much a product of glass and aluminum as of bricks and steel. But she liked them.

The Lake ran to the horizon behind the sheers. Anticipating the morning's sunrise, she was glad to see the blackout curtains behind them.

She went next to the bedroom, grabbing her roller bag on the way and lifting it onto the bed once she got there. The California king was enormous, its cream-colored duvet a quiet companion to the stars of the space—more original art that hung from the walls or sat on the chrome and glass coffee table in the corner by the two modern side chairs.

Whoever decorated these spaces recently had not forgotten the bathroom. The honed floor was of the same neutral palate as the other rooms. There was a walk-in shower. And there was a soaking tub! Farieh looked immediately at her phone—she still had more than an hour before she was due downstairs. The sound she nearly suppressed came out as a whoop as she rushed back into the bedroom to lay out her dress for the evening. Then she stripped out of the clothes she had traveled in and was eyes-closed in the tub before the water was high enough to cover her ankles.

Steven had said he would knock on her door at 6:25. As ever, he was precisely on time. In Lawrence, as he was asking her to accompany him to Chicago, he had told her this was the most important meeting of his life.

Impressed with Steven's organizational skills, his ability to recruit talent, and with his overall business acumen, Abdul had brought him into their family business more than a year ago. Steven told her he had felt more at home there than he had ever felt with his own family. He also told her he had "been successful." Farieh did not know what Steven *did* for Abdul and his father, but she knew he was talented: he was smart, he was articulate, he planned well, and he could focus. And when he wanted to be charming he could be that too. Steven's confiding the importance of this meeting to her was the first time he had displayed anything like vulnerability.

Farieh's vulnerability was Iran, and Mehri. Vulnerability had found no place in Farieh's growing up. She was too busy, too successful, too happy, and loved. But after introducing itself in Tehran last summer, vulnerability had become her boon companion.

She was surprised when Steven had exposed an uncharacteristic anxiousness as he talked with her about the meeting. Surprised by it when it happened, Farieh had thought about it several times since. He was trusting her to help him make a good impression. To herself, she committed she would do so.

Steven was reading messages on his phone when Farieh opened the door to her room, and he glanced up at the sound of the latch. When he saw the woman in the doorway he could not look anywhere else. Farieh had wound her thick auburn hair into a simple chignon. Asymmetric and sleeveless, her dress fit closely to her waist before it relaxed into a high-low skirt. It was a riot of candy-apple red satin without bows or beading or any other decoration. The four-inch heels of her matching Stuart Weitzman pumps made her just Steven's height.

The middle finger of her right hand supported a simple gold ring. A bright gold bangle—flat and nearly an inch across—circled her left wrist. Her neck supported a gold omega.

Farieh's pear-shaped, emerald earrings were more outspoken. But Steven was drawn to the far-more-brilliant green of her eyes. He could only stare at her, and he did stare—for seconds—until she stepped across the threshold and took his arm and said, "You look very handsome, Steven."

As the elevator doors opened at the floor for NoMI, Farieh exited first, turning left toward the restaurant. Still inside the car, Steven watched every head in the bar turn to follow her. Abdul had been talking with the maître d', Robert, and he took a moment to introduce him to Farieh and Steven as they reached his desk. Then,

Robert in the lead, they all made their way toward the center alcove on the east wall where NoMI's finest table looked out over the park. The view jumped across Michigan Avenue before settling on the original Chicago Water Tower, brightly lighted in the cool, fall evening. Hassan Barakzai, Abdul's father, had arrived from Afghanistan the day before. Now rested, his glass of Louis Roederer Cristal in front of him and his back to the window, Hassan stood when Robert entered the room and nodded in the maître's direction. He stood much taller when he saw Farieh.

Hassan Barakzai was only a moment shy of six feet tall, as lean and hard as a ranch hand who had grown up in the summer heat of southwest Afghanistan. Brown-skinned at birth, his face had darkened from years of living and playing in the sun and looked like the leather of his favorite pair of cowboy boots. Hassan smiled at all of them as they approached the table, his even teeth bright against his face, his expression mirroring the breadth of his outstretched arms as he embraced his son first and then Robert, whom he had known for years. When Abdul introduced Steven, Hassan took his right hand in both of his and said, "Steven, welcome. It is my pleasure finally to meet the young man from Kansas who has so impressed my son."

Farieh had been standing behind Steven. Abdul led her gently toward his father, pausing when she was just even with Steven on his left side. "Father, this is Farieh Bukhari, Steven's friend. She is from Tehran, but she has come to the United States to study engineering at the University of Kansas." Abdul could have introduced her as Marie Curie or Katherine the Great—it would not have mattered; it would take Hassan another hour to master her name. But Farieh needed only that moment to capture his senses. Hassan had known beautiful women before, many of them. He was mildly surprised she was so tall. He was not prepared for her eyes.

Farieh's dress bared her left arm and shoulder. Never thinking not to do so, Hassan reached out and touched her just above the left elbow in a gesture natural for a daughter or a niece. Realizing he was blushing at the impropriety, he turned away from her and with a sweeping gesture invited his guests to sit with him.

Robert came to everyone's rescue by seating Farieh and introducing them to the menu. Farieh was no stranger to fine food, but ordering dinner at NoMI at Robert's lead was like watching her mother shop at De Beers in London. Each moment presented something exciting. And if the final list was simply too much it did not matter; everyone was pleased.

Each of the salads was served with an envelope. Inside was an ivory-colored 8" x 4" card made of cover stock with elaborately embossed pomegranates in red and black along its borders. Following a heading, in English, were seven numbered questions in Dari. The heading read:

DO YOU NoMI?

Hassan held his card up to the three others, this time smiling like the Cheshire Cat. "I have created a small amusement for us as we wait for our entrees. There are several questions here that will be answered first by Steven and then by…" A pause; Hassan could not remember her name. "…his lady. The winner will receive this gift." Hassan held up a small box, giftwrapped in red and black. "Steven," he went on, "the questions are in Dari. I am hopeful one of the two of you will be able to read them. If not, it will be my pleasure to translate them for you."

The first question read:

1.  MY NAME IS "HASSAN."
WHAT DOES IT MEAN IN AFGHANISTAN?

Farieh translated the question into English for Steven, as she would do with each of the questions going forward.

Steven had looked up the father's name as soon as Abdul told him the meeting was set. Farieh had not looked it up, but she knew the answer.

Steven responded first: "Hassan" means "beautiful."
Farieh spoke right after him: "I agree."
"A good start!" said Hassan.

## 2.  WHERE AM I FROM?

Again, Steven had looked it up: "Kandahar," he said.
Farieh spoke quickly: "I do not know, Hassan. If it is Kandahar, you have a beautiful home."
"Well done, Steven," said the host.

## 3.  MY LAST NAME IS BARAKZAI.
## WHAT IS MY TRIBE?

Steven had *not* looked this up—it never occurred to him and he said he did not know.
Farieh answered next. "I do not know the tribe from your name. But as you are from Kandahar, which is close to the eastern portion of my country, you may be Pashtun."
"Just right!" replied an excited Hassan.

## 4.  WHO FOUNDED MY CITY?

Steven did not know and guessed: "The prophet, Mohammed," as much a question as an answer. He added: "May peace be upon him." It was the wrong answer, but Hassan thanked Steven for his courtesy.
Farieh was ready the moment Hassan turned to her: "Alexander the Great, just before he wisely led his army out of Afghanistan to avoid losing it."
Hassan *loved* the answer, which was correct factually and politically brilliant.

## 5.  WHAT IS THE NATIONAL SPORT OF
## AFGHANISTAN?

Steven did not know, but his guess this time was more confident: "Soccer." Wrong again.

Farieh answered, "Horses and goats."

Hassan allowed it—telling her the actual name was "buzkashi."

## 6.   WHAT IS THE PROPER OBJECT OF POWER?

Chasing the first thought that dropped into his mind, Steven thought Hassan might be working a ruse. Knowing Abdul was an avid gamer and assuming Hassan was aware of that, Steven decided Abdul's father was making a wild departure from his culture and his own age. Hassan had thought about his audience and had chosen a subject that was keen not only to his son but to many young Americans as well—video games. Hassan was asking his two young guests, but mostly Steven, his potential business colleague, about his son's favorite game, "Control." Believing Abdul's father would think him a seer if he could penetrate the ruse, and knowing the answer because of all the gaming he had done himself, Steven could barely suppress a smile as he answered: "The slide projector."

Having no idea what to make of the answer, Hassan struggled to respond gracefully and turned to Farieh.

As mystified by Steven's answer as was Hassan, Farieh answered more traditionally: "The proper object of power is peace."

Hassan looked at Farieh for a long time before returning a smile that made real the meaning of his name.

Farieh smiled back, then read the last question on the card.

## 7.   WHO IS THE MOST BEAUTIFUL WOMAN
## IN THE WORLD?

Steven professed he had no idea and added that even if he did, he would not presume to suggest an answer to Hassan.

"A wise answer, Steven," replied Hassan. But he was plainly looking for a different one. "Farieh?"

Speaking more softly than before, Farieh made her final answer: "In your eyes, it is your wife—Abdul's mother."

Hassan was so taken with Farieh's response he could say nothing for several seconds. Then he took a sip of his tea before returning his eyes to the young woman across the table, remembering her name as he did so. "You are wise so far beyond your years, Farieh. And if I had what the people in the United States call 'a short list' of the most beautiful women in the world, you would be on it."

Hassan lifted the small black and red box from the table and handed it to Farieh. He was again excited. "This is yours," he said. "You must open it!"

Beneath the heavy paper was a black felt box perhaps five inches square, its top hinged like the box jewelers use for an expensive ring, but larger. Farieh lifted the top and saw it held a bird with a gold-colored head. It was an eagle, the national bird of Hassan's country. Farieh smiled at Hassan as she grasped the head of the bird and pulled. But it was far heavier than she had anticipated, and wedged into the custom lining, so she needed her left hand to hold the box while she pulled at the bird with her right. As the eagle emerged she saw it was skillfully crafted from its beak to its feathers to its talons. The artist had as faithfully captured its stern visage, and every part of it was the same gold color.

The eagle was now free from its confinement and Farieh could turn it and hold it up to the light. Four inches tall and three and one half inches from beak to tail, it reminded her of the metal Jayhawk she had seen at Framewoods in Lawrence. But close inspection showed the bird represented here was real, not mythical. As that reality became apparent another crowded in: the eagle was not just gold-colored; Hassan's eagle was *made* of gold.

Farieh had never received a gift like this. She tried to find a word, anything that might convey her feelings, but nothing came. As she dropped her head, hoping Robert would come to her aid, she missed the darkness that had come between her and Steven, and the resentment that moved it across his face.

The entrees were served and the conversation turned to "business." But if there was commercial business discussed Farieh missed it. The conversation was all about Hassan: his boyhood, his education, Hassan's wife, their son—Abdul was their only child, and Hassan's fascination with buzkashi—a sport for mounted players in which the object is to carry a goat around a marker at one end of the field and then throw it into a scoring circle at the other end. A player is called a "Chapandaz." Hassan was a master Chapandaz, known throughout his country like famous football and basketball players are known in the United States. Farieh learned Hassan's life revolved around four things: competition, beautiful horses, beautiful women, and money.

Farieh ordered no alcohol and drank none—not even the champagne. Toward the end of the meal she excused herself and went to the restroom. While she was gone Hassan reached across the table, rested his hand on Steven's, and complimented him on his "magnificent lady."

They were too full for dessert. Hassan summoned the check with a flourish and paid it with an even grander one, and then they were standing and walking slowly to the elevator. Farieh said "Good night" to Hassan and Abdul and Steven as she walked out of the elevator on her lower floor. When Steven called a few minutes later he seemed distracted, even put out. When she asked whether anything was wrong he told her "No." Briefly, and in the same flat tone, he followed up: he was tired, he had to meet Hassan and Abdul for breakfast. With no change in affect he told Farieh the evening went well. On the flight to Chicago he had promised to take her shopping at Watertower Place if the dinner was a success. He had not forgotten the promise and he repeated it over the phone, telling her to be ready at 11:00. Then he hung up.

Farieh looked absently at her phone as she swayed between strong emotions. On one side was her elation with the dinner: how she felt as she had finished dressing and had looked in her floor-length mirror that one last time; how every head turned at the bar as she and Steven walked out of the elevator; how the table settings and the flowers in their crystal vases winked back at the low lights along the east wall; how the colors of the food surpassed even the radiance of the flowers; and how Hassan—a man as old as her father and the most virile and worldly of Afghans—had behaved throughout the evening like a school boy with a new kite.

There was another side. While the evening's brilliance had pushed Farieh's vulnerability to the farthest of her inner spaces, it stirred now. Farieh sensed the movement. But she had drawn deeply from other emotions tonight, and she was too tired to react to this one. Pulling off only her shoes, she crawled into bed and fell asleep.

Steven and Abdul joined Hassan for breakfast as Farieh eased through the morning in her hotel room. Toward noon they folded in the 90 minutes at Watertower Place that Steven had promised, then lunched at RL, then walked across the street to the hotel and the black GMC that would take them to Midway. The Citation made short work of the 400 air miles between Chicago and Kansas City, and Abdul's Porsche pulled up in front of Miller while there was still light in the sky. Steven, who had been riding in front with Abdul, got out first, opened the door for Farieh, and went to the back to pull her roller bag out of the Panamera's low trunk.

Used to the seating arrangement by now, Farieh had been on her phone during the drive in from the airport; she was pleased Steven would get her bag and open the door for her. Wearing a baby-blue puffy jacket, hot-pink Converse All-Stars, and the torn jeans popular with her American contemporaries—not the flared linen slacks and high-collared shirt Steven had just purchased for her at Eileen Fisher, Farieh got out and led Steven down the sidewalk to the front door. She stepped up onto the porch, turned, and opened her mouth to thank him, but he was already moving toward the curb. All she saw above the collar of Steven's jacket was the back of his head.

Steven lowered himself into the front passenger seat and closed the door behind him. Because he kept his eyes on Abdul he missed Farieh's wave and the perplexity that had dislodged her smile. "Thanks for driving, Abdul, and for dropping off Farieh."

"She's dynamite, Steven. Beautiful, smart as hell, and amazing with my father."

"I'm glad you think so," replied Steven. "Don't get me wrong; I'm glad we were so successful with your father. But I can do without a bitch who shows me up every time she opens her mouth. No matter how fucking smart she is!"

Farieh had not overreacted to Steven's indifference. She knew this had been an important meeting; she could imagine there were many details for Steven and Abdul to work out once they got back to Lawrence. But she was disappointed all the same, and she decided to address her disappointment by going to a movie. Jamie was game, they grabbed two other women from Miller, and they made a Sunday evening of it. When the movie had finished they stopped off at IHOP and spent the next hour seeing who could pile the most whipped cream onto the top of a chocolate soda before it slid off onto the tabletop.

It was nearly midnight before Farieh was ready for bed. She picked up her phone out of habit, looked at her calendar, and saw staring back at her the reminder her paper for Helen Lochlear's seminar on 19th-Century British Thought and Literature was due at 8:30 Monday morning. It's not like she had not started the paper; it was nearly done. But the section that was not done was the one she had had trouble with: whether England's Langham Place Circle, the first organized movement for British women's suffrage and Britain's first "feminist movement," had looked to Jeremy Bentham for any of its ideas. She did not know when she left for Chicago and had figured she would turn her attention to the paper Sunday afternoon, when she got back. But her discouragement with Steven had led to the movie, and then the whipped cream, and now the day was gone. She was tired.

Like every other KU student, Farieh had many thoughts about AI. It was obvious how it might help her with her assignments. But she knew some departments—the honors program, for example— were absolutely opposed to it. She had never used it before.

She went to the closet, retrieved her robe and put it back on, stepped back into her slippers, picked up her laptop, and headed for the dining room. She would try it tonight. It would save hours of time. She could have stayed up all night; but she was already tired, and there was no way an all-nighter spent on a topic she was unsure of would lead to "A"-quality work. She would use AI only for that one section of the paper. Also, she would write her own introduction to the AI section, and her own transition out of it. The AI section would be two paragraphs, max. All the rest was her own work.

# CHAT GPT

"Farieh! Glad you could come on such short notice."

There had been hardly any notice. Farieh's honors advisor was again her teacher. She had sent a text to Farieh at 2:10—not 20 minutes ago—asking whether she could stop by her office at 2:30. Farieh had been able to do so and had quickly responded, "OK." Arriving first, Farieh had just settled into the Poet's Corner with a small handful of peanut M&Ms when Helen Lochlear rushed through the door opening on her way to her antique desk, whose pile of papers she immediately added to. But she pulled one back and thrust it at Farieh. "This one is yours."

Professor Lochlear could focus on a student like the world had no other work to do at that moment than to solve a 20-year old's problem. But she could also be "busy," and she was "busy" now. Farieh had barely taken the document when Helen turned to the filing cabinet, a quarter-sawn oak beauty she had rescued from an estate sale, and stopped in front of it, hands on her hips. "Provost, Provost, Provost. Where IS that file?!" Then she remembered, pulling out the top drawer and removing a file close to the front. "Budgets! I thought we were DONE with budgets! But NO! Liberal Arts is still over and the Provost wants *everyone* to find another $1,000 they can do without and join her at Strong at 2:45 with their report. This is getting closer and closer to grade school teaching, where my cousin has to buy her own *paperclips* and *staples* and *manila folders* if she wants to keep anything straight.

"Oh, your paper." There was the slightest pause in the commotion that had walked into the office with her teacher. "I don't know which AI program you used, but you used one. This was bound to happen: two students in the class type in the same query and the program produces two documents that contain at least one sentence that is the same in each—verbatim. I know we talked about AI, and how you are not to use it in this class, which is about your own writing. I'm not mad about it; you just have to do it over—has to be your own work."

And then her teacher stopped talking rapidly and stopped moving rapidly. In fact, she stopped moving altogether. And when she spoke again she was looking directly at Farieh.

"I was too quick with this. I have seen AI-generated papers before, but I was surprised to see one from you. Please don't do this again, Farieh.

"Many KU faculty are so intrigued with AI they encourage their students to experiment with it. I understand that. But this is an honors class. The honors program regards the use of AI as cheating. We actually see it as worse than plagiarism. With plagiarism, the student is doing at least some relevant work to find the other paper, read it, confirm it fits, and copy it. With AI, the work consists of loading the parameters and pushing a button.

"This is a conversation you will get only once. If there is a next time the consequences will be different, and you will not like them.

"Okay!" Helen's original mood had snapped back and she was moving toward the door. "Thanks for coming on such short notice. The budget process calls—off to see the wizard!" Alone again in the Poet's Corner, Farieh watched her mentor march out into the hallway, bright scarf rippling. Daunted, the hallway made no challenge to her passage.

*There will be no next time.* The thought came just behind the warmth of the embarrassment that had already covered Farieh's face. *Besides, this was nothing. Two paragraphs. Professor Lochlear was not even upset. Had she been upset she would have given me an 'F,' and a long lecture. I'm fine.*

*There will be no next time.*

Farieh edged past the Poet's Corner, then walked out into the same dull hallway. Her face had cooled, so she was able to muster a determined look. But Wescoe's walls recognized the faux fortitude, and they greeted her indifferently.

# Christmas Party

Farieh! What a nice surprise!"

Helen was unloading her backpack onto her desk when she had noticed her favorite student. Her annual winter trip to Costa Rica, which attracted its full complement of students almost the moment it slipped onto the electronic list of KU course offerings, was not set to depart until just after New Year's Day. There was still more than a month before anyone had to leave for the airport. But Helen had just learned the graduate assistant she was counting on to help her, who spoke Spanish like she had been born in Madrid and who had been a whiz at scheduling the events in San Jose and the travel away from the capital, had been invited to study at the University of Barcelona starting January 15. She had accepted, had decided to take the first two weeks of January to travel around Catalonia, and had bailed on Costa Rica. Farieh's being there on the couch in the poet's corner perked up a November afternoon that had gone cloudy.

Helen poured tea out of the electric pot. "Scone?" She gestured to the tray on the table in front of them. "They were fresh at noon."

"Sure," replied Farieh. "It was all I could do to wait until you got here to have one!" As Farieh had last talked with Helen about AI, her anxiousness was mostly a product of not knowing how her mentor would receive her. The warmth of Helen's welcome released the buoyancy Farieh had held in check.

"They're blueberry," said Helen. "They take me back to the pies at the State Fair in Hutchinson." She put one on a porcelain plate for Farieh and a second on a not-quite-matching plate for herself. "No clotted cream this time. I didn't know you were coming!" Helen set the plates on the table and sat down in her chair, so close to Farieh their knees touched.

It was a long minute before they spoke again, both of them trying to maneuver a sip of the very hot tea around a first bite of the pastry.

"Bummer you got stood up on Costa Rica." Having gone to Costa Rica with Professor Lochlear last year, right after her first semester at KU, Farieh knew how busy she was when she had students in tow in a foreign country. Her teacher needed another person, and Farieh was concerned for her ability to recruit someone else so late in the year.

"It'll be fine," replied her advisor. "Let's talk about Christmas!"

"What *about* Christmas?" asked Farieh. It was a holiday she did not celebrate, but her advisor's enthusiasm had her attention.

"The chancellor is having a party! Just the honors faculty—first time ever for that. Some of my colleagues are so flabbergasted they are talking about buying a dress for it!"

"Lord have mercy," deadpanned the young visitor, who had become intrigued with American dialect and was trying out expressions like they were different-colored sneakers. If there was anyone who would not need a new dress for a party it was Farieh.

"I know!" said Professor Lochlear. "But there's other news about Christmas. Guess what?"

More enthusiasm! In the moment before she answered, Farieh recognized she and her mentor were moving on a different plane than usual. Professor Lochlear was dealing with her colloquially, in a tone that suggested a peer relationship, even a girls' friendship. It was not something Farieh had been looking for from her mentor, not something she had encountered before. But the familiarity was affirming, and that was worth whatever strangeness came with it.

Still feeling playful, Farieh guessed: "You and your husband are going to skip the party and go to Paris!"

"From your mouth to God's ear," said Helen Lochlear. "But, no. The other news is that the honors faculty decided to invite undergraduate honors students to the party—a kind of reward for significant contributions to the program. One each from each class."

"That's terrific," said Farieh, instantly curious who would represent the sophomores. "Who will be invited?"

Never taking her eyes off her student, Professor Lochlear blew across her tea cup, took another small sip, and answered. "The sophomore class will be represented by Ms. Farieh Bukhari."

Helen watched for the reaction. She was pleased to see how quickly excitement had formed in her visitor's eyes and face and was delighted to observe even Ms. Farieh Bukhari was speechless for a moment. But only a moment.

"Oh my God!" Another affectation. "Whatever will I wear?!"

Both women had to put their cups down they were laughing so hard.

"There's not much time to sort that out," said the teacher, still smiling. "The party is this coming Friday, Stop Day. It will be at The Outlook, a pretty easy walk for you. 7:00 p.m. A reception first, then dinner at 8:00. Probably a buffet. The Outlook doesn't really have table seating so we'll catch our food and either plunk down in an empty chair or stand. I'm planning to eat standing up."

"Sounds like *great* fun!" Farieh was still excited.

Helen Lochlear had not seen much of her mentee since their lunch in London at the beginning of the summer. Farieh had seemed moody, even withdrawn, during the opening weeks of fall semester. She had visited Helen's office only once before fall break, and she had stayed maybe 10 minutes, barely time to say, "Hello/Goodbye." Helen had asked about Farieh's parents. She knew about the trip to Tehran; she wondered what was going on in Farieh's relationship with them and whether that had colored her return to Kansas. But her inquiry had been a brief one: "What do you hear from your parents?"

And Farieh had replied as briefly: "Really nothing since I got back."

Helen left it alone.

Since October Farieh had been far more energized, regaining the spontaneity that had been a hallmark of her freshman year. Her appearance in the Poet's Corner today was further proof of that. Helen's experience suggested two explanations—either a fascinating new class or a new boyfriend. Helen did not know Farieh's schedule, but she doubted academics had anything to do with the turnaround.

*So, a boy! But who was clever enough to cut through the cloud Farieh was walking through when classes started? And how did he keep her attention until now? And what does he look like? Richie Armstrong may have seemed a 'mascot' to Farieh, but he was as tall and handsome as they get around here. What an interesting conversation this would be!*

Helen was not going to go there without an engraved invitation. She went back to the party.

"Why don't we go together? I will pick you up at Miller at 7:00. Coming into the party with you will make it easier for me to introduce you to some of our new honors faculty—scholars who were not here last year when you had your freshman seminar. I can also introduce you to the chancellor. We don't always see eye to eye on what should be funded at KU. But he's energetic and a good conversationalist, and he's certainly easy to look at."

Farieh blushed very slightly at Helen's last remark. As she covered her face with her napkin to hide it she noticed the clock behind the desk.

"5:30. I'm already late for dinner. But I do have to go or I'll miss it entirely. Thank you, Professor Lochlear. This was lovely." Farieh stood up from the couch, slung her backpack over her left shoulder, and moved around the corner of the table. Quickly hugging her teacher, she backed past the table to the office door and was gone in a moment.

Helen Lochlear stood on the east side of her office. The window there looked out over the lawn Wescoe shared with Flint Hall and allowed her to watch Farieh as she hurried across the front of Watson, the main library, and then around the south side of Fraser toward her scholarship hall.

Helen had had brilliant students before, many of them. Marshall and Rhodes and Truman Scholars by the basketful. Her graduates included popular novelists and famous scientists and professional athletes. But she had never had a student who combined the intellectual capacity, the openness of personality, the physical grace, and the sheer star power of Farieh Bukhari. Farieh had overcome the slow start to her sophomore year. Helen thought she seemed happy this afternoon.

The party at the Outlook was three days away. Helen was excited for her colleagues and for herself. The chancellor's hosting them was a recognition they all craved. But she would also get to watch Farieh, who would engage that faculty and the chancellor in a setting new to all of them. It would be leveling. Yet Farieh would be so much more than a peer on Friday night. She would be dazzling.

# Friday Night at The Outlook

The thermometer had sunk almost to zero, leaving the small, Friday-night space between Miller and The Outlook crystalline cold. Farieh and her mentor joined a line of people in heavy coats and scarves and gloves, most having walked several blocks from the parking lot at the Union. Helen wore her own heavy coat, a knit hat pulled over her ears, and a very red scarf from her very large collection of scarves.

Farieh had left her coat in her room. It was perhaps 25 paces from Miller's sidewalk to The Outlook's front door and she had decided she would not need one. Farieh stepped onto the porch of the large, white residence and through its entryway wearing what she had worn for her dinner at NOMI in Chicago: a sleeveless satin dress with four-inch, matching heels. The ring, the bangle, and the omega, all simple, were in place on her finger and wrist and neck as they had been in Chicago. The emerald earrings, which had never been simple, stayed behind, replaced by small gold studs. Helen Lochlear's prediction was accurate. At just over six feet tall, auburn hair tucked behind her ears, sheathed in red, and all of it set off by gold jewelry too impeccable to be costume, she was dazzling.

Farieh parted the crush of guests inside the door like they were photographers at the Oscars. The turning of heads and the abrupt lowering of the din of the conversation were so obvious that the chancellor, standing 20 feet away with his back to the front door, turned out of his conversation with the chair of the honors program to look. What he saw interrupted his conversation for more than a moment. He knew of Farieh Bukhari; he had been told she would be here tonight. He was not ready for this.

He was rescued by Helen Lochlear, who had found a place for her coat and was back at Farieh's side, introducing her to the man in a blazer standing between Farieh and the approaching chancellor. When Bob Barkett reached them it was Helen who spoke first, thanking him for the party and introducing both Farieh and Professor Ahmed Zaidi. Chancellor Barkett knew the law school teacher and greeted him warmly. Before he could say anything to Farieh, Professor Zaidi had jumped in to amplify Professor Lochlear's brief mention of the young woman.

"I have only just met Ms. Bukhari, chancellor. But I have told her about my seminar for next semester. Even though it is a law school class and she is only a sophomore, I have invited her to join it. I hope she does."

The chancellor turned to Ms. Bukhari and had barely uttered, "Thank you for coming. It's very nice to meet you," when he felt a tug on his arm. It was his administrative assistant, Jill Swanson, reminding him he was to address everyone in two minutes. He turned back to the group, excused himself, and followed Jill toward the east end of the living room.

Helen Lochlear *did* know everyone. By the end of the evening Farieh had met most of the honors faculty, all of its new members, and their spouses and partners and significant others. Professor Lochlear had all of their names at the ready. Farieh had been as dazzling in her conversation as she had been in her arrival, moving from small talk about the increase in KU's enrollment to the future of AI to a spirited exchange with Zaidi and others about Palestine and Israel and what was the proper role for the United States in that conflict.

It was just as cold on the short walk back to Miller Hall as it had been on the way to the party. But as it was hours later and there were no clouds, the sky was a fairy necklace of stars. Helen Lochlear stood on the sidewalk as Farieh stepped up onto the scholarship hall's porch. "Good night, Farieh. I thought you were a splendid addition to the party."

"I had a wonderful time, Professor Lochlear," said the sophomore. "You have made so many things possible for me at KU. Thank you for all of them, and especially for tonight."

"See you soon!" said the mentor. "Clotted cream next time?!"

"Yes!" laughed Farieh, turning toward the front door.

# Miller – After Midnight

The dream was always the same. She was in Tehran and was waving goodbye to Mehri, who had driven up to visit her while Farieh was home from school in Kansas. They never had much time. The protests did not stop for their reunion and Mehri had to get back. As Mehri drove away from Farieh's house, down its long drive, Farieh was waving vigorously. Mehri had stopped at the street and was looking over her right shoulder to wave back a final time. She forgot to check for traffic from her left. Only Farieh saw the speeding SUV.

Farieh pulled back the cover, stood up carefully—Jamie was still sleeping, and pulled on socks and jeans and sneakers and then a sweatshirt. She added her parka and a knit cap to glove liners and gloves before easing through the door. At the back end of the hallway was the metal door that opened onto the narrow landing of the fire escape. She would take those black steps down to the path immediately behind the scholarship hall, walk a few more steps toward its neighbor on the north, Watkins, then turn right. 21 narrow steps ran down between old stone walls toward a pair of iron gates at the bottom. Especially late at night, the scene might have been stolen for the campus from a hilly arrondissement in Paris. The stony passage opened at the bottom onto a small fountain whose nearby benches allowed Farieh to sit in the dark and grieve Mehri's death.

She had been here so often the darkness no longer bothered her. She could move straight to the stone bench now without fear of someone else. There had been regulars from The Wheel who had needed a place to sleep off a last call, and they had made her uncomfortable earlier in the fall. But they had stopped coming when it turned cold.

Farieh had dressed well enough not to notice the 24 degrees. As she took her seat on the bench and folded her hands in her lap she stared up through the branches. A crescent moon highlighted the few high clouds tracking south to north that would alternately obscure and reveal the morning's stars. Farieh hoped Mehri had found her stars, and that she was looking down on her from one of them.

# Part II
## Winter

# Miller Hall: January

Morning comes early to the south side of Miller Hall. Especially in winter, when the large trees surrounding the chancellor's residence do not provide the protection against the sharp white of January that they offer against the softer light of spring. Farieh and Jamie shared a room on that south side. As it was the only room on the second floor that had two windows, sleeping in was a struggle. Yet Farieh had shown little interest in early rising since Steven stood her up for Christmas, and she had covered the sheers with layers of trash bags to create passable black-out curtains. There were floor vents centered beneath the curtains. When Farieh saw the forced air parting her curtains when the heat came on, allowing the outside's intrusion she had worked so hard to prevent, she solved the problem with duct tape.

Jamie had organic chemistry second semester and had signed up for the 7:30 a.m. lab that met twice a week. It was a cold walk in January, and sometimes wet. But come April she would be glad to get lab out of the way before the heat of the spring afternoons made even the new spaces in Gray-Little Hall intolerable.

Jamie's early departures left Farieh alone in the room. Ordinarily she had nothing she wanted to do so she lay in bed. This morning she got up. She had missed breakfast again and she was hungry; she was used to that. But she was also restless. She pulled on sweat pants, pulled her hair out over a hoodie, slipped into her black Chuck Taylors, flipped her parka over her shoulder, and walked out into the hallway on her way to the front stairs. Madison Hartley, who was coming up the stairs, made an excited, "Farieh! Where have you BEEN?!" But Farieh moved past Madison and down the stairs to the front door without a word—not to Madison, and not to the several women in the living room who were as curious about her as Madison.

*Gloves!* she thought. It was cold—close to freezing; she had left hers in her room. But she continued north toward Jayhawk Boulevard, her mind settling down around a hot tea at the Union, her hands in her pockets.

Except during the first week of the semester, the street-level seating areas of the Union were rarely crowded. Even on a game day in the fall, some tables would seat individuals and small groups while others sat empty. Farieh ordered Chai tea at the on-line screen, added a granola bar, paid, moved right to pick up her drink, then turned for the farthest empty table, almost to the stairs. Reaching it, she put her tea down and took off her parka, but she did not sit. For a few seconds, and then a minute, and then five minutes, Farieh stood by the table and stared west through the stairwell, watching as the Union's windows tried to coax the flat light of the short January day into the space built to memorialize a war her classmates had never heard of.

Farieh never sat down. Her tea had reached room temperature when she walked away from the table to the stairwell and followed it to the bottom. There she could exit onto Mississippi Street, directly across from the Spencer Museum of Art. One of her favorite places her freshman year, the Spencer would have been as welcoming today. But Farieh was not hunting the warm interior of the cool, classic structure or any of the outspoken pieces that had moved her as a freshman. She had her tea; beyond that, she did not know what she wanted.

She walked north on Mississippi and passed the football practice fields. Memorial Stadium, now "The Booth," had become a construction site. The west-side stands would be the first part of the Gateway Project that would celebrate the recently-brightened fortunes of Kansas football. Farieh's brand of football was different from what the men played at Kansas. She barely glanced at the stacked lumber and steel as she approached Don Fambrough

Way before crossing it on her way to 9th Street.

*Was it there all along? Was I so wrapped up in the warmth of my family and the ease with which we lived that I missed the government, and the Guard, and the sufferance of them by my parents?*

At the 9th Street intersection, The Big Mill had taken a sleepy corner and transformed it into a haven for lovers of thick-crust pizza. But Farieh paid no attention to it either—not the place and not the smells of baking dough and marinara still hanging in the air from the night before. In her mind she was all the way home now; she might as well have been walking the streets of Tehran.

She searched for a transition, for a time—even a moment—when her parents had become hardened to liberal thought, to change, even to young people. Maybe they had been that conservative the entire time: supportive of the regime yet holding their political opinions to themselves and their close friends, sharing none of them with Farieh and her sisters.

What she remembered now was July. Her parents had been impatient with the protests to the point of anger. Anger! From the two least-angry people in her life. She remembered trying to talk with her father and mother over breakfast, the most relaxed time of their family's day, a time of easy conversation surrounding tea and Lavash and feta and quince jam. Arms folded across his chest that morning, her father had listened grimly. Unlike conversations that ran back to Farieh's earliest childhood, her father's expression did not change that morning. There was no affirming nod of his head; no smile crossed his face. There was certainly no laugh. Only a furrow across the bridge of his nose. Her father never interrupted, never asked to clarify, never sought to explore a point or to challenge something Farieh had said. When Farieh let out a sharp breath that signaled her frustration, her father had pushed back his chair and stood, leaving the room to Farieh and her mother. Had Farieh not been so upset she would have recognized his walking out as a first in any conversation she had ever had with him.

Her mother had sat across from her, watching and listening as Farieh tried to engage her husband. She seemed to understand when Farieh identified the ways in which the government had failed the young people of Iran as to a liberal education, access to social media and other modern communication, foreign travel, and jobs. But when Farieh moved past the well-worn criticisms of the regime's general policies to a condemnation of its more recent response to the protests, her mother became rigid. Her father's unexpected walking away had distracted Farieh, and she had not noticed the mien change in her mother. It was when Farieh castigated the Guard for their "brutality" with young women whose only crime was not wearing a head scarf that her mother, too, had stood up from the table and left the room.

Farieh and her parents had argued before over many things. Over Farieh's choice of clothes or classes, for example, and even occasionally about the economic policies of the government. But her parents had seemed to have limitless patience. No one got mad; no one ever quit the conversation. Last summer her parents had not only quit the conversation, they had walked out. Farieh had never felt alone in her family's home before. In truth, she had never felt alone anywhere in the world before. But she was by herself in the kitchen last July. And when she wandered into the living room and saw the newspaper's coverage of Mehri's death, she knew just how alone she was.

It was late afternoon when Farieh returned, walking off the sidewalk and onto the porch and through Miller's front door. Madison Hartley, now in the entryway using the mirror to check how her hair and her ball cap were getting along, saw Farieh's image move past her own reflection and spun around to greet her. Surprise and concern replaced the geniality of the morning: "Farieh! Are you okay?!"

Farieh wished *she* had thought of a hat, to say nothing of the gloves still lying on her dresser. She forced a wan smile as she closed the door behind her, careful it did not hang up on the small rug that slid around the entry hall like a saucer sled. She had forgotten socks, as well, and her ankles glowed pink over the tops of her sneakers. "My feet are cold," she said, moving past Madison and up the stairs.

# Biomarkers

Farieh had been in the same seat last fall. Then, for the first time since arriving at KU the year before, she had been excited about something other than English literature. The auditorium in the new Integrated Science Building, named Gray-Little Hall for a former chancellor, was not that large—only 330 seats. The seats turned left and right toward one another, enabling the students to "collaborate" in the midst of a presentation. But Farieh had faced only forward last fall, captivated by the lecture on medicinal chemistry. The ISB's enormous clean room was being used to create new tools—nanodevices, which the presenter described as "circulating biomarkers"—that could be implanted in the body and then withdrawn along with blood or urine or spinal fluid to provide a liquid biopsy to aid in diagnosis and disease management. For Farieh, who had not done any reading in current science since arriving in Lawrence at the start of her freshman year, these new ideas were exhilarating.

But that was months ago, when Steven had been as exciting as the ideas. Even the weather had been welcoming then: an Indian summer had winked at Halloween and carried its warm days and blue skies nearly to Thanksgiving. How different the ISB was now, its large and "welcoming" lab windows shrouded in frost, its underground passageway to the Burge Union the only alternative to snow-covered sidewalks and daytime highs in the 20s. Farieh had barely heard this afternoon's lecture. Her mind had been somewhere else from the moment she had taken a seat, and now it was time to leave.

*Why doesn't Steven call me?*

Farieh asked herself the question a dozen times a day. Her last real contact with Steven had been in Chicago—"the most important meeting of his life." From her perspective, it had gone well—very well. Setting aside her disappointment in not seeing Steven after the dinner, the dinner itself had been dazzling. Steven had spent much of the next morning in his meeting with Abdul and Abdul's father, and they had toasted the success of the trip on the flight back. Since, he had been a stranger. Worse than that over Christmas, when he left her alone at Miller with her bags packed. He may have been busy since the meeting, he probably was. But not honoring his promise to take her to Chicago to meet his parents, and announcing the change of plans with a text? That was horrible. She had always thought of Steven as a nice person. Too busy, but nice. Yet nice people did not do things like that.

She pushed the thought aside, put on her parka, pulled her stocking cap over her ears, and had one mitten on when she moved through the east door onto the sidewalk that ran south across the building from Irving Hill Road. She was not ready for the wind! So she retreated into the entryway to fish out her scarf, adding it and the second mitten before she ventured out again, hunched down into her shoulders, genuflecting to the cold. The sting of the wind made her put on her sunglasses, an otherwise empty gesture in a late afternoon whose light was also fleeing the cold and had nearly made it over Daisy Hill to the west.

Miller seemed far away. But standing outside Gray-Little would not get her there, so she moved down the steps and across the parking lot, opting to walk through the space between the parking facility and Allen Fieldhouse. She thought it would be less exposed and warmer. She could not have been more wrong. The slot between the buildings was a wind tunnel.

Farieh's eyes were watering behind her sunglasses. But when she reached into her backpack for a Kleenex and dabbed at them she realized it was not the cold. She stopped, and her doing so caught the attention of the basketball manager who was pushing through the locked field house doors on her right. "Farieh! You must be freezing! Here—come inside."

Farieh had never met the young manager. But nearly everyone involved with KU basketball knew Richie Armstrong and the tall, olive-skinned girl he had become infatuated with his freshman year. Grateful for anything that would stop the wind, Farieh walked past him into a space that was nearly as dark as the outside but much warmer.

"Are you okay? Can I get you some water? Hot chocolate?" Tommie James, the young manager, could not have been more attentive. But Farieh wanted only the space and not the attention and she told him she was fine. Tommie did not believe her. Yet he had never met Farieh, and he was self-conscious to see her upset, so he took her at her word and pushed out through the same door he had just opened for her. The blast of cold air did not last as long as the sneezes it prompted from Farieh. When at last she stopped sneezing she was grateful to be indoors.

There was little to see: an expanse of polished concrete floor; a glow from the southwest cast by the entrance to the men's locker room. There was likewise no place to sit. The 16,300 seats were on the other side of the wall and the doors to the basketball court were locked. But Farieh did not care that the space was spartan and dark. It was warm. For the next few minutes, that was enough.

Her eyes wiped dry with another Kleenex, Farieh pulled out her cell phone. At the start of her sophomore year at KU there were dozens of numbers Farieh had committed to memory. On a bitter day turning into an even colder night in February, she could recall only two. One was Steven's. The other belonged to Jamie. She dialed Jamie. When she answered Farieh could manage only her roommate's name.

"Farieh! Where *are* you?!"

Jamie's voice settled Farieh. "Allen Fieldhouse," she answered.

Not knowing what to make of the answer, or what to say

next—for she identified Allen Fieldhouse with Richie Armstrong, whom Farieh had managed to avoid since her return last August, Jamie paused before settling on a response that was clinical in its focus: "Where? I'm coming for you. Right now. Where will you be—which entrance?"

Farieh knew she was inside, at the north end of the building, on the ground floor. She also knew Jamie could not get close to her location without entering the parking facility, whose levels she was not familiar with. "Meet me in the parking lot just up the slope from the Wagnon entrance, on the north side."

"Right," said Jamie. "I'll be there in five minutes." She was.

"You must be frozen!" she said as Farieh got into her front seat.

"I was," said Farieh. "I was so cold I didn't even know I was crying. A basketball manager let me into the field house."

Jamie reached across the console to squeeze Farieh's forearm. Neither said anything else until they were back in their room at the scholarship hall. They had removed their parkas and were sitting cross-legged on Jamie's bed, facing each other. Jamie reached across the small space and took Farieh's hands in her own. "I know it's Steven. Can you talk about it?"

She did.

"I like him. It's important to start there. His experience—I assume much of it is business experience—puts him far ahead of any undergraduate I've met. He speaks with an understated authority, which is so different for guys at KU. But he doesn't speak very often. He's too busy listening to me. Steven is a fabulous listener. He'll listen to me talk about politics for an hour. Not U.S. politics, Iranian politics! Then he'll ask a question that tells me he heard everything I said, one that indicates he knows so much about Iran and wants to be sure *I* get it right! Why would he learn anything about Iran if he didn't care for me?

"But then a week will go by, or longer, and I won't hear anything from him. I text him about something almost daily. Like anyone else, I want to hear something back. Maybe not a short story, but something! But no reply seems to work for Steven.

"There are things about him that worry me, what you and my sisters would call 'warning signs.' I can see now his almost complete lack of conversation after the dinner in Chicago had to do with me and not with his preoccupation with Abdul's father. But he won't talk about it, even now. I've tried. His standing me up over Christmas was awful. I had never felt that kind of hurt before. Still, I remember in London my father kissed my mother goodbye one morning and did not come home for dinner. It's not that he was late, he didn't come home at all. When she rang his office that evening to find out when to expect him, the phone forwarded the call to his cell phone. And when he answered it he was in Cairo!"

Jamie, too, was a skillful listener. She asked an occasional, clarifying question, but never more than that. Farieh moved on from her father's unannounced trip to Egypt to other stories about Steven, stories Jamie knew. Farieh paired each with a seeming attempt to mitigate what, to Jamie, was irreducibly-oafish behavior. Jamie listened to all of them. When Farieh at last wound down, went to the bathroom, and came back, it was Jamie's turn.

"Okay. You have at least thought about these times with Steven, or the lack of them. That's good. But you tell them like you were writing a newspaper story. You give me the facts then try to figure out what Steven had in mind. You have said nothing about *you* so far. What were *your* reactions? Take Chicago—the dinner at NoMI. How did you *feel* about it when it was all over? You present Abdul's father like he's the featured actor for that beer commercial, 'the most interesting man in the world.' Is that what you thought? I listened to all of that the day you got back. My immediate impression was 'Mafia Don'!

"What about Quebec? That's a hell of a first date with a guy you barely know.

"And what about the flowers? You meet a guy at a random house party, you talk for 15 minutes, he dips out early and leaves you alone at the barbecue grill. Next day, it looks like Owens Flower Shop had a fire and moved its sales floor to Miller Hall. Who *does* that?! It's all so over-the-top. Or is this the way you roll?!"

*Oh, Jamie,* thought Farieh, *I do love you!*

"I *have* thought about it," Farieh responded. "All of it. It *is* over the top. But none of that makes Steven any less intelligent, or less handsome, or less giving. He can be selfish. I get that. And he is not very giving of his time. I get that too. But I can handle this. I just want to believe the time thing is temporary."

Jamie had nothing more to say. Farieh had taken tsunami warning signs and worked them into a forecast of light rain. If that's where she was, there was nothing more to do this evening than find a pizza—they had missed dinner. They decided on Papa Keno's. It was freezing; they would walk to the Massachusetts store anyway. They needed to get out of the room.

# University Scholar

Freshmen students invited into the honors program at KU are a select group—fewer than 10% of an entering class of more than 4,000. But theirs is not "the" select group. Each year in the spring, 15 sophomores who have distinguished themselves for their intellectual achievement and their "curiosity" become "University Scholars."

There are prizes for the winners. There is a scholarship in the amount of $1,500. Each student is paired with an Honors Faculty Fellow, one of KU's very finest teachers, whose job it is to support the student's academic interests. Each student joins the other 14 in an interdisciplinary seminar on "a topic of contemporary interest," a seminar unlike any other because of the care with which it is led and because of the crackling intelligence of its participants. But the real prize is the recognition.

Most of the University Scholars are women. Farieh Bukhari, from Tehran, Iran, was one of them. And in February, Farieh and her 14 colleagues were introduced to the university community at a reception hosted by the honors program at the Nunemaker Center.

The former KU chancellor, who was always invited to this reception, had never attended it. Because she never attended, no one thought to provide a seat for her successor. Bob Barkett, the current Chancellor did not mind. He moved inconspicuously to the common area at the back of Nunemaker's upper level and took a place behind the 20 or 30 other guests, nodding politely to the ones who turned and saw him.

Barkett had started out at Purdue, alma mater for America's most famous astronaut. Completed in 2007, Neil Armstrong Hall was architecturally dramatic and proud of its namesake—right down to the replica of the Apollo 1 command module suspended from the ceiling of its atrium. But the school of engineering at Purdue had snoozed into the twenty-first century's third decade, its attention not turning fast enough to AI. Its many successful alumni were used to its ranking behind Stanford and MIT. And they understood CAL, whose #3 position some attributed to the proximity of the Lawrence Livermore National Laboratory. They understood the vicissitudes of ratings slumps, which rarely cost the Boilermakers more than a place or two. But when the school fell from fourth to 10th, settling in behind not only Michigan but also Illinois, the shocks spread from Bechtel to Benesch to Caterpillar.

Bob Barkett had been at Nvidia, happy to lead his team of bench scientists and ethicists to corral AI for one of the world's leading chipmakers. When Purdue called him to become Dean of Engineering he said, "No! Not today, not tomorrow, not ever!" But it was his classmate and best friend Charlie Buchholtz on the other end of the call. Charlie's second call was to tell Bob he was in California, sitting just outside Bob's office in Santa Clara. When Bob looked out through the glass wall and saw Charlie simpering back at him beneath a Purdue ball cap, the hook was set.

Bob Barkett needed six months to recruit the new faculty he wanted; he took another six months to modernize the curriculum— stuffing it with courses in computer analytics and AI. He took the next year to recruit the students he wanted to teach. He had never spent so much time in airports and bad diners. But when the ratings came out at the end of those 24 months the Boilermakers had jumped up—from tenth all the way to third!

Kansas was one of the most aspirational STEM schools in the country, but with far less to brag on than Purdue. When the Jayhawk search committee began pecking around for a new chancellor the search chair mentioned the job Bob Barkett had done in West Lafayette. Kansas caught him on a day when his desk was clean and Bob was feeling he had done what he had set out to do at Armstrong Hall.

The KU search committee was surprised when he said "Yes" to being considered; they were stunned when they met him. Movie-star handsome at 6'1" with thick brown hair running just past the top of his shirt collar, Barkett was more inclined to jeans and boots than a jacket and tie. The committee discovered that when he showed up for his first interview at the Alumni Center.

But he could talk. Billie Thompson, the committee's senior member, had grown up on 12,000 irrigated acres just outside Garden City. Barkett knew computer science like Billie knew pivot sprinklers and feed lots. And while he was careful not to show off his understanding of AI, there was no limit to his enthusiasm for it and his belief in its potential to revolutionize human history. A taller version of Brad Pitt mashed up with Steve Jobs and Phineas T. Barnum, he was irresistible.

Why would Barkett come to Kansas? There was a science element to the chancellor's position, at least to hear the search committee tell it. They told him Kansas wanted to become one of the premier STEM schools in the Midwest. The university needed a star to attract the right people to Lawrence and they felt he'd be perfect for the job. They had wisely included the current Dean of Engineering on the search committee. Barkett liked Jim Abrams from the first handshake and was confident he could work with him. When Barkett had set sail on the good ship AI during that first interview, it was Abrams who held up the committee's end of the conversation, nearly matching Barkett's enthusiasm and sharing his view that ethics was a critical component of any successful use of the new tool.

Money wasn't an issue. Barkett had plenty; whatever KU wanted to pay him was fine by him.

And moving to Lawrence wasn't an issue. West Lafayette wasn't far from Indianapolis. But it was twice as far away as

Lawrence was from Kansas City. Barkett liked the Chiefs more than he liked the Colts. He also liked Lawrence. He had done his own research on the free-state origins of the place and had reviewed his notes carefully during the hour-long flight from Indy. He liked the craft-brew and blue-jeans vibe of this Midwestern college town. He liked its being the sole blue dot in a state map awash in red ones. And he liked its history, which went back to some seriously-bad times during the Civil War. Bob Barkett talked about all of that with the Kansas search committee.

What Bob didn't talk about was the part of his undergraduate years at Purdue that did not relate to engineering. He had played basketball in high school and was pretty good. Not good enough to be recruited by what would now be called a "Power Four" school, but pretty good. He had played in Purdue's intermural "A" league all four years. The Purdue alum he admired the most—who had become neither an astronaut nor an engineer—had been a basketball player at Purdue, a guard. He had been an All-American three years running. But he wasn't remembered for his time at Purdue, as impressive as it was. What John Wooden was remembered for was his time at UCLA and the record for NCAA Tournament Championships he set while he was there, a record as untouchable as any in sports.

Bob Barkett was as tuned in to college hoops as he was to semiconductors. He knew who the best coach was and where the best college basketball was played. He also knew the KU chancellor got tickets to the games. All of them. From the first exhibition skirmish with Fort Hays State to the deciding game of the Final Four. And he knew where the seats were located: center court at Allen Fieldhouse and courtside for every game away from it. Trips to the State Farm Classic and other tournaments were cherries on the top of the sundae.

That was the thought that nearly had him laughing out loud during the "compensation" discussion. The search committee must have felt basketball tickets were unworthy of mention to a prospective chancellor; they were included in the handout but never spoken of. For Bob Barkett, basketball tickets were the only part of the compensation package that moved the needle. He accepted the offer the first time the search committee made it, and he arrived as KU's newest chancellor within the month of doing so.

Bob Barkett had been KU's Chancellor for four years. He had never heard so much about a student as he had heard about the young woman from Iran who was a newly-minted University Scholar. He had met her at his Christmas party but had not been able to talk with her. He was hoping for that chance today. That's why he came.

The program was short. Within a few more minutes the guests had worked their way down the receiving line to shake hands with the members of the new class. As most of the guests were faculty, and as it was still the middle of the afternoon and they had classes to teach and labs to plan, most of them left soon after. The chancellor stayed. He congratulated several of the new University Scholars and chatted with the faculty members he knew as he kept his eye on the tall woman with the olive skin and the green eyes, biding his time until she was clear of her well-wishers.

Farieh had turned right to retrieve her cup of lemonade from a nearby table and did not notice the approach of the chancellor. When she turned back left he was right in front of her. "Hello," he said. "I'm Bob Barkett. I'm the chancellor at KU. We met at the Outlook at the Christmas party. Congratulations on being selected as a University Scholar! That is the highest recognition we can give an undergraduate during their sophomore year."

"Thank you very much," she responded. "I'm Farieh Bukhari." She was almost nose to nose with the chancellor but made no attempt to widen the distance. She knew full well who he was. That he was here, talking with her, was an opportunity she had not anticipated. "Has anyone offered you something to drink?" she asked. "They are serving water, soft drinks, coffee, and lemonade."

"Coffee sounds good," said the chancellor. "Thank you!" Farieh led the chancellor to one of the small tables at the back and gestured for him to sit down, which he did.

"Would you like cream or sugar?" she asked.

"Cream," he replied.

Farieh was gone only a moment, returning with a paper cup of coffee, a small plastic cup of creamer, and a wooden stir stick.

"Here you are," she said as she took the chair across from him.

Barkett had given some thought to this encounter, and he had a few questions in mind. Before he could ask the first one, though, Farieh had asked one of him: "I know you came to Kansas from Purdue. How did that happen?"

Barkett had to smile. Farieh was everything people said she was. He looked at his watch before responding. "Do you want the long version, or the short one?"

"Long, please," said Farieh, smiling back at him as she sipped her lemonade.

"I was Dean of Engineering at Purdue. Not the President; not the Provost. But as so often makes a difference with academic searches, I knew somebody.

"Jim Hite chaired the search committee at KU. We were at Purdue at the same time. Jim was in engineering; I studied history and philosophy. We persuaded ourselves we had plenty of time for our fraternity and our intermural teams along with everything else we tried. Some semesters we were right!"

*He's self-deprecating,* thought Farieh. *That's a positive.*

"I was a good student. But if I had a strength it was my ability to get along with people and help them get things accomplished. I was class president my senior year and took a seminar led by a professor at the School of Engineering, who was terrific. It was a small group—only eight students. Our conversations never seemed to end when the bell rang so we just hung out and kept going.

"Very early into the class another history major talked about career paths for graduates in the field and what they got paid. There weren't many openings in history. A person who could find a job could expect to earn what today would be around $45,000. Our teacher, Professor Herrick, was excellent at starting discussions and listening. But she couldn't help herself this time. She told us engineering graduates were making what today would be around $98,000! I had had to borrow money to go to college and that really got my attention. I was good at math, and I had done well in the several science courses I had taken, so I asked her whether someone like me—a history major—could get into one of the masters programs in engineering. She was encouraging, I applied, and I got in."

Farieh shifted her position, had another sip of lemonade, and could not help but smile. It was clear she was getting the long version. But she knew the importance of the conversation. The person on the other side of the most powerful academic relationship she could hope for was barely two feet away, sharing his story. It was worth her while to listen.

"That I got in did not mean I was fully prepped for graduate school in engineering, of course. I looked over the program areas and decided systems engineering was a more promising course for me than electrical or biomedical or some other tech-heavy program. I liked it, did well, and a year or so later I went back to Professor Herrick for another talk. My teachers were encouraging me to stay on for a Ph.D. But I was broke. Once again, she steered me in the right direction. She told me universities and their colleges were increasingly looking to fill their senior leadership positions with people who had practical experience. Medical schools were looking for clinicians; business schools wanted candidates who had led major companies; engineering schools wanted candidates who had built things. She kept her eye on job openings. Nvidia, then a fledgling chip maker, was interviewing on campus the following week. Professor Herrick encouraged me to sign up, I liked them, and when they offered me a job I took it.

"I spent the next 20 years trying to understand what the company made and trying to communicate that to their customers. I traveled all over the world working with the best-possible design teams, with the C-suite of Fortune-500 companies, and with senior government officials. That's when Jim Hite called me the first time. He was at KU then, on the engineering faculty, and had seen the Dean's position at Purdue had opened up. He thought I should look at it.

"One downside of my work was being away from home a lot, often far away. Our three kids were all teenagers. Nancy—my wife—and I talked about it. We agreed a position that would let me be home more often would be a good thing for the family, so I applied. I don't know who was more surprised when I got the job, Purdue or me!

"We were at Purdue five years. It was Midwestern; that appealed to Nancy, who is from Iowa. I could walk to work every morning. Meetings were held at Neil Armstrong Hall, at the student union, or somewhere else in West Lafayette. I was still traveling. But it was one or two days out and then home.

"We did two things there I am especially proud of. We brought AI awareness to the school of engineering and we created the Engineering and Polytechnic Gateway Complex. We were in the middle of construction for the Gateway Complex when Jim Hite called again. This time, he said, it was personal. Jim had been appointed Chair of the Chancellor Search Committee at KU, and he wanted me to apply for the job."

Farieh changed her position again. They were the only two people left in Nunemaker. A transitional comment seemed appropriate.

"It sounds like we're closing in on Kansas," she said as she finished the last of her tea. "Am I right?"

This time it was the chancellor who smiled. "I told you earlier I had liked graduate school. To be able to work in an academic setting at Purdue was a joy. Nancy and I loved the pace of things;

we loved being close to the campus; we loved how our children thrived there. I loved my colleagues, too, and their diverse interests, and the depth of their expertise. The most routine break for coffee at the Union could introduce me to an artist or a discipline or an entire culture I knew nothing about.

"As the engineering dean, I was back in the middle of all of that. But I was also able to watch the president. Purdue's was excellent, and working with her told me I wanted to be one. Jim's call came out of nowhere. Now I'm here. Nancy and I have never been happier."

As the chancellor reached for his very cold coffee his cuff rode up his arm, which revealed his watch. "Good grief!" he said. "I have talked us nearly past my next meeting, and it's at Strong Hall. I am so sorry, Farieh, but I have to leave." He stood up. "It's been wonderful meeting you and talking with you."

Farieh stood with him. "I suspect they'll wait for you, chancellor," she replied, smiling again.

The Chancellor of the University of Kansas made a nearly-imperceptible bow, then hurried to the west-side door of Nunemaker and through it to the parking lot. As he got into his car his mind swung instinctively toward the next meeting, but it stuck on his conversation with the young University Scholar: *She hardly said a thing.*

# Professor Ahmed Zaidi

Ahmed Zaidi had been raised in Islamabad. His parents had no money. But they had books and they had time and their son grew strong from both. At the urging of several teachers he went to Cambridge for his undergraduate studies, getting a First in history. Homesick his entire time in England, he had returned to Pakistan and had cast about for several years before deciding to study law. He was admitted at Quaid-e-Azam University and again graduated with highest honors before enrolling as an Advocate and joining a law firm in his hometown. He loved his city and his firm, and he loved the law.

On his 32$^{nd}$ birthday he became restless. A month later he left his money with his parents and flew to the United States. To everyone's surprise, he stayed in New York City for nearly a year and worked a mishmash of jobs dramatically beneath his station as a lawyer. At the end of that year he applied to the international law course at Georgetown and was immediately admitted to the two-year program. He knew he had made the right choice after his first day of class. Several months of studying within hailing distance of the Capitol revealed something else: Zaidi felt an obligation to bring the insights he was developing to more than a single law firm's privacy-obsessed clients and to more than a single government's self-absorbed foreign policy. He would teach. He decided the United States was the most advantageous place to do so.

Academically, Zaidi was as successful at Georgetown as he had been everywhere else, and he was again on his way to getting first honors. He filled out the Faculty Appointments Register form for the upcoming AALS Faculty Recruitment Conference and sent it in. It never registered that as he was still a year away from completing his degree, he was a year early.

Zaidi did not know much about the Recruitment Conference other than its trade name, the "meat market." He knew it was a required first step for getting a teaching position in an American law school and that it was held annually in Washington, D.C. He read the Register form carefully and was meticulous in completing it online. But he did not pay the same attention to the "Helpful Hints" that accompanied the application materials, and he did not rush to the AALS website, "Becoming a Law Teacher." Because he had not yet published anything, his Register form was thin; few schools contacted him ahead of the conference. When the conference began that October he had only three interviews scheduled. One of them was Kansas.

Andrew Stevenson sat alone in the small room with its small desk and its three small chairs, his colleague on break. Thinking their next applicant might already be there and not wanting to give up the few minutes that might extend an already-short interview window, Andrew got up and opened the door and looked. Sure enough, their next appointment was already seated opposite the door.

Andrew's immediate thought was: *This will be different.* He saw no anxiousness, no trying-too-hard-to-please expression, no smoothing of an already-flawless jacket. The composed, brown-skinned man in his 30s reached for the file on the chair next to him, stood up, and extended his hand to Andrew as though they were *already* colleagues and had known each other for years.

The back and forth of the interview was the same. Barely pausing for a breath as Virginia Shelton returned to the room, Ahmed Zaidi was quick to his feet and warm in his welcome, dealing with her as though Virginia was the guest. Kansas had a teacher of international law, a very good one. But he was leaving the next year to return to the Philadelphia area, where his wife's family lived and where Villanova wanted him so badly it would nearly double his salary. Kansas needed someone for the international law spot, and before ten minutes had passed Andrew Stevenson knew this brilliant young Pakistani was the person to fill it.

Those 30 minutes were also different for Zaidi. He had never met a man in cowboy boots before, and certainly not someone Andrew's size. Ahmed was of average height and build for a young Pakistani male, which made him 5'8" tall and 140 pounds. At 6'2" in his boot socks and crowding 250, Stevenson was a giant. He was also patient. Ahmed's first year at Georgetown's law school had prepared him to be interrupted at any and every moment of a conversation; Stevenson was content to listen. Only when it was clear Ahmed had finished his thought did either of the Kansas teachers follow up with one of their own, or with a new question to explore what Ahmed had in mind. For those 30 minutes Ahmed Zaidi felt more respected than he had felt since he had arrived in the United States over two years ago. He became so relaxed, so caught up in his enjoyment of the conversation, that he failed to note the hands of the large round clock on the wall in front of him had moved past the half hour and that his time was over. It took Andrew's standing up, and Virginia Shelton's joining, to remind Ahmed he needed to stand up himself, thank them, and leave.

Ahmed Zaidi had other encouraging interviews at the "meat market." But when the school of law in Lawrence offered him a position for the fall semester still a year away, subject only to the satisfactory completion of his LLM at Georgetown, he accepted by return e-mail, then telephoned Andrew Stevenson to tell him directly. That was 10 years ago.

# Tea at DeBruce

Jamie waited for her roommate in the lounge just past the law school office. She knew Farieh liked to talk with her professors after class, and this class was no exception. In fact, her seminar in International Law from Ahmed Zaidi had required only one session to become Farieh's favorite class this spring semester, and Jamie was used to the wait.

It wasn't long before Farieh's unmistakable accent, boosted by her unmistakable energy, sounded up the stairwell from the lower level where Green Hall kept its classrooms. Jamie stood up out of the soft chair, walked past the bookcase, and stepped into the main hallway in time to see Farieh reach the top of the stairs. Her face was turned toward her teacher, her left hand accentuating her argument as her right hand managed her laptop and her jacket.

Professor Zaidi stopped briefly as they reached the first floor. He smiled helplessly as he shook his head at his Iranian prodigy, then—still smiling—brought the conversation to a close and moved left toward the elevator that would take him upstairs to his office. He walked right past Jamie, who was smiling almost as broadly as he was. Farieh could do that to you.

Jamie walked to the head of the stairs to greet her roommate. "Another professor vanquished?" she asked.

Farieh laughed. "No," she said. "Hardly! I have almost no success with Professor Zaidi! He knows everything about international law and international politics, and he is impossible to argue with because he is so unfailingly polite!"

"What was it this time?" asked Jamie.

"The Taliban! I take the position they are lawless suppressors of women who should be stamped out of existence. But Professor Zaidi counters with the peace they have brought to Afghanistan and how peace is a prerequisite to meaningful social progress in any society, eastern or western. I agree with that in concept, and I told him so. But I think Afghanistan under the Taliban is different. So I said, 'But what about the decades in which the Taliban controlled Afghanistan before 9/11? There was a peace of sorts after the Russians left. Yet Afghani women led a primitive, brutal existence, most of them not even aware there was an alternative. That changed with the United States occupation. Girls were finally educated, and women could pursue careers. But since the United States' withdrawal, the Taliban's suppression of females—women and children—has been appalling.' That took us to the top of the stairs. You saw the rest."

Jamie had seen the rest, and she could see her roommate was again building a head of steam, so she jumped in to remind her they were going to have tea. It was a beautiful day, probably 65 degrees, so they carried their jackets as they walked past the court room and out the front door.

The DeBruce Center was barely a block away to the south, across the street toward the Allen Fieldhouse parking facility then just east and down the steps. KU's best coffee shop was just inside the doors on the right. There was seldom a line at this time of the afternoon and they moved right to the counter to order. "English Breakfast," said Farieh, reaching into her billfold for a credit card.

"I'll have a vanilla latte," said Jamie.

"I thought we were having *tea*!" kidded Farieh. "What's with that?!"

"Best latte in town," said her roommate, reaching for her own card.

They took their drinks and moved back across the entrance before walking down past several layers of the tiered seating to a spot in the center, right next to the window wall that ran the length of the building on its east side. Jamie put her jacket on the table next to them as she walked past it; Farieh added her jacket and her books. Jamie moved to the bench on the south side of their table. Farieh pulled back the chair across from her and sat down, plainly still absorbed in her conversation at the law school. "I wonder what it would be like to *go* to law school," she mused. "The law school is like its own world at KU. The teachers seem more energetic, more engaged, so much more—I don't know, up to date. I walk into that building and it's like I'm in downtown Chicago or New York City, not in the middle of a Midwestern college campus. The pace is quicker, the intensity goes up, the people walking around are diverse—especially the faculty, and the women students have much more to do than check out the cute guys. It's just different!"

"What's wrong with cute guys?" mugged Jamie. "Steven is cute; you didn't seem to mind checking him out!"

Jamie expected a spirited retort. Instead, she got a mood shift, from upbeat and bantering to subdued and pensive. And Farieh had said nothing.

"Well *that* wasn't the transition I was expecting," she continued. "What's up with you and Steven?"

Farieh once again said nothing. So Jamie reached a hand across the narrow table to lift Farieh's chin. "Hey," the roommate continued, "talk to me. I know you've been having a hard time with Steven. But you make me nervous when you run off like that."

More moments went by before Farieh lifted her eyes, as well. "I don't know. I haven't seen Steven for weeks. When I text him he rarely responds. It's been mostly like that since before Christmas break. I understand he's busy; he's made that all too clear. But he never has time for me. The last time I saw him we were supposed to go to a show at Liberty Hall. We had barely walked in before he got a call and became anxious about something—he never tells me what it is—and told me he had to take me back to Miller. He drove off as soon as I got out of the car. Didn't even walk me to the porch.

"I don't claim any super powers in the way of instincts; I don't think he's seeing someone else. But he's not seeing me.

"I'm sounding far more observant than I am. I've never had anyone like a 'boyfriend' before; I have no idea how someone like Steven should behave. But his behavior sucks as far as I'm concerned. There a strong part of me that wants to send him a text and end this stupidly one-sided relationship. There's another part, just as strong, that has enjoyed seeing him and talking with him, that believes he's smart and talented and creative, and that wants this to be a real relationship for two equal partners. As you can tell, I'm stuck."

It was Jamie's turn to sit back, but carefully, as there was no back to the bench. Farieh had come back from her summer in London different than Jamie had expected. She had gone to one of the world's great cities, her first time there in years. After the month-long party that was the British Summer Institute, Farieh had spent two weeks with a sister she loved dearly. Then she went to Iran to spend time with her parents. Jamie expected her to be bouncing when she saw her again that summer. But Farieh was anything but bouncing.

Jamie learned about Iran when they went to the Bird Dog. In the weeks that followed, Farieh went to her classes, helped with the meals and the cleanup at Miller, and studied at her usual spots in the evenings. But the fire that had burned so brightly her freshman year seemed to have gone out. Until October, when she met Steven at a house party. Farieh had come home that night like a surprise winner at the CMAs, smiling a smile that rocked her whole face. Steven was "the nicest man" she'd ever met, and "the best looking." She "had never felt like that with anybody." Jamie had watched all of it from the middle of her bed in their room. She was relieved to see Farieh happy.

She met Steven a few weeks later. He was as handsome as Farieh had said; he was also four or five years older. While he wasn't the "nicest" man Jamie had ever met, he was polite, although in a polished kind of way. Steven called up something in Jamie, and it took her a while to put her finger on it. It was one of her grandmother's favorite expressions: "If it seems too good to be true, it probably is!"

Jamie watched their time together that fall: Steven enjoyed lounging in Miller's living room. His red Tesla S Plaid—ever present at the curb—begged impoundment. The flowers he had sent at the beginning had overflowed the living room.

Jamie remembered the fairy-tale trip to Quebec. She remembered how focused Farieh was on being helpful to Steven in Chicago. But Chicago ended indifferently. And then came the holidays. Steven had invited Farieh to spend the holidays at his family's home; Farieh was excited to go. Jamie remembered the December Friday when classes were finally over and Farieh had sat with her luggage in the living room, waiting for Steven to pick her up. And how he was late. And then he was later. And how he finally sent her a stony text to let her know something had come up and the holidays weren't going to work after all. It took days for Farieh to pull herself together.

Jamie's grandmother might have been sitting beside her in the DeBruce Center as she listened to her roommate that afternoon. The "too good to be true" part that had been lurking since October had become the reality, at least from Jamie's perspective. Yet here was her brilliant roommate, drawing down all of that intellect to rationalize a guy Jamie was convinced was a bum.

Jamie had grown up in a family who knew how to care for people. She loved her parents for that. She loved them now for teaching her how to listen to people, and how to respond to them. She was not sure Farieh was "hurting" now. "Confused," maybe; "disappointed," for sure. She chose her words carefully.

"Not being able to understand someone you care for is hard. I'm sorry that's where you are now. I don't know what is happening to Steven. We'll have to hope it's something that will change for the better, and soon. Does that sound okay?"

It did. They stood up together, picked up their laptops and jackets, and headed for the north door.

# A Slow Saturday Night

Steven and Abdul sat on the small balcony that jutted west away from the wall of Steven's apartment. There was little room. But it was just them so the space for two chairs and the small table that held what was left of their dinner was enough. Uber Eats had delivered it an hour ago. They had finished in 20 minutes and had talked the rest of the time about the expansion of their business. It was a slow night in February. It had rained off and on since noon, and the basketball game was away.

The Chicago meeting last fall with Abdul and his father had been huge for Steven. They had brought him into the business; his attention to the smallest detail and his knack for hiring the right people had bolstered all of their Midwest college operations. Abdul and Steven were talking tonight about expanding into Colorado and Wyoming and Montana. They liked the idea. But as neither believed they could take that step now the conversation had slowed and then stopped, with both men staring out across the metal railing.

"What are you thinking about?" It was Abdul who asked the question.

"Farieh," said Steven.

"Farieh! I thought she was old news—over—done."

"She is." Steven looked out over Massachusetts Street as though he were counting the buildings. It had last rained at dusk and the night air had settled soft around the downtown. But there was nothing soft in the expression on Steven's face. "I'm thinking about giving her to somebody."

Steven's speaking of Farieh like chattel did not surprise Abdul. Steven was appealing when he wanted to be—attentive, helpful, charming. But he had parchment-thin skin when it came to his view of himself. He could stand being attacked; he understood losing, although he hated it. Embarrassment was way too much. Despite the success of the Chicago meeting it was Farieh's upstaging him in the game with Abdul's father he remembered, and the sting of it was as fresh as this afternoon's paper cut.

Abdul shifted his body toward Steven. "Who?"

"Saladin," replied Steven, holding onto the "S" a moment longer than necessary.

If there was a Number 2 in Steven's operation it was Saladin. Abdul shifted back until he was once more aligned with his business partner. They were quiet, again staring west into the night. This was Steven's town, and it was Steven's call. Abdul had only to acknowledge it.

"Perfect," he said.

# The Wheel

I t's from Steven!"

Farieh and Jamie were sitting cross-legged on Jamie's bed. It was late evening in February and their heavy socks were pulled up over their pajamas. They had been talking about the other girls in the scholarship hall. The rarity of a gossipy conversation had made it all the more interesting, but Steven's text killed it.

"Steven!" The disdain was unmistakable, but Jamie couldn't help it. "You have barely heard from him for months. What does *he* want?!" Jamie had not stopped hoping Steven was out of Farieh's life, and she was disappointed he had shown up again.

Farieh scrolled through the message. "He wants me to come to The Wheel next Tuesday. Says he will be there with friends, and he wants me to meet them!"

Jamie knew Farieh could not help her excitement. Still, it sickened her a creep like Steven had any hold over the most talented young woman Jamie knew, and it was all she could do not to sound as angry as she felt. She took a deep breath. "Okay," she said. "I guess you'll go, right?"

"Yes," said Farieh. "I have barely talked with him this year. Of course I'll go!"

*You have barely talked with him since he stood you up over Christmas break last year. With a text!* Jamie was getting angry again. She dropped her legs over the edge of the bed and stood up. "I have to pee," she said. Mostly, she just wanted to get away from the thought of Farieh and Steven. "Be back in a minute."

# The House of the Lambs

East 1900 Road runs south from the highway bridge that crosses K-10 a mile east of Lawrence. After skirting a small golf facility on the east side, it moves steadily up and down low hills past dark green cedars and an occasional pole barn or frame house, which show up on both sides of the road. Scattered across the adjoining fields farther south are much larger homes and their more elaborate horse barns, including several behind very strong brick walls. These residential sites evoke Lexington, Kentucky—but without its fences, and Johnson County, Kansas—but without its density. Farieh could see all of this from the backseat of her Uber. Even this close to midnight, the moon was bright enough that the houses and barns and the occasional stock pond stood out clearly from the empty fields.

The farther south she went the more rural the surroundings became. From Farieh's perspective, someone who had never traveled this road before and had never traveled any road outside of Lawrence that did not lead directly to Kansas City or its airport, this could have been northwest Iran—except for the Wakarusa River, which she had crossed not even half a mile south of K-10.

The clouds crossing the face of the winter moon dimmed its light as Farieh walked past the rural mailbox. It stood at the top of a long gravel driveway leading downhill to a copse of bare cottonwoods and the watercourse that had to flow beside them. The Uber had stopped at what the driver had insisted was the right address: 852 East 1900 Road. But there was only a mailbox, and it was now past midnight, and the clouds and the moon made for an evening more suited to phantoms than a party. Farieh asked him to wait as she got out to read the writing herself. Sure enough: "852."

Calmed, but not by much, she thanked him, wrapped her red coat tight around her shoulders, and started down the driveway in her Adidas cross-trainers. The Jimmy Choos she had brought for the party sat in her over-the-shoulder bag.

She had looked back at the paved road half a dozen times before the Uber crested the hill to the north and disappeared toward K-10. When headlights jumped out of the darkness in front of her she was so frightened she could not make a sound—nothing.

"Farieh! Is that you?"

She did not recognize the voice calling her. But any voice speaking her name at that moment was welcome, and this time she was able to respond: "Yes! Who's there? Where am I?!"

"It's me, Tom," said the young man who was leaning out of the passenger-side window. The car pulled even with her on the gravel driveway and stopped. Tom got out, opened the back door next to her, and said, "Hop in!"

Farieh remembered a "Tom" from the group at The Wheel last night. Steven's text that she join him there, her first contact from him in weeks, had surprised her and excited her at the same time. She had been there 30 minutes when Steven and his posse arrived.

Tom had been quiet, at the edge of the circle surrounding their table, not saying much. It was when Farieh had noticed Steven was no longer there and had got up to leave herself that Tom peeled off ahead of her, holding the door for her as she walked down the steps onto the sidewalk alongside 14th Street. She remembered he had bounced down the steps after her, arriving at her right side and immediately introducing himself. "I'm Tom," he had said, like so many young men at KU who seemed to feel a first name was all anyone would ever need. "Steven asked me to make sure you knew about the party at Lambda House tomorrow night. Midnight. They all start late; you'll get used to that. He would really like you to come. Here's the address." Tom had held out a small card that read "852 East 1900 Road." It was in Steven's handwriting, followed by: "I hope you can make it! Steven." She had taken the card and looked at it closely and put it in the pocket of her jeans. When Tom made to leave Farieh thanked him. As she watched him walk east toward Massachusetts, she thought Tom had said "house of the lambs."

When Farieh stepped into the back seat she could see yet another car just behind them, but with its lights still off. Tom got in beside her. "Who's in that car?" she asked.

"That's Greg," said her companion as the late-model Mercedes E300 eased away from the mailbox and turned south onto 1900 Road. "He'll get the next guest. The party isn't really at this address. In fact, no one lives here. We checked that out very carefully several years ago when we started up again at KU and decided to meet this far out of town. The Lambda house is several miles from here. But we ask our guests to come to this address and be dropped off to make sure no one is following them. We have another car in another driveway about a half mile to the north, right at the crest of the hill, to make sure of that. But we also want to make sure our guests don't know the house location; only members know the actual address. That's why we'll ask you to wear this." Tom pulled a carefully-sewn felt mask out of his jacket pocket and put it on her lap. It was red—bright enough she had seen it clearly in his hand; but in the dim light of the back seat it disappeared against her coat.

"Like Mardi Gras," observed Farieh.

"Right," smiled Tom. "Just right."

Farieh found the mask and pulled it over hair so thick the elastic barely stretched around it.

"Put your head back and relax," said Tom. "We'll be there in just a few minutes."

The Mercedes traveled south on 1900 Road for two miles before meandering southwest for another two, finally turning west through nondescript barbed-wire gates in a nondescript barbed-wire fence onto a nondescript gravel road. But the gravel extended only as far as the hillcrest, maybe 500 yards farther west. Once past it and out of sight on the far side, the Mercedes rolled to a stop and Tom took off her mask. The ribbon of asphalt straight ahead of her ran between wide, grass shoulders. Though brown now in winter, it was apparent they would be carefully mowed and maintained come spring. Just outboard of the grassy shoulders, branches from rows of adolescent pin oaks dappled the moonlight onto the roadway's surface. There was nearly half a mile of this before the roadway finally swooped to a stop in front of 14,000 square feet of house whose slate roof was dotted with broad, stone chimneys. The house of the lambs was large.

When she moved through the entryway she encountered a towering timber frame sized for a cathedral. Iran had palaces in her cities; her timber-frame structures were in the mountain communities. And while Farieh had grown up in those mountain communities and had been to beautiful mountain houses, she had never seen anything like this.

Steven greeted her just inside the front door. The dazzling Lambda House had overwhelmed her senses and Farieh was relieved to see him. His smile and quick embrace chased both the awe and her anxiety. "Where *am* I?" she asked as she stepped into her stilettos.

"You'll need to leave your phone." His voice was matter-of-fact.

Still unsure of herself, still glad to be with Steven, asking "Why?!" did not occur to her. But when she reached into the bag she was surprised to find nothing in it but her card case, a comb, a lipstick, a mirror, and the cross-trainers she had just placed at the bottom.

"I don't have it!" The excited exclamation rang true enough to Steven. But he waited patiently as his flustered companion searched every pocket in her jacket, and her bag twice more, before conceding it wasn't there.

Steven said nothing—only took her red jacket from her shoulders, draped it across his arm, shouldered her bag, and invited her to follow him.

As they walked past the small entry table, Steven spoke to the young woman seated behind it: "No phone."

The tables in the low light of the great hall held up mounds of cheeses and fruit, sliced meats, baguettes and croissants and beautiful whole-grained loaves, salmon and shucked oysters and caviars, together with silver bowl after silver bowl of condiments and a garden full of flowers cut into crystal vases. In front of a fireplace tall enough for even Farieh to walk into was the bar. Lined end-to-end with premium bourbons and other American spirits, the finest whiskies from Scotland and Ireland and Japan, and French champagnes, it was flanked by enormous copper tubs filled with ice and beer.

Farieh assumed the great hall was important to their route, yet Steven slowed for neither the architecture nor the many hungry guests. They were as quickly through a white kitchen, crowned by its own timber-framed ceiling, and then into the library. There had been people in the kitchen, too, but Steven's pace had not allowed her to meet them.

The library was empty of people. Large oriental carpets rested on a gleaming oak floor that might have been stained and varnished that morning. 19th-century furniture from both England and New England ran in every direction. A leather-topped partner's desk—tooled, not stamped—commanded the room from the far end, illuminated by what had to be a Tiffany dragonfly lamp. And there were books—thousands of them—climbing up from dark mahogany cornices to a ceiling vault that was 14 feet higher. The books on the top shelf rested behind carved capitals crowning fluted walnut columns that rose up from black marble scotia. But the columns were only varnished, not stained. In the soft light of the library, and especially at the top where the ornate capitals greeted the fluting, the columns seemed to be cast from honey, and they quite literally took Farieh's breath away. Her gasp caught Steven's attention.

"It's something, isn't it? Let's sit over here," he said, guiding her by her arm to a leather love seat just to Farieh's left. Farieh sat facing the partner's desk; Steven sat at a slight angle to it, facing Farieh.

"This is Lambda," he said slowly.

*Oh*, she thought. *Not 'house of the lambs' after all*!

Steven continued. "Lambda is a collegiate secret society dedicated to one goal—pleasure. It attracts the most attractive, most adventuresome students on campus, people who are often the brightest students, as well. We do not discriminate in any direction. Our members are straight, queer, and questioning; black, brown, yellow, and white; Catholic, Protestant, Muslim, and Jew. Everything and anything. We get along because we recruit diverse people of high-quality who adhere to a code of conduct.

"After graduation, Lambda members tend to become the highest of high achievers. Those who value their Lambda membership—and we believe that is most of them—give more than generously to sustain the undergraduate chapters.

"Like most KU fraternities and sororities, Lambda has a house. You are sitting in ours. But just as Lambda differs markedly from fraternities and sororities, so does its house differ markedly from theirs. As you will see as we walk through it, this house is much more than a magnificent estate. It is purpose-built to accomplish its goal.

"Lambda was active at KU until the AIDS epidemic. The medical advances since those early days made chapter activity possible again. KU's chapter was reorganized about a decade ago; the land was purchased next; the house was completed two years after the reorganization. We believe we have the most beautiful house in the nation." Steven paused; Farieh had a question.

"Tell me about the code of conduct," she said. "That seems at odds with the rather narrow goal of the society, doesn't it? Why do you need a code?"

"We believe people who are allowed to care only about their

own pleasure can hurt others. The code is simple: A member may do anything she wishes with another member so long as the other member gives a knowing consent to the activity."

"What counts for 'a knowing consent' here?" asked Farieh, her voice carrying an unmistakable sarcasm.

"The term means the member whose consent is being sought must understand what is being asked of him. As you will see when we walk around the rest of the house, our members engage in activities that others—people on the outside—may regard as dangerous. Drug use leads the way, probably. But no one may impose drug use on another member. Not directly; and not indirectly, either, by lying about its side effects, for example. Members are allowed to invite others to use drugs with them, but only if they say what the drug is, say where they got it, say what it does, explain the side effects and the possible health risks, and answer every question the other member asks. If the other member hears all of that and doesn't want to use, that's the end of it."

"So what else goes on here? You've told me about getting high."

"Lambda is mostly about getting high and having sex. But with sex, too, the same code applies. Just as we have members who are really out there in terms of their experiences and their personal preferences, we have other members who are less so. So long as the member understands what is involved—what is being asked of them, and so long as they consent, then the activity can go forward. Otherwise, no."

Farieh's patience had run out, and her next question was as emphatic as it was immediate: "How do you *enforce* this?! When the two people are a man and a woman, of different size and strength and sobriety, and the man says the woman consented and the woman says she didn't, *then* what?! In a setting like this…" her right arm swept out across the library and back to the great hall, "consent must be *assumed*!"

"An excellent question," said Steven, oblivious to his

condescension. "We don't 'try' disputes here. If a member says another member made her engage in an activity she did not consent to, that other member is expelled. No trial; no mediation; no informed neutral; none of that. Just expulsion."

Farieh was quiet for a moment. Then she asked, "What about false accusations? Is Lambda somehow immune to them?"

"Probably not," answered Steven. "But Lambda has determined over the years that rigorous membership selection is the best guaranty that any complaint made will be legitimate. And we feel we are better off siding with the member who makes the complaint than we are to side with the other person, or to subject everyone to a trial and a verdict."

Farieh was again quiet, thinking about what Steven had said and the context in which he had said it. "Okay," she said. "I agree with you."

Steven stood up. "Let's see the rest of the house."

They moved past the partner's desk, out of the library, and into a hallway that ran 15 feet to a six-panel door that looked mahogany but was actually faux-painted steel. Just in front of it sat a young man in khakis, a button-down shirt, and a pullover who stood on their approach. "Hello, Steven," he said, his voice at least as deferential as it was welcoming.

"Anthony, this is Farieh. Farieh is not a member; she's my guest for the evening."

Anthony extended his right hand, Farieh reciprocated. "Very nice to meet you," he said, releasing her hand and turning to open the door. This time Anthony's voice had been as warm as his smile.

As they moved through the door opening and as Anthony took his seat behind them Steven spoke again. "Anthony is the Guard."

Farieh fairly smirked at the term. "Guard! You said this place was built on *consent*. Why on earth would you need a *guard*?!"

"I told you consent was the essential element to our code of conduct. This door is the threshold to the most important part of the house, and the Guard stands and greets everyone. If a member is being brought into it without their consent, that can show in a facial expression or in body language that the Guard will pick up. That gives us an important moment before anything . . ." Steven paused, "awkward might happen."

The door closed quietly behind them and ceiling lights came on overhead. They were red, just bright enough to reveal a long hallway running away from them both left and right. Regularly-spaced doors and a deep-pile carpet made it look like a fine hotel, except for the lighting. Steven turned left and gestured for Farieh to follow him. All of the doors were closed. Next to each, at a height perhaps five feet up from the carpet, was a 12" x 12" window, most of them shuttered from the inside. Steven saw Farieh looking at the first shuttered window and explained. "There is a 'performance' aspect to what happens at Lambda. Not for everyone, but for many of our members. We have 12 rooms, all of them the same and all of them different. Each has a large bed with side tables and lamps, a sofa, two large, overstuffed chairs, a glass-top table, a fully-stocked bar/refrigerator, and a bathroom with a tub. But the color scheme and the furniture design is different room to room…"

"Like a bordello," Farieh interjected.

"If you wish," he responded, then went on. "The tables are glass-topped . . ."

Farieh interrupted again: "For the cocaine."

"Yes," said Steven, "for the cocaine. But we were talking about the windows. The shutters close automatically when someone enters the room and locks the door, and they open automatically when someone leaves the room. If the people inside wish others to be able to watch them, they can open the shutters from the inside."

They had come to the second room, whose shutter was also closed. But the third room was unshuttered, and it was occupied, and Farieh could not keep herself from looking. A bearded, powerfully-built male whose naked body seemed to be covered with hair was having sex with an equally-naked young woman. Her snow-white body accepted him with a rhythm in keeping with the feral rapture on her face, which she had turned to Farieh.

As they moved on to the end of the left hallway then back toward the center, Farieh saw little of it. The exhibitionist couple had shaken her. Did Steven expect *her* to become a member of this sex club?! In her eyes they had been a couple since October. Steven had been patient and sharing at the beginning, along with funny and ridiculously generous. Their difficulties had started during the trip to Chicago to meet Abdul's father, and they had continued into the holidays. Steven had promised to take her to meet his family over Christmas and then had canceled—abruptly— the day they were to leave. Since then, he had been so preoccupied with other activities he had had virtually no time for her. But she was also busy, and she was not interested in a new relationship, and he had invited her to this party. And while there was so much about this evening that was odd, Farieh was willing to attribute it to Steven's vastly broader experience.

They came to an unshuttered room that was empty. Steven opened the door and gestured for Farieh to follow him in. It was furnished in the Arts and Crafts style, a large king bed in the center of the far wall, the obligatory glass-topped low table, large leather chairs with wooden arms. A closet stood to the left of the bed, its door open, and a bathroom door opened off the bed's right side. Farieh walked to the closet. A hooded blue robe hung from a solitary wooden hanger, women's size 4. She returned to the center of the room and followed Steven as he walked out of the room.

When they again reached the center of the hallway, just opposite the door to the Guard, Farieh thought they would return to the library. But Steven turned her toward a door she had not noticed, and she followed him through it. The lighting brightened slightly to reveal a large "common room" decorated with at least a dozen comfortable couches and with elegant card tables and chairs.

Four enormous flat-screen TVs anchored both sides of the far corner. A large bar was straight ahead. To the right was a kitchen island, an overhead light fixture in bronze and black, and half a dozen bar stools around the island. The couples who were sitting were talking intimately, and they wore only a robe, the same robe Farieh had seen in the closet: cashmere; almost-entirely blue—lapis, actually, with a crimson band around the front of the hood.

Farieh asked, "Why the robes?"

"We make them for the members. They receive them the evening they join Lambda."

"All right," said Farieh as she considered his response, which jostled against her observation of just minutes earlier. She asked another question: "Is wearing them significant in any way?"

"Yes," said Steven. "First, a robe says you are a member. If you are here, past the Guard in what we call 'the back of the house,' a robe also says other members may approach you."

Farieh turned on Steven: "What if I don't *want* anyone to approach me?! What if I don't *want* sex with someone I don't know?! Or drugs?! Or whatever else is going on here? What *then*?!"

Steven was as patient as Farieh was agitated, but his patience was forced and the tone of his voice had changed to something as cool as the outside air. "Then you stay in the front part of the house—either the great hall or the library or the kitchen, and you never go past the Guard."

"I'd like to leave *now*," she said. "I have 'consented' to as much as I can handle from Lambda!"

"I understand," replied Steven. "It may have been a mistake to invite you here this evening. It's this way." Steven turned and walked toward the door they had used to enter the back of the house.

They passed the Guard, retraced their steps, and were in the library when Steven's cell phone rang softly in his jacket pocket. He answered, spoke briefly, then said, "I have to take this—I'm very sorry. Please make yourself comfortable. You may want to find a book—we have many of them, as you can see. I will have someone bring you something to drink." Then he turned for the kitchen, leaving her alone in the library.

Farieh drifted to the nearest shelf and had just removed a leather-bound volume when she heard someone clearing his throat behind her. When she turned she was greeted by another young man in khakis, button-down shirt, and a pullover, this time holding a small silver tray on which rested a Baccarat champagne flute. "We ordinarily serve Veuve Cliquot," he said, extending the tray toward her. "But if you'd like something else I can get it quickly."

*Of course you can!* thought Farieh to herself. She took the slender glass while he watched her. "I'm sure I will take no time with this," she said peremptorily. "Please bring me another one!" Steven's absence had made her anxious, and her impatience slipped out before she could manage it.

"Of course," said the young man. He was back in seconds with another flute, and this time a small plate of canapés. He put both on the coffee table, next to the cat palm in its perfectly-sized onyx vase, right in front of the leather chair into which Farieh had slumped after putting her first glass on the same table. Then he bowed briefly and left the room.

Farieh stared at the shelves for the next several seconds, trying to get a handle on her anger. Her mind would not let her focus on the Baccarat or her book but raced back to the bedrooms on the far side of the Guard, then returned to the crystal flutes in front of her. And then her mind gave way to a different place—she was back on campus—and to a different voice. Colin "Chip" Hanson, her honors instructor in organic chemistry, had begun their seminar not with alkenes and bonding but with something far different. Professor Hanson had needed only a few minutes to demonstrate just how much he cared for his students. Farieh's near-photographic memory worked almost as well for auditory learning, and she called up the lecture just as he had delivered it:

"Gamma-hydroxybutyrate, or 'GHB,' is a central nervous system depressant. When added to a beverage such as champagne, the clear, odorless liquid is at first a relaxant. But most people who take it feel they have more energy. They become happier, they lose their inhibitions, and—depending on the circumstances—their playfulness will often expand into increased sensuality. Most young persons who take it are intoxicated not only by its chemical properties but also by its reputation. For persons taking it for the first time, 'Ecstasy' is an especially powerful drug that trashes inhibitions and paves the way to sex. But whether you use it may not always be up to you. That's why you need to be aware of its state—its form or appearance and how it is used—as well as its pharmacological activity. Ecstasy is not merely provocative. Taken unawares, it can be dangerous."

Farieh had just finished scrolling through Professor Hanson's first-day remarks when yet another young man appeared in front of her, and he was not dressed casually. Polished Allen Edmonds boots glowed beneath charcoal slacks; and the herringbone sport coat that covered his white-on-white shirt had to be custom-made as there was not a wrinkle in it across his powerful shoulders. He was as tall as Steven but had a deep tan. He was as handsome as Steven, but differently. Steven carried himself lightly, and his sense of humor was never more than a half step away. This fellow was all business, his smile a thin straight line across perfectly-white teeth. He was saying something to her but she did not get it all. She had once again been in the back of the house, staring at the seemingly-misplaced robe in the one empty bedroom, women's size 4, so she asked him to repeat it. He did.

"I'm Salah al-Din Abadi, Farieh. My friends call me . . ."

*Saladin.* Farieh said it her herself, soundlessly finishing his sentence.

"You left your scarf in the common room; Steven asked me to help you retrieve it."

Farieh lowered her head to her book to mask her reaction.

While she did not recognize the picture on the puzzle carved into this rural landscape in southeast Douglas County, its pieces had come into focus. She had not worn a scarf.

Her head still down, her eyes were drawn to the champagne flutes where an intrepid fly walked the rim of the closer one as though a celebrated tightrope artist. But it lost its balance abruptly, falling straight down onto the table and lying there still as the dead, whose company it had just joined.

Farieh closed her eyes. When she blinked them open her mind insisted she return to the back of the house, to its one empty bedroom, and to the single garment in its closet. The robe had *not* been left there by mistake. *She* wore a size 4.

She looked up. Her new companion was exactly where he had been, his expression—lips barely parted across dazzling front teeth—the same. As he began to speak Farieh's words darted ahead of him. "Thank you, Saladin. But I have not had the chance to drink the champagne or eat any of the food they brought me. I would like 15 minutes to do that, and to read some more of this book. I'm sure the scarf will wait for us." Betting the rest of her evening that the tactical politeness of the members would bind Saladin for at least that long, Farieh purred a question at him: "Will that be all right with you?"

Saladin bowed slowly. "Of course," he said, stepping back from her to make a stage exit from the library into the hallway that led to the back of the house, never turning his back to her, never taking his eyes off of her.

Farieh had looked up at him with her question. As her eyes followed his all the way out of the library she knew he would mistake the cause of their radiance, which had nothing to do with him—only his departure.

Again alone in the library, Farieh focused as she had never focused before. She swept the room; empty. She reached forward casually, lifted the flute whose contents had toppled the fly, and emptied it into the cat palm. Then she emptied the second one.

Then she stood up, walked to the French doors at the far end of the library, and removed her shoes. She pulled the cross trainers from her bag and replaced them with the Jimmy Choos; but she put the cross trainers on the floor, not on her feet.

Nearly dark now but for the desk lamp and the reds and ambers playing out of it through the dragonfly's wings, the library separated her from the hallway to the back of the house. Farieh covered the distance quickly before making a sharp stop at the door frame. She could not walk boldly into the hallway and confront the Guard; he may have been read in on Steven's plans for her. So she mussed her hair, grabbed the door frame, and prepared to swing herself around it in a slightly-drunken pirouette.

Farieh knew how to pray. She had been taught prayer by her mother and grandmother well before she had been taught to read. She prayed in two forms: she recited the Quran for its teachings and for its comfort, and she prayed for specific help in her life. But she had prayed little over the last few months, until tonight. For the past hour, ever since asking to leave the house of the lambs, Farieh had prayed constantly; but her prayers had been unfocused. Now she knew what she wanted: she wanted the Guard to be asleep. She stumbled into his hallway and looked up, having no idea what she would say to him. When she saw his head lolling against his chest and his magazine fallen to the floor, she thanked Allah for his blessings.

It was a quick thanksgiving! Farieh was up in a moment, back into the library, and once again across it to the front of French doors that opened out onto—what? Hurrying into the cross-trainers as she shouldered her bag, Farieh hopped sideways to the first window on her left and looked. Dawn was still an hour away, but her herald suggested the presence of an outside patio that bordered the library and wrapped around its corner to the front entrance. And there she knew she would find the driveway that led away from the house of the lambs. She did not remember where the driveway would lead. But wherever that was would be better than here.

Farieh pulled down the handle, pushed open the door, and ran.

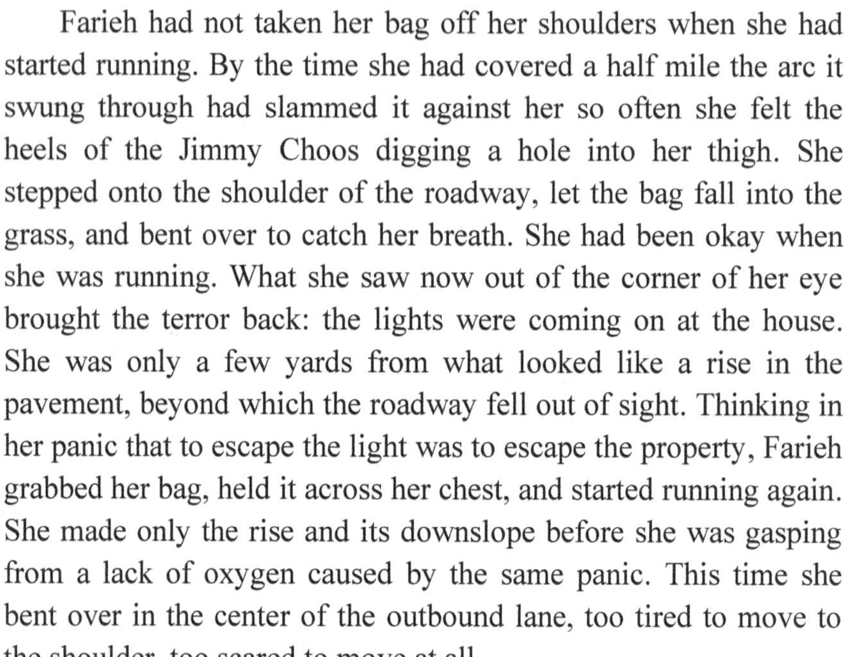

Farieh had not taken her bag off her shoulders when she had started running. By the time she had covered a half mile the arc it swung through had slammed it against her so often she felt the heels of the Jimmy Choos digging a hole into her thigh. She stepped onto the shoulder of the roadway, let the bag fall into the grass, and bent over to catch her breath. She had been okay when she was running. What she saw now out of the corner of her eye brought the terror back: the lights were coming on at the house. She was only a few yards from what looked like a rise in the pavement, beyond which the roadway fell out of sight. Thinking in her panic that to escape the light was to escape the property, Farieh grabbed her bag, held it across her chest, and started running again. She made only the rise and its downslope before she was gasping from a lack of oxygen caused by the same panic. This time she bent over in the center of the outbound lane, too tired to move to the shoulder, too scared to move at all.

The truck crested the hill behind her. Screaming disc brakes tore the air first, then joined the screech of its big tires as they locked up on the cool pavement. Farieh was powerless to move out of its way as the screams crested over her. Yet the driver had seen her red jacket, and that saved her.

Nearly immobile before the truck's arrival and frozen in place afterward, Farieh looked like a statue in the high beams of the Autocar trash truck. The driver opened his door, stood out on the step rail, and yelled down to her: "Hey, there! That's not a great place for a selfie, you know. I coulda run right over you!"

When Farieh neither moved nor spoke in reply the driver stepped off the rail and walked over to her. He wore scuffed, steel-toed boots and a gray Carhartt over a gray sweatshirt, and his

"Chiefs" ball cap made him six inches taller than Farieh. With his freckles and the gap between his front teeth and his 300 pounds he could have passed for a cast member of *Ozark*. He took off his hat, held it over his chest like someone had just started up the national anthem, and touched her gently on her left shoulder. "Hey," he said, softly this time. "You okay?"

Slowly coming back to the present, Farieh breathed deeply and turned toward him. That she had yet to say anything did not seem to bother him. "Well, I'll be," he whistled. "You are *one* pretty gal! What you doin' out here by yourself at dawn's early light? The British ain't comin', that's for sure. You waitin' on somebody else?"

Farieh turned her head and looked back down the illuminated roadway, the distance she had to travel before she even made it off the property at last made clear by the high beams. "I need a ride," she gasped, the tremor in her voice almost a match for the big Autocar's idle, "can you give me one?"

"Why sure, little lady. Bobby V. Hinshaw to the rescue!" And with that he drew his ball cap across his waist, made a low bow, walked to the passenger side, grabbed the door handle, and opened the door. "Right this way!"

Farieh followed him to the step rail and stopped. She had never climbed up into the cab of anything bigger than the compact pickup her family kept at their mountain house in Iran, and you could fit that in the front seat of this thing. Her forehead barely reached the bottom of the seat cushion. She had no idea how to get into it.

"Let me hep yuh," said Bobby, offering his right hand to her left hand and—when she took it—securely placing his left hand underneath her right elbow. "Use your right hand for that grab handle 'round the mirror when you get to it and hold onto the grab handle until your butt hits the seat. Goin' up!" With that he lifted her straight up off the ground, Farieh's cross trainers barely brushing the step rail as they raced past it. She caught the grab handle, and the upward momentum swung her right into the cab. As Bobby let her go she dropped onto the seat like a stone.

"There's a bag here in the middle of the road!" Bobby was yelling again. "Bet that's yours. I'll hand it up." Then he walked through the high beams and got into the truck on his side.

"Where to, little lady?" He pushed in the heavy clutch, pushed the shift lever into first, and started the Autocar toward the gate.

"Are you going to Lawrence?" Farieh's question was so quiet Bobby barely heard it.

"Yep. I go to Lawrence. In fact, I run the Greek houses next. If you're in one of them I can prob'ly take you right to your front door."

"Not a Greek house," said Farieh, "a scholarship hall— Miller."

"I know them too," said her knight errant. "I run them tomorrow. But I can't take the truck up on campus; chancellor don't like it. All right by you if I drop you off in the Kappa parking lot?"

"Yes," replied Farieh, "that would be fine."

*Fine*, she said to herself, smiling as she watched Bobby negotiate his truck through the barbed-wire gates. *You have no idea Bobby Hinshaw how 'fine' that would be!*

It was nearly 5:30 a.m. when Farieh walked into her room and leaned back into the pillow. She did not have the energy to take off her shoes, but she couldn't stop herself from checking her phone. She had another paper due. Today. By 5:00 that afternoon. Honors 19th Century British Literature. Helen Lochlear. She tried to call up the assignment from memory and to think about how she would manage it, but she was too tired. She would find a way to do it later. She fell asleep.

# Rain

Farieh had seen rain like this before—in the spring of her freshman year. It had been April, and she had just pushed through the front door of her scholarship hall on her way to the Union when she saw a wall of gray just past the porch. It wasn't a dull gray. Thousands of clear beads moved on its surface; thousands more moved inside it. Teardrop-shaped, the beads bore downward and splattered as they hit the ground, bursting sideways and upward off the hard surface of the sidewalk. All the way to the street from the covered porch, tiny translucent geysers sprang up from the pavement to rush past or intercept the beads falling toward them. And when they crashed together, as they did constantly, their mid-air explosions joined the barrage along the sidewalk. Her freshman year she had turned around and gone back to her room, glad the trip to the Union could wait.

But Farieh was a sophomore. She had the same honors advisor who had inspired her as a freshman, who had led her on last summer's intellectual frolic to England, and who was again her favorite teacher, this time in a seminar about women writers. Her advisor had asked her to come to Wescoe Hall for a conference. She was due there in 10 minutes, she would be late if she did not step off the porch, so she stepped off—into a rain so furious she felt like she was walking into the ocean's surf during a storm. Farieh's jeans and sneakers were soaked before she could look down to notice them. Her umbrella failed next, twisting into a bright blue flag that announced her coming to anyone foolish enough to be out looking for her. No match for the wind when untied, the hood of her Sierra Designs jacket nearly flipped back from her forehead. Dropping the umbrella, Farieh was able to secure the hood beneath her chin and protect her hair. Five minutes later, after running most of the way to Wescoe and clearing its few outside steps onto the safety of its porch, her shoulders were dry, and her hair. But she looked like she had been wading in her clothes.

Once inside she walked directly to the bathroom, where she took off her jeans and socks and wrung them out in the sink before putting them on again. She held her sneakers beneath the dryer for minutes before stepping back into them. They weren't dry yet; but at least they didn't squish when she walked out into the hallway that led to Helen's office.

Helen's door was open and she was standing where Farieh expected to find her—in the poet's corner, the space created at the far end of the office where Helen's favorite overstuffed chair and her students' favorite couch came together at a 90-degree angle. Farieh had sat or sprawled on the couch dozens of times her first three semesters at KU.

Helen looked up as her student crossed the threshold, took her glasses off, and frowned at the drops of water that trailed Farieh into the office. She managed "What on earth?!" before her embarrassed visitor was able to speak.

"The rain is horrible, Professor Locklear! I was drenched the moment I stepped off the porch at my scholarship hall. I am so sorry to track the water into your office."

"It'll be fine," said the advisor as she returned her glasses to her face. "This will take only a minute." Stepping toward Farieh, she extended her arm and gave her the document she had been looking at when Farieh walked in. It was a letter—short, typewritten, on university letterhead. Farieh read it.

```
Dear Farieh:

    Your paper on Pride and Prejudice was nearly
identical to the paper submitted by another
```

student. The other student's name is not important. Neither do I believe you copied the other paper. I was able to create a third paper that mirrored the first two using Writesonic: the structure was the same; the arguments were the same; nearly all of the quoted material was the same.

We talked once before about using AI resources to create work you were supposed to do yourself. You apologized, said you had used AI for only one section of the paper, and told me you would not use it again. I accepted your apology, and your commitment. But I cautioned you there would be severe consequences if you did it a second time. After your paper of last Friday afternoon we are to that point.

I have reviewed your situation with the Executive Dean of the College. We agree the appropriate response by KU is to remove you from the honors program. Although you will be permitted to complete the courses you are enrolled in this semester, you will not be able to enroll in honors courses next summer, or thereafter.

You will receive an "F" on the Austen paper you wrote for my class.

You have the right to appeal this decision to the Provost. The appeal procedures are on the university's website. If you have other questions about this decision, please direct them to the Office of the Executive Dean.

Very truly yours,<br>
/s/   Helen Lochlear

Farieh looked up. Her advisor's arm was again extended in her direction; this time Professor Lochlear's hand held an envelope. As Farieh took it from her Helen spoke to her in a voice so soft Farieh could barely make out the words. "The first letter is the official response from the university, Farieh. I am your advisor in the honors program, so I signed it. This second letter also comes from me, but it is personal. I want you to read it, but I don't want you to read it here. Please take it with you; please read it in a private place." Her face set hard into the expression that comes after one clenches their teeth to check any show of emotion, her advisor added, "Please take care of yourself."

Professor Lochlear turned away from her student and walked back to her chair, where she stopped and stood with her back to Farieh for a full 10-count. When she turned around her student was still standing there, so she spoke again, this time more audibly: "You may go."

Farieh had almost passed Flint Hall before she was aware she had left her advisor's office in Wescoe. She was wet, she was getting cold, so she ran across Sunflower Road and past Watson Library, cut through the lobby of Fraser Hall, and ran the rest of the way back to Miller. Her teeth were chattering as she pushed through the front door and took the stairs two-at-a-time toward her room. Inside, she stripped out of her clothes and pulled her robe out of the closet and wrapped it around her, reaching behind her head to pull her hair away from her back. Both were wet. Only when she had tied the robe around her did she finally stop what had been constant motion since she had started running.

The envelope that contained Professor Lochlear's handwritten letter lay where she had dropped it before she tore out of her clothes. She picked it up and removed the folded sheets of paper and held them, taking in their cream color and their weight. Farieh held the letter a long time. When the crick in her neck told her she needed to move, she got up and walked to the cluttered desk by the window and stood by its small chair. Had the chancellor been sitting in his second-floor office in The Outlook, he could have looked out his own window to watch as Farieh pushed the ends of the papers back away from the folds.

```
Dear Farieh,

    You are my best student. You were my best
student last year, as well. Only a few times in my
```

decades of teaching have I encountered someone with
your gifts-the power of your intellect, the sweep
of your curiosity, the ease with which you interact
and communicate with everyone-distinguished
scholars, senior administrators, fellow students,
even shopkeepers in London and pub owners in Skye!
You are lovely in every way, from the graciousness
of your manner to the wide-ranging elements of your
wardrobe.

You are also a joy to be with. Whether I have
joined you in a group of two or am one of many
people in a large gathering, there is no one's
company I would rather share.

And you have promise. Oh, my, do you have
promise! I have frequently entertained myself over
a cup of tea, musing on the hundreds of things you
might yet do in college and the wonderful things
you will achieve afterward.

The honors program is the best academic and
leadership vehicle we can offer students at KU. For
someone like you, it is the only program certain to
challenge you. I have watched you carefully, and I
believe you have been challenged. Your work and
your growth your freshman year were remarkable. At
the end of last semester when the rosters came out
for spring, I was thrilled to see you had enrolled
in my seminar.

But there is a darkness now. It was clear our
first day of class in January, and it has
continued. You are as smart as ever; your comments
are as often incisive and as often imaginative. But
the joy-the bright bell of your presence-is too
often silent. You greet people differently. You
rarely stay after class. And I have not seen you in
my office this semester, until now.

You are one of at least a thousand KU students
who have written a paper using AI. As you know,
some KU teachers not only allow it but encourage
it-usually in controlled situations where all of
the students are using AI. The honors program does
not allow it, and you know that too. That you would
put a paper at risk with AI was a mistake. That
this was your second mistake and that it has cost
you the honors program is a tragedy. But I am far

more concerned for you than for your place in the
honors program.

You must confront the darkness. It may come
from your family. If it does, you must sit with
them and talk about it. It may come from a
relationship. If it does, you should weigh it
carefully; and perhaps you should end it. This last
statement may strike you as hasty in the extreme,
coming from someone who knows nothing about any
relationship you may be a part of. But you are
young and smart and resilient. I have watched
hundreds of talented young women agonize over
bringing a difficult relationship to a close. Most
have ended them. All who did so have thrived.

I will not be your advisor next year. But I
will watch for you, and think warm thoughts about
you, and be glad for your successes. And if you
should ever want to join me in the poet's corner,
there will be tea and scones for you when you
arrive.

With warmest-possible affection and good
wishes,

/s/   Helen Lochlear


Farieh set the letter on the desk. Her hair was still wet and the strand of it that had strayed beneath the collar of the bathrobe loosed a drop of cold water down the middle of her back. Shivering in response, she wrapped the robe more closely around her and walked to her bed. Although it was still mid-day she wanted to sleep; but she had to do something with her hair. She got up again, lifted a towel out of the clothes hamper in the closet, ran it vigorously across the top of her head, then pitched it back into the hamper. When she got back to her bed she climbed under the covers. But still she sat upright, looking out the window.

Academic success had come fast. Already in the honors program when she arrived in Lawrence, she had surprised the Department of Mathematics by offering to test out of her entire undergraduate degree a few days after classes started, then dazzled the entire university by doing so in a stand-up, chalkboard tour de force in Snow Hall. Her exceptional freshman grades reflected her exceptional papers and tests. She went to England and Scotland the next summer, returned to Lawrence, and capped her first semester as a sophomore with her selection as a University Scholar. It had all come so easily it was easy not to grieve the loss of a part of it.

Fatigue, embarrassment, resignation, hurt. All of these circled the afternoon. But not loss. Loss would come later, next fall; she would miss the honors program next fall. She would miss the challenge Professor Lochlear had spoken of. Mostly, she would miss the camaraderie: working with her friends to understand and solve the problems Lochlear and the other gifted teachers presented, laughing with them over tea in the Union, walking home with them as the light in the sky above Daisy Hill gave way to evening.

Now she was mostly cold. Her hair splayed as she fell back against the pillow. She tugged the covers up to her chin to answer yet another shiver that raced from her shoulders to her knees. The last thing she saw before her eyes closed was daylight on the other side of the window. It was still raining.

# Miller After Midnight: Steven

She remembered flying back from Chicago—the last time she had seen him excited. He had talked non-stop about the "amazing success" of the evening, but to Abdul—who was seated just across the aisle—and not to her. Steven spoke of "supply chain simplification" and a "much more robust distribution" and the "potential for markets we have never dreamed of." Both young men were drinking the champagne that had been laid in the night before in anticipation of this very conversation. But they were barely making time for it.

Farieh was on her phone, two rows behind them. As she knew almost nothing about Steven's work, other than the demands it made on his time, these terms meant little to her. But she understood Steven's excitement, which was mirrored by Abdul's. Farieh was pleased for Steven. This most important meeting of his life had gone well, and she had helped. Yet he did not share his excitement with her during the 45-minute return flight. If he had known of the needs she had carried to Chicago, he ignored them.

At first, Steven had been a distraction from the emptiness of her thoughts of Mehri. He became more than that when he asked her to accompany him to the meeting with Abdul's father. For the first time, he needed her support; he had counted on her to give it. She had supported him. She felt she had done so flawlessly: wasn't Abdul's father beaming at the end of the evening? Yet here was Steven, bragging to Abdul about his own role in it, saying nothing about her, saying nothing to her. At the time, she saw it as an oversight, the product of a craved success having wildly exceeded expectations. But it was impossible to miss, and it stung, and she did not know what to make of it.

She had seen Steven hardly at all in the several weeks after Chicago, which worked well for Farieh because she had so much to catch up on before finals. And then it was the morning of December 23, when Steven was supposed to pick her up on his way to the airport for the trip to meet his parents, the one he had promised on the way to Chicago. She had waited the entire day for the cruel text that came late in the afternoon: "Something's come up. Can't do the trip home after all. Will call after the holidays. Steven."

Only two people shared Miller's empty spaces with her that Christmas break. Beth stayed because her parents were divorcing. Jamie stayed to be there with her roommate.

Farieh found the steps and the gates and the bench in the early morning of the 24th. She sat for a long time, hoping the feelings she had felt for Steven during their weekend in Quebec and during their magical dinner at NOMI  would find her. But the canceled holiday had laid siege to the tower of her affection, and the feelings were inside, silent. She would call to them.

Farieh reached into the pocket of her parka for the small notepad and ballpoint pen she had put there when she left her room. One failed start followed another. There were many words, but she could not fit them into anything she liked. Finally she wrote them out just as they appeared to her:


## A SONG FOR STEVEN


Mercury's winged chariot bridges cities,
Even countries,
Within the span of a breath
Of the god.

Snow everywhere.
Yet not inside;
Not within a chateau

Built too late upon the plain
To impact any battle but that,
Now,
Lends its peace to every visitor.

Morning.
The sun arrived early.
I watched it play across the water
Before it jumped ashore
To peek around slate roofs and chimney tops.
The touch of my hotel robe
Made me want a different touch,
And to make real the hope of a kiss to follow.


The holidays came. Steven did not call. January became February. Cryptic responses answered her long texts when a response came at all. And then The Wheel, and a familiar sidewalk, and a young man she barely knew holding out a piece of paper. Steven's signature at the bottom. The invitation led her to the country house, where Steven poisoned the feelings she had tended so faithfully since Quebec.

Once again it was well after midnight. Once again she sat on the bench. Once again she had been there for a long time. She reached for her notebook and pen.


## A SONG FOR FARIEH


Dark passageways that were too long
Too soon replaced the kinder spaces with

Their gleaming lights,
Their flashing crystal, and
Their winter flowers bright as summer.

My feelings for you waited too long, as well.

What did you leave for me?

Not the taste of you I wanted
But the toxic draught you planned.

# A Long Walk Home

Green Hall is expressionless from morning to dusk, its charcoal windows accepting little of the day's light and giving nothing back. At night, if there were trees around it, a passerby might miss its ordinary outline altogether. But as there are no trees at night it stands out, though without distinction, barely second place to the architecture of the School of Engineering that sits across the street to the north and is itself no threat for the Pritzker Prize.

Farieh's classmates in her international law seminar had opted for a single night session that semester and they had just had it. As usual, she stayed behind to engage Professor Zaidi on his presentation. Tonight he had addressed the utility of economic sanctions as a means of changing nation-state behavior, concluding they were ineffective. But Professor Zaidi had opened his evening schedule for only the class, and it closed as soon as he had finished. He apologized to Farieh for not having time to talk with her, but he left. It was 9:30.

Farieh walked out of Green Hall through the lower doors, crossed Irving Hill Road, and continued east on the sidewalk in front of the Allen Fieldhouse Parking Facility. She would ordinarily take the other way back to her scholarship hall—to Slawson Hall, up the hill, then east down Jayhawk Boulevard. Tonight she decided to take the back way: through the neighborhood south of the chancellor's residence, up the hill on the chancellor's back drive, and around the corner to Miller.

*What did I do to Steven?* As soon as the question formed she was embarrassed by it, embarrassed at blaming herself for the terrifying behavior of the male in her life. But the question had simply appeared. She was alone; no one had challenged her with it.

*And why would I do this to me?!* Farieh recognized this was the better question.

She was walking in an April evening that had turned past indigo to black. Though the light spilling toward her from a dozen streetlamps held back the darkness, she felt no freedom in it. The thoughts of Steven would have been there in the dark as well as the light.

*Maybe this is a tape I have been laying down for years as my friends and my sisters and my aunts talked about their own boyfriends and their own husbands. Now I have a boyfriend—or had one. And he treated me badly. And I am asking myself the same questions I heard over and over in Iran. How stupid!*

She walked the length of Capitol Federal Hall and past the north end of the Ambler Rec Center. The lighting from the vast parking lot that joined the two made for a confident transition to University Place.

A residential enclave immediately south of the campus, University Place presented short blocks and mature trees and charming homes in a variety of traditional styles. Though there was much less light here, there was enough that Farieh could see the houses clearly and the occasional bicycle or scooter leaned up next to a side door. The miasma of the asphalt repair work in the Ambler Center parking lot was gone now, replaced by something familiar to northeast Kansas on an April evening. The night air in University Place smelled like sheets: pinned to a clothesline in late afternoon and left until morning, clean and crisp with a hint of moisture.

*Why do women look like property to men? Especially rich men? Something they can pull down from a shelf to amuse themselves and then either put back for next time or pitch away? If we let them know they hurt our feelings, we're clinging. If we get angry and, God forbid, express ourselves in that way, then we're bitchy. If they acknowledge our feelings it is only to recoil from them. They want a pretty face, someone who looks great in a little black dress. But a real relationship?*

Farieh had turned north, moving past the picture-book residences toward the university. Her anger was cooling, but not just cooling. New thoughts were pushing it out altogether. She had had other things to do this semester, important work. Not classwork, although she certainly had that. The work she was thinking of was personal.

Farieh had sensed from New Year's Day that she and Steven would fail. The realization lay so deep in January that some would have called it unconscious. But it grew, winnowing through her thoughts, insistent. Her mind and her heart made less and less space for Steven and his indifference. In their place she found Mehri. Mehri had been there the entire time. Farieh's personal work of the spring was for Mehri.

Farieh had been asked to organize a student response to the Kansas Legislature, which was once again mucking around with diversity on college campuses. The conservative-dominated House and Senate seemed evenhanded about it; any limiting legislation would apply to all the Regents' schools. But the undergraduates in Lawrence knew KU was the real target.

Farieh had been monitoring the Kansas House of Representatives, whose leadership was zealously opposed to diversity, equity, and inclusion on Kansas campuses and who had sponsored several bills to limit it. Farieh and her group had worked with the Democratic caucus and with pro-diversity organizations in the state, such as the ACLU and the NAACP, to resist the legislation. One bill, a budget rider, was the front runner, and it was heading for a final hearing in a week.

Farieh helped the House Minority Leader find a speaker to attend that hearing and oppose the bill. Farieh was excited about him. He was clever and well-prepared and articulate. But he was more than that. He could identify with his audience, speak to their feelings. As a result, he had had real success stopping similar legislation in other states.

The speaker was critical. Still, the consensus within her group, and at the Capitol, was that the bill would likely pass. It was a numbers game; the conservatives had the votes.

If the bill passed the House and Senate, getting the governor to veto the bill was their last chance. KU's opposition to the bill at that point would be important, maybe decisive. She would do everything she could to make it happen.

Farieh and her group would approach the university. They would ask KU to support a veto. If the school sat on the fence, which she expected, she would take things up a notch: she would lead a sit-in at the Chancellor's Office.

No one in Farieh's group believed a sit-in would work. But Farieh believed it was a necessary next step on the way to an all-out protest. Farieh was already working on the details of the protest. They would do the sit-in first.

Protests were disruptive. They could get out of hand. But in her heart, Farieh knew how the university would respond to the milder parts of their plan. KU would do nothing. There would have to be a protest.

She had climbed the south slope of Mount Oread and had just passed The Outlook, where the lower, public floor of the university's official residence showed dark to the outside. On the north side of the second floor, where the chancellor lived, a single light shone in the window facing Miller Hall. *Probably his office,* she thought. *Probably he's working.*

Farieh had met the chancellor early her freshman year. As a first-semester sophomore, she had attended his lively party for the honors program in December. Two months later, she had spent nearly an hour with him at the University Scholars event. He was handsome and thoughtful and she liked him. She hoped he would not be angry with her once the protests started. But that would be up to him.

# Part III
## The Protests of Spring

# Trinity Episcopal Church

They met in the library at the downtown Episcopal Church because Farieh chose it. It was the right size for the seven of them, it was downtown and close to the apartments and scholarship halls where they lived, and it was the right price: free. The Episcopal Church, including Trinity in Lawrence, had supported social causes for generations. Trinity was a traditional church with a small, downtown footprint. For Rebecca Seacrist, who attended the church and had recommended it to Farieh, that meant the church and those who chose to meet there should be well beneath anyone's radar.

Rebecca's instincts were accurate. They had been there since January, meeting for hours in the small, book-lined space just south of the sanctuary. They had become more than friends, almost sisters, but this was no start-up social sorority. Their meetings were serious from the start, and they had become only more so. The young women were animated, challenging, occasionally angry, and frequently noisy. There was shouting, the occasional fist slammed on the table, and the occasional slammed door. That no one had interrupted them was a blessing.

They had come together to talk about what was happening at KU. They were disappointed, upset, suspicious—pick an adjective. With surprisingly little pushback from the Board of Regents, the Kansas Legislature seemed intent on reducing university education to a STEM-oriented exercise shorn of humanities and with as little time to a degree as possible. Three years was the actual goal for an increasing number of legislators.

Having grown tired of signaling its discontent with

progressive incursions into the state's educational system, the conservative majority had acted. Transgender students were now legally restricted to bathrooms and to participation in sports only if consistent with their gender at birth. The Legislature's effort to eliminate abortion through a broad constitutional amendment having failed, the conservative majority had launched a multi-pronged statutory attack to restrict it. Eager to join the anti-woke crusaders in Florida and other Southern states, conservatives were gearing up to stamp out diversity, equity, and inclusion on Kansas campuses.

Both sophomores, Rebecca and Farieh had met briefly as freshmen in honors program orientation. They liked each other and became Facebook friends. And while they did not share classes or other activities their first year at KU, they kept up with one another. Farieh had welcomed Rebecca's invitation to a meeting in early January and her suggestion that Farieh bring several of her friends. Their topic: protecting what had been a vibrant culture of diversity from the Kansas Legislature.

When all of them had gathered at a deserted Union that Friday afternoon there were seven. They were not of like mind. Rebecca, who had played soccer and had run track in high school, could understand the concern by high school girls and their parents if they had to compete against transgender girls who had gone through puberty as males. Farieh, who grew up Shia in Tehran, did not understand how anyone could be "in favor of" abortion. None of them wanted quotas, or any kind of forced representation of minority or disadvantaged groups. But each of them believed strongly in community. Each believed women and Blacks and Browns and gays and straights and any other group with a lawful purpose were entitled to have a community at KU. Each believed KU should be able to support those communities, free from any meddling by Topeka.

They mostly watched and listened the first several weeks. By mid-February, the thrust of the conservative's legislation had become clear. Seeking any kind of commitment to "diversity" would be outlawed as a consideration for recruiting, hiring, retention, and promotion. A teacher who intended to teach about "diversity" would be required to say so when she posted her syllabus, to post all materials touching upon it online, and to produce the material in paper format when requested. Staff members who planned to mention "diversity" in recruiting, hiring, etc., were required to do the same.

Enforcement was left to any student who felt aggrieved by something. The student's complaint went straight to the Board of Regents. Once it reached them there was no threshold it had to clear, no requirement of logic or probable cause. The Regents had to investigate every single complaint and make a report of each investigation. A finding of a violation led to a range of serious sanctions capped by dismissal.

The seven women immediately saw the peril was not in the burdensome posting requirement but in the complaint process, and especially in the appeal. If the student did not like the report from the Regents, they got *an automatic appeal* to the state's Attorney General. While the Regents were seen as politically-moderate and genuinely concerned for the state's universities and their students, the Attorney General was the state's most outspoken opponent of diversity. Any appeal to his office required him to conduct yet another investigation and make yet another report. And a report of violation from the AG carried the same range of penalties for the offending teacher or staff member.

The final threat was overlooked by everyone but Farieh. "What does 'diversity' mean?" she asked. "I can't find a definition for it in the bill. If there is no definition, the people complaining and the Attorney General can define it any way they want!

"Also, our teachers and staff will not know what's okay and what's not okay. If they want to be safe, they will have to stop talking about diversity in any context. And that, I'm sure, is *precisely* what the bill drafters had in mind."

The discussion that followed was a short one. All of the women agreed the legislation was chilling and needed to be opposed and defeated.

Knowing what the target was, Farieh and Rebecca and their friends tried to formulate a plan of action. Their committee-of-the-whole approach failed. So they broke up into two smaller groups, one led by Rebecca and the other by Farieh, in the hope two groups would generate more ideas and more ideas would generate at least one good one. That went better. By March, they were onto something.

Farieh would deal with the Legislature. She would meet with the Democrat leadership in the House to plan the opposition. When a hearing was set, she would help them find a speaker to oppose the bill. She had heard of someone from the East Coast. It was a stopgap, but it was a chance.

Rebecca would oversee the next phase, which assumed the bill would pass and be sent to the governor. She would coordinate actions on the KU campus to generate university support for a veto from the governor. Without breaking the law, violating any student code of conduct, or engaging in any form of violence, they would confront the university administration. They would drive KU toward supporting a veto. Or, they would drive the university to suppress the students trying to get its attention.

It was Farieh who reported first at their next meeting. "We've got a speaker for the House hearing! His name is Charles Willoughby. He's from Washington, D.C. I had heard of him, but I didn't know where to find him. My sister has a friend on the ACLU staff in the District, her name is Jackie, and she located him for me. Jackie was excited we were interested in him; she actually heard him speak. 'Fabulous!' she said.

"Jackie's grandfather was a Baptist minister. Pops—that's what she called him—always told her that when he preached the Gospel, he liked to 'put the hay down where the goats could get it.' Jackie loved the expression, and she told me: 'Willoughby preaches a different gospel, but he puts the hay down in the same place!'"

# Speaker of the House

Paul Carlton had been asked a hundred times whether he might run for governor. "Nope," he'd always say. "This job's too important, and it takes too long to learn it." He meant every word.

He was from Goodland, as safe a Republican district as there is in Kansas. He had been elected and re-elected a dozen times. He was conservative, but more so fiscally than socially. He could talk with the progressives in the legislature, and he understood them, but he didn't always agree with them. Sometimes he couldn't agree with them. DEI was one of those times. He wasn't going to the barricades to fight DEI—diversity, equity, and inclusion. But many of his colleagues were already there, especially Gerald Hampton, the Speaker Pro Tem, whose intelligence and energy made Carlton's job so much easier than it might have been. Gerry had asked his help with a rider to the Omnibus Budget Appropriations Bill he said would ban the consideration of DEI in the hiring of faculty and administrative staff, and Paul said he would give it. The actual rider was just vague enough to threaten any consideration of DEI by Kansas's state-supported colleges and universities, even in their classrooms and student organizations.

Stamping out DEI on college campuses was a Republican issue. Republicans had prevailed on it from Florida to Texas to North Dakota, and Kansas Republicans were determined to enact something in their state this spring. Hampton thought his tacking it onto the omnibus bill was clever, and he was right. There was too much in the budget bill that people wanted. Besides, the omnibus bill was automatically fast-tracked, which made the mounting of a successful opposition difficult.

There was only one hearing left before the House Committee

on Appropriations would vote the bill up or down. Today was Thursday, March 6. The hearing was set for Tuesday of the following week, March 11. Because he had talked with his wife that morning about their grandchildren, Paul also knew spring break for most of the Kansas public schools was March 17-21; but he had no idea why he had thought of that. He looked up from the pile of papers on the quarter-sawn oak desk he had inherited from his grandfather, rang for his communications director, William Prescott, sat back in his chair, and waited.

Prescott knocked lightly on the tall oak jamb and entered the Speaker's office quietly. It wasn't quite dark at 6:30 but it was headed that way. The Speaker's desk lamp was on, and the Speaker was rocked back in his chair with his eyes closed and his feet up on the desk. But that didn't mean he was asleep.

"Billy?" he asked without moving, his eyes still closed.

"Yes, sir, Mr. Carlton. You called for me."

"I did!" Carlton swung his boots to the floor and moved his chair a few inches closer to the desk. "What does 'Don't call me Frances' have in store for us next Tuesday?"

"Don't call me Frances" was the Speaker's pet name for Frances Costello, the House Minority Leader. Costello had been called "Frankie" since grade school. At the statehouse, almost everyone called her that, including Paul Carlton. But she could be prickly at any time, and damned difficult in a tough floor debate, and the Speaker enjoyed using his own name for her in close company.

"I don't know," replied Billy Prescott. "I looked over her witness list for the hearing; she was required to submit it today, of course. Only one name on it—Charles Willoughby. I don't know who he is."

The Speaker was now looking at Billy over the top of his wire-rim glasses, which he did when he got an answer he didn't like. Paul Carlton liked Billy Prescott, who was the most effective person he'd ever had in the communications job. But Billy was only 25. And despite what were now three full years working in the Speaker's Office, he could be gun-shy. Carlton liked to tease him.

"I don't know who he is, either, Billy. Which one of us should look into that?"

"I am *so* sorry, Mr. Carlton. That's me, of course; certainly not you. I'm really sorry. I'll have that for you right away." And with that the young communications director wheeled around and hurried back to his own office. Carlton looked at the large wall clock left of the door, another heirloom from his grandfather: 10 minutes to 7:00. He took off the glasses and returned his attention to the papers on his desk.

Billy Prescott's next knock came just over four hours later, at 11:00 p.m. It was quite dark now yet the only light in the Speaker's personal office came from the same desk lamp. It was a soft light, a glow really. It did a good-enough job with the desktop but only suggested the rest of the room. Billy's knock was louder this time, even authoritative, and Paul was fully alert when he heard it. "What have you got for us, Billy?"

"Willoughby's a regular on the ACLU circuit and has appeared frequently before legislatures considering anti-DEI legislation. He wasn't there for Florida or Mississippi or Texas. But somebody found him. And since *he* weighed in the ACLU has been successful in more of these contests than unsuccessful."

"Okay, he's successful. What do you know about the man? What's the back story on Charles Willoughby?"

"He's a stud, Mr. Carlton!"

"Whoa, there, Billy! Take it easy. What's got a jaded old communications guy like you so excited about an ACLU mouthpiece?"

"That's just it, Mr. Carlton. I've never met him, of course. But he comes across as a regular kind of guy. Brilliant; no question about that. But just a guy. Let me give you some examples.

"He went to an Historically Black University, Howard.

Graduated with highest honors; double-major in history and engineering. Played the shooting guard on the basketball team. He's 6'4". The team picture says he's handsome. Class President his senior year. Turned down a Rhodes Scholarship because he wanted to get married!

"Went to law school instead—Georgetown. Graduated with honors—Order of the Coif. Could have been the number-one student in the class, but I can't tell that; Georgetown doesn't rank its law students. Private practice for 15 years, alternating between high-end commercial litigation and appellate court advocacy. Now seems to spend all of his time with one cause or the other, often with the ACLU.

"Oh, yeah, I forgot. He has a monthly podcast. I listened to one of them; they're great. On top of everything else, he's funny."

"Okay," said the Speaker. "He's smart and he can shoot and he's a comedian. What else?"

"To me, his personal life is even more impressive than his professional life. He's still married to the same woman, and they have three kids. Two of the kids, a boy and a girl, are out of the house and appear to be highly-successful. The third, another boy, is a high school junior. Public school, not private; National Merit Semi-finalist. And Willoughby coaches his summer baseball team. He and his wife are church members. Capitol Hill United Methodist. They sing in the choir there—no, really! As I said, the guy's a stud!"

"When's the hearing again?"

"It's next Tuesday, Mr. Carlton."

"Is Willoughby employed somewhere? Is he represented by a speakers' bureau?"

"Yes. Washington Speakers Bureau."

"Do you suppose they'd talk with us about him?"

Billy Prescott paused just a moment, then went on as rapidly as before. "My experience with these organizations is they're pretty tight-lipped about their talent. But Willoughby seems to be all about transparency, and I suspect he has directed his handlers—within reason, of course—to give out whatever information people want to have about him."

This time it was the Speaker who paused, thinking about where to go with this. The rock star who had emerged that evening was a real problem for his friend Gerry Hampton. "Call them tomorrow morning, Billy, as soon as they open." Carlton paused again, as though he were not sure how Billy's conversation would go, which he wasn't. A moment later he had the answer. "I want you to tell them you have an important opportunity for Mr. Willoughby next week Thursday, that it's in Salt Lake City, and you want to know whether there is any way he can arrange his schedule to handle it. As soon as you get them on the phone and have an answer I want to hear from you."

"What's the opportunity?" asked Billy. "What am I supposed to tell them?"

"If my instincts are correct you'll never get to that point. If I'm wrong, tell them it relates to the Sundance Film Festival. Or make something else up. Tell them you were calling just to check availability and you'll be back with the details in an hour."

"Okay. Got it."

The Speaker had returned his attention to the papers on his desk so Billy was forced to clear his throat to get his boss' attention. "Will there be anything else tonight, Mr. Carlton?"

Carlton looked up at his young staffer. "No, Billy. You've been terrific. There's a real bullet headed our way. You figured that out, and we may be able to deflect it. Thanks for staying on so late tonight. See you tomorrow morning, just as soon as you get the information from the speakers' bureau."

"Right," said Billy Prescott as he stood up out of his chair and made for the door. "Good night, Mr. Carlton."

The Speaker stayed at the Cyrus Hotel on Kansas Avenue when the legislature was in session. He could walk there, and he did, soon after Billy had left.

Billy lived in Lawrence. His after-midnight departure from the capitol meant he did not get home until close to 1:00 a.m. He had to be back in Topeka by 7:00 in order to dial up the Washington Speakers Bureau when it opened at 8:00 Eastern Standard Time. But he made the call and got the information and knocked on the Speaker's door jamb at 7:45.

"Billy!" Paul Carlton was unreasonably chipper for Billy Prescott at that hour. But Billy set that aside as he made his way into the office and took his seat across from the Speaker.

"What have you got for us this morning?"

"You were right, Mr. Carlton. After they told me Willoughby couldn't make the gig in Utah they were eager to explain why not. Seems he has booked a flight to London with his wife and the boy who is still in school, and they leave at 8:05 on Thursday morning for a long-planned spring break holiday in England. According to the woman I talked with, who just had to share this, Willoughby secretly arranged for the other two kids to meet them in London. Willoughby's wife and youngest child don't know about it; it's going to be a big surprise."

The Speaker was so tickled with himself he stood up and shouted, "Perfect!" Then he sat back down in his chair and continued with his communications director. "Billy, I want you to wait until 4:30 this afternoon, then send a text message to 'Don't call me Frances.' Tell her the Speaker has been forced to postpone the Tuesday hearing until Thursday morning. Don't make any explanation; just tell her it's off. Tell her I am aware everyone will be disappointed. That's it. Got it?"

"Yes, sir!" said Billy, smiling almost as broadly as the speaker.

When Billy made to get up from his chair Paul Carlton held his hand up to stop him. Carlton was smiling again, but he had replaced his victory-lap grin with something warmer. "You did outstanding work last night, Billy, and I know I kept you way past the time Mary expected you. It's Friday. In the hope you and Mary are able to reconfigure any plans you already have for this evening, I am going to suggest dinner at your favorite restaurant in Lawrence, The Wine Dive. It will be on me. I'll call them and let them know you're coming. Does 7:00 sound all right?" Billy nodded it was. "Good. Dinner, wine, whatever you want. They received a Wine Spectator Award recently, so I know the wine list is excellent. I hope you and Mary have a great evening!"

Billy got up, shook hands with his boss, and made his way to the corridor through the same tall door frame. He marveled again at Paul Carlton. At his imagination and his tenacity, for starters, and at how he could work his people so hard, then find just the right way to say, "Thanks!" Billy Prescott did not know how long he would stay around Kansas politics; but he liked the guy he worked for.

Frances Costello stared at her phone so hard her granddaughter would have expected a pony to jump out of it. Remembering Charles Willoughby's service had a 24-hour hot line, she looked it up and dialed the number. A male voice came on the line. "This is Washington Speakers' Bureau's after-hours service, how can I help you?"

Frances identified herself, asked how she might reach Mr. Willoughby about an engagement they had planned for next week, and asked about the person who kept his schedule in the event Mr. Willoughby was not available.

"I'll need to put you on hold for a moment, ma'am." Frances had barely checked the time when a new person was speaking to her: "How can I help you?"

Frances told her about the postponement of the Kansas hearing and asked her to confirm Willoughby would still be able to come on Thursday. There was a pause as the woman pulled up Willoughby's calendar on her computer, then a longer pause. "It appears Mr. Willoughby will be traveling that day for another engagement."

When Frances asked whether Willoughby might be able to travel through Topeka on his way to the other engagement she drew a kind-hearted laugh. But sensing the desperation in the question, the assistant added: "Mr. Willoughby will be traveling the other direction that morning—to London—for a spring-break trip with his family. I am so sorry."

There was nothing more to say.

# Thursday Morning 10:00 A.M.
## The Old Supreme Court Chambers

Richard Swanson had made his career in accounting. He ran for the House seat from his district in West Wichita, got elected, and was an immediate hit. Smart, careful, and with real-world skills in budgeting and finance, he was appointed to the Appropriations Committee his first term, became the chair four years later, and had enjoyed the ride ever since.

The pro-tem's career in aviation had made Gerald Hampton an easy guy for Swanson to share a Scotch with, and they had become good friends as they made their way up in Republican politics. Swanson's principal responsibility this Thursday morning was to see that the Omnibus Appropriations Bill cleared his committee and made its way to the Senate, where it was already greased for passage and a quick walk to the Governor's Office. Hampton's anti-DEI rider was the principal item on the morning's agenda; Swanson was determined to help his friend with it.

Frances Costello had filed her list of speakers for the hearing the week before, and she had been quick to talk with the press about Charles Willoughby: his background, his eloquent manner, and his success in beating back anti-DEI measures in other states. The *Capital-Journal* had been so impressed it ran his picture on the front page of the Friday paper alongside its interview with Costello. Swanson had seen the story and was intrigued enough to forward it immediately to Hampton, along with the suggestion he take it seriously and get his own supporters lined up. When Hampton reported back not two hours later that Swanson would need "a good-sized barn" to hold all of the rider's supporters, Swanson scheduled the hearing in the old courtroom of the Kansas Supreme Court.

The well of the courtroom was large enough to accommodate his committee, his staff, and anyone who might come to speak to the bill that morning. The seating area behind the bar, the largest one available to a House committee, could handle the expected audience. But what Swanson really liked about the space was not its size but how it looked. Its frontier elegance elevated the Appropriations Committee whenever it met there.

The construction firm from Lawrence that had renovated the Capitol had done an exceptional job with the courtroom. The oak paneling and wainscoting gleamed under the television lights; the stencils were magnificent—as bright and as cleanly executed as when the building was first completed more than 120 years ago.

There had been a few witnesses identified for the omnibus bill, itself, but each had withdrawn in the face of the negotiations that had preceded the hearing. That left Hampton's anti-DEI rider. Swanson had exercised his prerogative as chair and had invited Frances Costello to call her opposition witness first. As Hampton had promised, the audience seats were filled. The hum of their whispers faded, then dropped to nothing, as Costello stood and moved to the lectern.

"Good morning, Representative Costello," said the chairman. "I understand you have an outstanding speaker for us this morning, a Mr. Willoughby, is that correct?"

Frances Costello was prepared to explain Mr. Willoughby's absence. As her efforts to find a substitute speaker on such little notice had been futile, she had also prepared to make this presentation herself. She had worked on it non-stop since Monday afternoon. What she was not prepared for was the chair's courtesy. It weakened the armor she normally carried into this Republican stronghold. Embarrassed and angry, she found herself incapable of responding in kind. When she did respond, she was loud and abrupt: "I didn't postpone this hearing—you *REPUBLICANS* did that. And thanks to YOU, Mr. Willoughby—who is every bit as outstanding as you say he is—cannot be here."

The audience burst into a chatter so distracting the chairman felt obliged to rap his gavel lightly against the sound block. "Order, please," he said, leaning into his microphone. Turning again to Frances Costello and taking an audible breath before speaking, he continued. "The committee is disappointed Mr. Willoughby is unable to make his presentation. We were very much looking forward to it. As he cannot be here, is there someone else who will speak against the rider?"

"Yes," said Costello. "*I* will speak against the rider."

"Very well," said the chairman. "We have allocated 30 minutes for speakers in opposition. Please go ahead, Representative Costello."

Frances got off to a poor start: she *was* angry, and she was *behaving* like she was angry. Ten minutes into an impassioned attack on the rider, her notes fell from the lectern's small ledge onto the floor of the courtroom, scattering in all directions. She was able to collect them, thanking the several people who had gotten out of their seats to help her. But when she looked at the pile they had gathered it was clear the papers were completely out of order. Not wanting to risk an additional 60 seconds of dead time while she rearranged them, she decided to move on without the notes.

After five more minutes she had gotten lost in her argument and had forgotten what came next. Now totally frustrated, the minority leader gritted her teeth and just resisted the urge to shout "*Shit!*" The choice she made was more polite, but no more effective. She heaved an enormous sigh, looked up at the chairman, said, "That concludes my presentation," and returned to her seat.

Gerald Hampton had been watching from the back of the courtroom. Never a fan, and feeling no sympathy for her now,

Hampton turned to the gentleman on his left—Paul Carlton, the Speaker of the House, who had joined him for the hearing. "That's 'Don't call me Frances' for you," said Hampton in a stage whisper. "She'd rather be angry than effective!"

The chairman waited until the minority leader had taken her seat, then he looked left and right along the ranks of his committee. "Under the circumstances, the chair does not believe it will be useful to call any of the people who are here to speak in favor of the rider to the Omnibus Appropriations Bill. Will anyone call the question?"

The question was duly called. No debate was permissible, and the motion carried. The committee approved the rider on a party-line vote; approval of the entire bill followed. The chairman made a few notes on the committee copy of the bill, gave it to the aid who was standing off his left shoulder, and instructed her to carry it immediately to the President of the Senate so it could be voted on and delivered to the governor that afternoon.

Returning his attention to the many people still sitting in the audience, Richard Swanson cleared his throat, sat up a little straighter, and addressed them. "Thank you for coming," he began. "Finishing the appropriations bill is one of the most important jobs of the Kansas House of Representatives. We are glad you were a part of our work this morning. We are adjourned." He rapped the gavel emphatically this time, stood, and walked past the bar of the courtroom to congratulate Gerald Hampton.

# North Star Steakhouse

The Omnibus Appropriations Bill and its rider cleared the Senate Thursday afternoon and was delivered to the Governor's Office by 5:00 p.m. As soon as he received confirmation of that the rider's author, Gerald Hampton, called his co-sponsors and his favorite lobbyist, Tom Dennis. "It's 5:00 o'clock somewhere!" he said to each of them. "And you know what that means: North Star!"

Both of the co-sponsors agreed to meet him there at 6:00. Tom Dennis, the lobbyist, had been down this road with Hampton several times too often. Pretending to check his calendar and pretending it showed a dinner meeting that evening, Dennis begged off. But he told Gerry to put the dinner and the drinks on his tab.

The Topeka institution just north and west of the city that everyone calls "the North Star" is actually the North Star Steakhouse. A five-pointed, back-lit star with a neon "NORTH" in the middle hangs on the front of a windowless building, just right of the red neon sign that declares the place "OPEN." There are no windows in the add-on entryway, either. Signage aside, this could as easily be a rural U-Store facility as a restaurant.

If the inside reminds guests of the 1950s, that's intentional. The tables and chairs are simple, the 4x8 sheets of paneling on the walls came out of your grandfather's rec room, and there are vintage jukeboxes on the inside walls of the booths. Today's menu is different than it was 80 years ago. There is a menu, for starters, not just a chalkboard for everyone to read as they came in. And there is more to look at than thick steaks and French fries with brown gravy. But the steaks and the fries and the gravy are still the best sellers by a mile.

The North Star serves alcohol too. If a guy wanted a Jack and Coke with his steak, or a Johnny Walker Black, or a Makers, this was the place to get it. And if his favorite lobbyist was spotting him the drinks, the North Star had a long list of more expensive whiskeys.

They were midway through the main course when the Speaker Pro Tem stood, hoisted his heavy highball glass, and invited his colleagues to stand with him. Gerald Hampton was drinking doubles. With his left hand on the back of his chair to steady himself he started with this: "Here's to us, goddammit it! Those candy-ass queers and their non-binary brothers and all those other DEI weirdos can go fuck themselves. Let 'em go back to San Francisco or Portland or Seattle or wherever the hell else they came from. We kicked their ass today, right?!"

Biding their time, the two men standing with him tipped their glasses in the pro tem's direction.

Hampton was still warming up. He called for another Scotch. Waiting for it, and moved by the camaraderie of the men around him, he offered another interim tribute: "You guys are the best goddamn team in the country!"

His colleagues continued to watch him. They had been with Gerry before on nights like this; they knew the big one was coming.

"Okay," Hampton said, "I've finally got it." He had his toast in mind, and he had his drink. "No more DEI bullshit! Not in MY state!"

Three 3-ounce pours of 18-year-old Glenfiddich were swallowed as one. Though Hampton's final toast had beaten back most of the din, conversations lingered in the corners as he slammed his glass onto the white tablecloth and sat down. The new sounds, like the thunk of a mortar round as it hits the bottom of its tube followed in quick succession by two more just like it, silenced the entire dining room. All eyes were on two young members of the Kansas House who were standing at the center table, congratulating Gerry Hampton.

# Martini Night

Thursday evening had become a sacred time for the secular on the nation's undergraduate campuses. Most KU students arranged their schedules to avoid Friday classes and would spark at the clueless advisors who suggested them. Those shackled with class on a Friday felt no shame at arriving unprepared, if they arrived at all.

Massachusetts Street filled early on a Thursday, especially on an afternoon like this one in April when a bright sun and accompanying clear skies had chased the rains of Tuesday and Wednesday. It was still 70 degrees at 4:00 p.m. and the sidewalks were full of students making their way from bar to wine dive to pub. The downtown restaurants would start to fill an hour later. At the Eldridge Hotel, still dominating Sixth and Massachusetts as it had during Quantrill's Raid 170 years ago, dozens of sorority sisters would grab large tables in the dining room to begin a happy-hour crescendo of cocktails and conversation.

Understanding what Thursday meant to their contemporaries, Rebecca and Farieh had chosen that afternoon for their meetings and had met at Trinity every Thursday since January, excepting only spring break. They began at 2:00 and were careful to finish by 5:00, as the church had its own Thursday schedule and parishioners would begin to arrive at 5:30.

H.B. 3105, the Omnibus Budget Bill, included an anti-DEI rider when the Kansas Legislature passed it and sent it to the governor. The headline from the *University Daily Kansan* that announced its passage asked a fair question:

IS DIVERSITY DEAD?

The young women gathered in the church library were all reading the *UDK*. They had known of the bill for weeks, ever since it had been introduced by the Speaker Pro Tem of the Kansas House, Gerald Hampton. Initially, they could not decide whether it was intentionally vague or badly drafted. But their early concerns no longer mattered. It had cleared the House that morning, the Senate had taken only a moment to approve it on a party-line vote, and it was on the governor's desk by 3:00. The *UDK* had printed its entire text after leading with the headline it had been saving for days.

The *UDK* was a KU paper. But the article had meaning for all of the state-supported colleges and universities because H.B. 3105 applied to all of them. If the governor signed it, or if he allowed it to become law, "diversity" could not be considered in any academic hiring decision. But the Legislature had not bothered to define the term, which allowed an interpretation beyond even the shifty imaginations of the drafters. Farieh explained that a plausible reading of the language meant no state-supported college or university could spend money on diversity. Further, no existing employee of a state-supported college or university—no teacher, no coach, and no staff member—could "support" diversity, whether with their leadership, their scholarship, their teaching, or their time.

Farieh had circulated the draft of the plan the previous Sunday, when the budget and its rider were still in committee. She spoke now to their list of action items for attacking the new legislation at KU.

The plan had few parts. First, Rebecca would approach the university directly and ask it to oppose the legislation. That was to happen tomorrow morning. Everyone was confident the chancellor and his team would do nothing, just as they had done for weeks as the rider made its way forward in Topeka. Still beholden to the Legislature for a substantial portion of its budget, KU was loath to oppose any legislation that did not directly cut its funding. With legislation like this, one of the many fronts of "the culture wars" being waged in the nation's red states, Farieh and her colleagues knew the university would not move a muscle. But they would give the university the weekend to respond. Their timetable had to be short because the governor had only 10 days to act before the rider automatically became law.

In the expected event the university did nothing by Monday, Farieh would lead a sit-in at the Chancellor's Office.

"Why a sit-in?" The question came from Wendy, one of Rebecca's friends. "Isn't that just a waste of effort? With the timetable we're working under, the university gets only two days to change its position once the sit-in starts. That can't be long enough to have any effect. The university will ignore the sit-in, and we'll have to move to the protest. Why not go there directly?"

The sit-in was Farieh's idea, so she responded. "You're probably right about the sit-in's having any real impact. But I see it as a courtesy—a necessary courtesy. We want people outside KU, and especially the media, to believe we gave the administration every chance to support us before we kick off something that *will* get media attention and that *might* be seriously disruptive."

Rebecca jumped in with the next part. If the sit-in did not work they would begin a campus-wide protest the following Wednesday. It would feature daily marches past Strong Hall to the Chi Omega fountain, then down the hill to the law school, where recruited faculty members would condemn the legislation. The marches would end in the grassy area east of Green Hall. The speakers would be the centerpiece, the Tai Chi sculpture the backdrop. That time of the afternoon, the adjacent parking lot could accommodate the media trucks and satellite dishes they hoped would swarm to Lawrence to cover the protests.

At some moment, as the protests interfered more and more with the daily business of the campus and as the media's scrutiny moved from novelty to nuisance, the university would change its position and ask the governor to veto the bill.

# I Have a Few Friends with Me

It was Monday morning. As expected, the university had made no response to their demand that it publicly oppose the anti-DEI rider and ask the governor to veto it.

Farieh walked past Strong Hall's own Jayhawk, the "Pterodactyl," on her way to the administration building's massive entry doors. Inside, she walked up the staircase and, at the top, turned left into the Chancellor's Office, which occupied the entire east half of the second floor.

She was wearing a head scarf. Rebecca had talked with her about it. She had been with Farieh the entire spring and she knew Farieh had not been covered their sophomore year, not since she returned from Tehran the previous summer. But in a protest that sought to preserve a space for diversity on the KU campus, Rebecca felt Farieh's head scarf would be galvanizing.

Farieh had never *not* worn the hijab as a KU freshman. But she believed whether to cover was a personal choice. Last summer had presented choices in every direction: how to manage on her own in England and in Scotland, whether to drink alcohol, and what to wear, to name only a few. She went abroad, she drank wine, and she left her head scarf in her hotel room. In Iran, she had covered out of respect for her parents. After Mehri's death she had worn the hijab only to keep herself safe as she fled back to Kansas.

Rebecca's proposal that she wear a head scarf now seemed superficial, and that made Farieh uncomfortable. But she understood how it made sense to the protests, protests she had helped to plan and had agreed to lead. She picked a yellow one.

Jill Swanson had served the chancellor since Bob Barkett had taken the position. Jill knew Farieh and smiled warmly as the sophomore walked through the door and up to her desk. The darling of the honors program as a freshman, "Farieh Bukhari" had been on everyone's lips by the middle of her second semester last spring.

The chancellor had entertained the honors faculty for dinner at his residence just before the holidays last December. The faculty had selected four students to accompany them, one from each class, and the chancellor had been caught off guard by the tall sophomore in the stunning red dress. In the few minutes he had had to spend with her that night, Barkett had watched her lead a conversation about whether women had been portrayed fairly in 19th Century English literature, then turn without pause to address the questions of the dean of engineering: *Will ethical standards impede the implementation of AI in developing countries? And, if so, should we relax them there?*

The chancellor had had a long conversation with her himself early this semester, when she was named a University Scholar. Bob Barkett had commented about her to Jill several times, and it was the chancellor who had noticed Farieh's name on Jill's calendar and highlighted it.

"Hello, Farieh," she said. "We are so pleased to see you!"

"Thank you, Jill," the young Iranian student replied. "I have a few friends with me. May they come in as well?"

Jill heard the question, but she had needed to check the chancellor's last appointment for the afternoon and she was not looking at Farieh when she made her answer: "Of course," she said. Her head still down, she did not notice Farieh's come-along gesture to the hallway. Neither did she see the first half dozen of the 30 students who would soon occupy the central corridor of the Chancellor's Office, from the west entrance door to the Office of the General Counsel at the east end. They came in quietly, several of them nodding respectfully to the startled administrative assistant as they took places along the walls. Once they had all entered, they sat down. It was Monday, March 30, at 11:09 a.m.

# The Administration Responds

She met with him in his private office north off the now-crowded central corridor. The chancellor had been entirely surprised by the sit-in and was behaving strangely, but Farieh made efficient use of the five minutes he gave her. She told him she wanted the university to oppose the anti-DEI budget rider in a public statement to the press, then follow that up with a written request to the governor that he veto it. Finishing just before noon, Farieh called attention to the time and told him the university would have 48 hours to make a decision.

The chancellor used the lunch hour to call his leadership team, and he presided over a brief meeting with them at his residence that evening. The Provost, the Executive Vice Chancellor for Finance, the Vice Chancellor for Strategic Communications and Public Affairs, the Vice Chancellor for Strategic Initiatives/Chief of Staff, and the Vice Chancellor for Legal Affairs/General Counsel were all in Lawrence that day and everyone showed up at 7:00. The Executive Vice Chancellor for the KU Medical Center lived in Kansas City, but he was the first to arrive at 6:45.

In fact, the university had little stomach for a confrontation with the Republican-dominated Kansas Legislature. The seven participants had barely had time for their soft drinks and coffee before it was clear all of them wanted to stay quiet and see how things went. Taking on the anti-DEI rider was not high on anyone's list. In fact, it was not even *on* anyone's list, so the leadership team did not need a long conversation to take a pass on Farieh's demands. With one exception—the man from the medical center in Kansas City, they were all out the door before 8:00.

Patrick McGinnis stayed. Pat had been a part of the search committee that had hired Bob Barkett. He had liked him when he met him in Lawrence during Barkett's initial interview. But he liked him even more the following week when, as incognito as he could manage it, he had traveled to West Lafayette to do his own walk-about of the town-and-gown scene at Purdue.

He was in Neil Armstrong Hall as much as any other campus building, but he had gone other places too. He hung out in the Student Union, drinking coffee and eavesdropping on student conversations. His advance work had identified two lectures that looked interesting—one presented by American Studies and one by the Department of Chemistry, and he attended both. He made sandwiches in his hotel room and carried them in his backpack and took them out as he sat on or walked through the lawns and malls and plazas. He paid attention to the way in which the students interacted—their body language, their facial expressions, their energy, whether they seemed to like each other. And he went downtown, in and out of at least a dozen retail places, talking with the shopkeepers during the day and with the restaurant servers at night. West Lafayette was upbeat, energetic, and confident in its future. He found the people at Purdue were even more so. He returned to the search committee excited about Bob Barkett. Once Bob took the KU job they had become friends.

There was a kitchen on the ground floor of The Outlook. It had a small table, and Pat knew that's where Barkett liked to be in the evening when he had something on his mind. Pat took a chair across from Bob. He had watched his friend run the brief meeting of a moment ago; he had noticed the chancellor said nothing about how *he* felt. So he asked him.

"What do *you* think about all of this, Bob? You said very little during the meeting."

"I know," said the chancellor. "What I think about it and what I believe we are able to do about it are poles apart. Have you read the budget rider?"

"No," said Pat. "I just heard about it yesterday."

"It's disappointing." Barkett's drink had been coffee, and he took another sip from the KU mug on the table. "Without making any attempt to define what it means by 'diversity,' the Legislature makes it nearly impossible for anyone at KU to engage in it. We're supposed to guess at what is or is not permitted; and if we guess wrong the penalties are serious.

"I happen to support diversity. I support it generally in society, I support it especially on a college campus, and I support it at KU. I think the bill's sponsors are culture warriors chasing headlines. They look at Florida and they want that kind of attention here in Kansas.

"When it was clear this rider was going to carry the House and Senate, I had our legal office pursue their back-channel contacts with the governor to get a read on his plans for it. I am almost certain he will use a line-item veto to kill it. Because of that, I don't think KU needs to do anything to challenge it.

"If we *do* challenge it, we guarantee a pissing contest with the rider's sponsors—who include most of the leaders of the Kansas House, the speaker pro tem leading the way. We have more than enough trouble getting money from the Legislature as it is. I'd love to take on the House over legislation this poorly considered. But it's dangerous, and it's probably not necessary.

"That's why I said so little during the meeting. The woman leading the sit-in—her name is Farieh Bukari—is very smart and highly capable. But she's also courteous, and the students who are doing this with her are anything but confrontational. I think we can wait this out."

"Okay," said McGinnis, pushing back from the kitchen table. "I'm glad to hear about your contact with the governor. That's good enough for me on a weekday night in Lawrence. I've got a 7:00 a.m. meeting tomorrow."

The chancellor walked him to the front door. "Thanks for

coming over for the meeting, Pat, and for staying. It's nice to have someone to share this with."

# The March to Green Hall

The sit-in had been deftly executed: 30 students had made their way into the chancellor's anteroom and were seated almost before anyone had noticed. And they were courteous. They did little more than sit there, talking quietly, reading or sleeping when they weren't talking, drinking a water or a soft drink brought in by one of their colleagues, and changing places with another student when their 12-hour shift was over.

There was plenty of commotion in other places. The staircases of Strong Hall and the long sidewalk running to its front door were sloppy with raunchy messages on placards and posters, with empty water bottles, and with sacks and sandwich wrappers from McDonald's. Inside the chancellor's suite of offices, though, it might have been a prayer vigil. The protestors were so quiet it was easy for Jill and the rest of the staff to forget they were there, and the administration did forget. It also forgot it had been given only 48 hours to meet the protestors' demand. When the clock ran past noon on Wednesday, the administration learned the students had more on their minds than courtesy.

While Farieh was managing the sit-in in the chancellor's office, Rebecca had approached students from all over the campus. What she wanted was a part of their afternoons, three hours—from 2:00 to 5:00 each weekday, when they might join her in a march down Jayhawk Boulevard to protest the anti-DEI budget rider just passed by the Kansas Legislature. They would start at the Union, march to Strong Hall and stop there for a short bullhorn-blast at the administration, then circle the Chi Omega fountain on the way to Green Hall, the law school building. They would stop there for the afternoon's address by an invited speaker and whatever interviews the assembled media wanted to conduct. Rebecca assured them they would be done by 5:00. Many of the marchers were well-briefed on the rider and thought a campus protest was an appropriate next step once the sit-in's deadline had expired. All of them thought three hours in the mild sun of a lovely spring day was too good to pass up.

The first placard moved through the doors of the Student Union at 12:10. Behind it were the 300 students who, since morning, had gradually assembled in the Kansas Room on the 6th floor and in the hallway just outside. Maybe 20 had been busy the entire time stapling the placards onto the laths that would carry them. When they finished their work there were 125 placards, designed just two nights ago by architecture undergrads and fabricated the night before by enthusiastic majors in visual arts. The others had just filtered in for the good time.

DIVERSITY NOW! and WE WANT A CHANCELLOR, NOT A COWARD! were the respectful messages.

There were a couple that read: STOP KISSING THE LEGISLATURE'S ASS!

Farieh and Rebecca had stressed making signs that were pithy and impactful but not churlish, and they had largely succeeded with the workshop participants. But there were thousands of marchers, and individual students had brought their own messages. Among them, FUCK TOPEKA! was the most popular by far.

The 300 who had been inside the Union walked out its east door into a throng of a thousand, and there were more students surging toward them from the Oread Hotel and the Union's parking lot. Not even a block away to the south, students from the Greek houses and the scholarship halls and the apartment buildings east of campus were cresting the hill at Jayhawk Boulevard and spilling across the intersection onto the lawns around Spooner and Danforth Chapel and Lippincott Hall. When Rebecca, wielding her bullhorn from the plinth for the Jimmy Green statue, had thanked them for coming and had jumped down to lead them west toward

Strong Hall there were more than 2,000.

Nobody with KU Administration at Strong Hall knew about the march when it started. Although Rebecca led it, it was Farieh who came up with the ruse to keep the preparation both efficient and out of sight. Wanting to assemble the signs and placards at the Union, she booked the Kansas and Curry rooms on the top floor under the name of a "new student group," "DEI Storm." And she staggered the arrival times for the students assembling them so they would arrive in small groups. It all worked; the Union staff was clueless.

Word was out by the time the throng of students passed Bailey. It was just another minute from there to the front of Strong Hall, where Rebecca jumped up onto the pedestal surrounding the distinctive bronze Jayhawk to address the crowd of young people pouring in behind her.

"NONE OF THE SPONSORS OF THIS BUDGET RIDER GIVES A *SHIT* ABOUT DIVERSITY," she said into her bullhorn, eliciting an immediate cheer.

"All they care about is PUBLICITY!" Another cheer.

"If this rider becomes the law of Kansas it's going to HURT PEOPLE!" Another cheer.

"What we want is a RESPONSE from Strong Hall!" Another cheer, but slightly softer because Rebecca had coughed in the middle of *response*.

"We want the chancellor to tell the Legislature, 'NO! YOU CAN'T DO THIS! PEOPLE IN LAWRENCE HAVE FOUGHT AND DIED FOR DIVERSITY SINCE BEFORE KANSAS WAS A STATE!" Another cheer—much louder this time.

"We're marching from here to Green Hall." She was looking over the heads of the crowd now, talking to the students right across from her who had gathered on the sidewalk in front of Wescoe and Budig.

"JOIN US!" she shouted. And then she jumped away from the big bronze bird to make a balanced landing and turn right for the fountain.

Rebecca did not know who her speaker would be. It was Farieh's job to arrange for that, and for everything else at the law school, including the media. Sure enough, once Rebecca had walked far enough down the hill between the School of Engineering and Slawson Hall and could see the parking lot and the lawn on the east side of Green Hall, it was clear her friend had been busy.

Five logoed television trucks and their broadcast antennas filled much of the upper parking lot. Just onto the lawn to the west was the aluminum skeleton for the tent the law school had first erected during the pandemic and had left up because outdoor classes in the fall and spring were so popular. There were chairs inside the tent, visible because the tent's skimpy fabric made only a roof and a short curtain extending just down from the roof. To the north of the tent was a large speaker's stand, its sound system already in place. Several people were standing at the foot of the speaker's stand, including Professor Ahmed Zaidi, the law school's Distinguished Professor of International Law, whom Rebecca knew about but had never met. As the commotion from the oncoming crowd of students reached him, Professor Zaidi looked up at them and smiled.

Rebecca led the students down the hill and through the intersection. That the tent would hold only a fraction of their number was clear in an instant, so they arranged and rearranged until they spread from the courtyard of Learned Hall, the engineering building, across 15th Street and onto the lawn of Green Hall, then past the lawn south into the law school's lower parking lot just across the street from Allen Fieldhouse. They engulfed the Tai Chi and packed the concrete sidewalk that led to Green Hall's front doors.

Rebecca had not dealt with television crews before and did not realize the broadcast teams wanted to know who the "leader" was. Neither did she appreciate the pace with which they wanted things to happen. Alerted to the event just after noon, several trucks and crews had already been there for hours. The sun was not hot in March, but there was no shade.

The students' surge would have carried her to the speaker's platform had she not wanted to walk there on her own. Once there she was surprised when Professor Zaidi introduced himself to her. *Farieh,* she said to herself, *you could organize a riot!*

Professor Zaidi gave her a 3x5 card on which he had written a few sentences of an introduction. She thanked him, confirmed he was ready to proceed, and walked up the steps onto a six-foot square platform. The lectern and the microphones were on its west side. She turned and gestured for Professor Zaidi to follow her up the steps, which he did. She introduced him, grateful for the small card, then exchanged places with him and walked down the steps, moving to the front of the platform so she could see him.

Ahmed Zaidi was standing by himself in the small square of the speaker's stand, just back from the microphones. But he was anything but alone. The nearly 3,000 students surrounding him enclosed the camera crews and the prime-time broadcasters with their sponge-wrapped microphones. Perhaps a dozen of his law school colleagues had come out from their offices before the students had romped down the hill, and they were standing at the edge of the sidewalk closest to the speaker's stand. As the mass of students had blocked the traffic approaching the law school from the north, south, and west, many of the drivers had gotten out of their cars and pickups and were standing next to them or walking to get closer to the speaker.

Directly in front of his microphones and not five feet away was the person whom Ahmed Zaidi had gone to yesterday for help with his speech, Andrew Stevenson.

"Almost no one will remember it," Andrew had told him. "But that doesn't mean it doesn't matter. This does matter. Be brief. Tell a story. Smile. Make it about you. Your law students like you; these students will like you too."

Ahmed nodded at Andrew. Nodding back, Andrew gave his friend a thumbs up.

Ahmed took a deep breath. The spring day was sunny but cool—in the low 60s. Ahmed took off his jacket anyway, placed it on the one chair on the platform, and loosened his tie. Then he took two steps forward to adjust the center mic. When he looked up he could not help but smile at the students who a moment ago had been jostling and shouting as they would do for a football or basketball game. They were quiet now, waiting on what he would say.

"CAN YOU FEEL IT?!" Ahmed did not realize it, but he was shouting.

"CAN YOU FEEL THE SPIRIT THAT IS LAWRENCE, KANSAS?!"

Only too keen to respond to his enthusiasm, the students cheered him. They were ready for someone with great energy, someone with passion. They were ready for Barack Obama. Malcolm X would have been even better. But what they got next was just the opposite. The brown-skinned man on the speaker's platform had stopped shouting and was speaking quietly to someone at the front of the crowd.

"Please tell me your name," he said as he continued to point to the student in the Kansas basketball jersey.

Don Bufford finally realized the speaker was pointing at him. "Don," he replied; "Don Bufford."

"Where are you from, Don Bufford?"

"Chicago. New Trier High School. I'm a junior."

"That is excellent," said Professor Zaidi. "Like me, you came to Kansas from somewhere else." Zaidi paused only a moment. "If I ask you to do a small favor for me, will you do it?

More comfortable now with the attention, Bufford answered right away: "Sure! You bet! What is it?"

"Give me just a moment." Zaidi asked that a second microphone be handed to Bufford, and Bufford took it. "I gave you the microphone, Mr. Bufford, so everyone could hear both of us. Now, the favor. I would like you to take your shirt off and hand it to the person behind you. Is that okay?"

Bufford was surprised at the request. It wasn't cold, exactly, but it wasn't summer, either. As to pulling his shirt off and standing there naked from the waist up—it was an odd favor, for sure. But he'd doffed his jersey often enough in football and basketball games to be getting self-conscious now. He pulled the jersey over his head, handed it to the young man immediately behind him, and looked back at the speaker.

"How to you feel, Mr. Bufford?"

The tone of the question was kind. Bufford felt the speaker was treating him as genuinely as he could so he answered as genuinely: "I'm cold."

"So was I, Mr. Bufford, when I arrived in America from my home in Pakistan. And I had brown skin. But you, Mr. Bufford— 'you' representing everyone here in the United States—helped me. At first you *gave* me clothing. When I had gotten back on my feet a little, you allowed me to buy it from you for very little money. I believe my brown skin made me a better candidate for your generosity. I wonder what my fate would have been had the law *prohibited* you from responding generously to my brownness.

"As I said, Mr. Bufford, I know what it is like to be cold; please put your shirt on. Thank you for helping me."

Zaidi turned his attention to the law school building, where he spotted a coed in a cowboy hat. He gestured next to her. "I am pointing at a young woman in a cowboy hat. Do you see me, young lady?"

The young woman nodded back as she shouted, "Yes! I see you!"

"Good," said Professor Zaidi. "Will someone take the microphone to her?"

When the young woman had the mic in hand Zaidi continued. "I have a favor to ask of you. Will you help me?"

The young woman took no time in responding: "Yes! What is it?!"

"First, what is your name?

"It's Jennifer," she responded, "Jennifer Sherwood. I'm from Chanute."

"I see you have a purse over your shoulder, Jennifer from Chanute. Is that where you carry your money?"

"Yes," she said, "in my wallet. It's usually at the bottom of the purse, buried under everything else." Nearly every woman student laughed.

"The favor I would like is this: will you please give your purse to the person behind you? If you know the person behind you, please give it to a person you don't know. Will you do that?"

Now that she knew what the favor was, Jennifer was in fact hesitant about it. There were at least a dozen rows of people behind her, and they were all packed together, and whoever got the purse would have a hard time running off with it. She turned around. Recognizing no one, she gave her purse to the person closest to her, a tall young man who was probably a freshman and who was also wearing a KU basketball jersey. Trying to be discrete, she inspected his face for something distinguishing. When she turned back to the speaker's platform she was both uneasy he had her purse and embarrassed she had studied him so closely.

Professor Zaidi understood Jennifer's uneasiness, and he asked his next questions to address it: "Jennifer, will you now give the mic to the young man who took your purse?" Jennifer did so and Professor Zaidi continued. "Young man, what is your name?"

"Robert! I'm Robert Sanderson, Professor Zaidi. I'm from Topeka."

Zaidi continued. "Are you a student here, Robert?"

"Yes!" said the young man. "I'm a freshman—College of Liberal Arts. I live in Templin, right up the hill behind the law school."

"Thank you for helping us this afternoon, Robert. Please

return the purse to Jennifer." Robert did so.

"Now, Jennifer, back to you. How did you feel when you *first* handed your purse to Robert Sanderson, before you knew who he was and where you could find him and before you got it back?"

"Nervous, I guess," said Jennifer. "Poor, maybe. I just got my check for next semester's tuition, and it's in my purse. If I lost it I would not be able to go to school next year."

"When I arrived here that's what I was, Jennifer—poor! I desperately needed a job. And I had brown skin. I had been told many people in the United States would discriminate against brown-skinned people. In subtle ways, maybe, but discriminate all the same. And I was really worried I would not find work. But I did!

"I worked first for a pizza shop, making deliveries. There was real irony in that. I was in New York City and I had no idea *what* the streets were or where to *find* them!" The crowd had been a little tense ever since Jennifer mentioned her tuition check, and they relaxed at this and laughed.

"My second job paid more. I became a server in—wait for it— a kosher restaurant in the Bronx!" The crowd loved this and laughed again, much more enthusiastically. "What was the connection? Pizza? Kosher? Neither one. It was the willingness of the owners to hire someone with brown skin, and quite likely with a different religion.

"The rider just passed by the Kansas Legislature would *prohibit* the University of Kansas from even knowing a job applicant had brown skin. At least as important, it would also prohibit teachers and student leaders and school-sponsored clubs and teams from acknowledging race or religion as a factor in any aspect of life here at KU. If the rider becomes the law of Kansas, KU will not be able to read about race, ask questions about religion, or use either as a criterion—or a suggested help—for hiring staff or coaches or for recruiting athletes.

"I need one more student. But this time I need someone who

actually *knows* the person standing behind them. That means I need two people. Will anyone volunteer?"

Hands shot up everywhere! Professor Zaidi selected two people close to him and asked that the mic be brought to the one in front.

"Okay," he began, "What are your names, and how is it you know one another?"

The person in front was eager to answer him. "I'm Julie Schmidt, Professor Zaidi. I'm from Liberal. Kaity—Kaity Pearson, who is right behind me—is my roommate."

"Perfect," said Zaidi. "Are you good friends as well as roommates?"

Both yelled, "Yes!"

This time it was Kaity who took the mic and spoke to Zaidi. "We're best friends, Professor Zaidi. I'm from Maine—Bangor, and I spent the second half of Christmas break with Julie and her family. I had never been to Southwest Kansas before. I had never seen a grain elevator or a pivot sprinkler or a feed lot or a wind farm. I had a *great* time."

"Wonderful," responded Zaidi. "What I want you to do now, Kaity, is pretend you don't like Julie. I want you to frown at her, then turn your back on her." Kaity did all of those things in a moment, crossing her arms across her chest in the process.

"Now, Julie. Everyone knows this is make-believe, but I want to ask you about your feelings anyway. How did you feel when Kaity frowned at you and turned her back on you?"

"You're right, Professor Zaidi. I knew she was acting. But Kaity is a really good actor—she's a theatre major; and I found myself wondering what it would be like if she *meant* it! For just a second, I felt like I didn't *have* a friend."

"When I arrived in New York, Julie, I didn't have a friend, either. It took time for me to find them. But no one was telling those New Yorkers they *couldn't* talk with me because my skin was brown, or couldn't text me back, or couldn't go to the park to play soccer, or do any of the things we *did* do that let us *become* friends.

"The rider just passed by the Kansas Legislature does not *say* it was written to prevent friendships between brown- and red- and yellow- and black-skinned people and other students at KU. But if the other students cannot acknowledge race, and discuss race, and pay attention to race—something that is *central* to the lives of people of color, then how can any friendships form?"

The crowd had become thoughtful, and quieter, ever since their laughter had faded from Zaidi's talking about the Kosher restaurant in the Bronx. Now you could hear a pin drop. As Professor Zaidi readied himself for his closing he stepped away from the microphone and took several large breaths. Then he leaned into the mic and projected his voice to the very back of the crowd.

"House Bill 3105 has the *potential* to do many things on the campuses of Kansas' colleges and universities. What it *will* do is encourage loneliness and discourage friendship. I know how I feel about it; now I have a question for you, and I want you to tell me—shout it out so I can hear you. Are you *for* this rider—or *not*? Yes or no?!"

NO! surged out of the throats of thousands of students who had been quiet long enough.

Ahmed Zaidi scanned the crowd in front of him. He had resumed his closing, but in his normal volume, and his voice had gotten lost in the shouting as the students answered his question over and over again. When he finally held his hands up the crowd grew quiet.

"Since I graduated from college, all I have wanted was to be a teacher. Now I am a teacher; for many of you I am *your* teacher." Scattered shouts from his students lifted from around the speaker's platform and bounced off the walls of the law school.

"Teachers have special responsibilities to their students. The most important one is to tell the truth.

"The truth is this: *Diversity is life!* We must welcome it; we must nurture it; we must celebrate it. And we must help the people in Topeka to recognize these things. *That* is our responsibility—all of us."

Bowing to the thousands of people surrounding him Professor Zaidi said, "Thank you." Then, to their tumultuous applause, he walked down from the platform into the arms of the students closest to him.

# Streaming Now From Lawrence, Kansas

Guess the folks in Lawrence don't like your rider."

Billy Prescott, the young Communications Director for the Speaker of the Kansas House of Representatives, was frequently back and forth to the office of the Speaker Pro Tem, Gerald Hampton. Billy was there Wednesday afternoon, staring at the screen of his laptop.

"What was that, Billy?" The question reflected the preoccupation of its author, who was staring at his own screen. "Sorry," he continued. "I'm pretty caught up in the Dems' reaction to the budget, which is all over the place like we expected."

"There's a rally of some kind at KU this afternoon, Gerry. The WIBW reporter says it was organized to protest your budget rider. Looks like they're having it just outside the law school. Nearly all students from the looks of it; somebody haranguing them from a small platform next to the parking lot. But there are LOTS of people there. Don't know how many thousands, but more than a couple, for sure. Here, let me show you." Billy stood up and carried his laptop around the desk so the pro tem could see it. When Gerald Hampton looked at the laptop the camera crew was doing a sweep of the crowd and had focused on the signs carried by the students. "STOP KISSING THE LEGISLATURE'S ASS!" hit a sour note with the Speaker Pro Tem, who had barely a short fuse for the university he regarded as the woke capital of the state. "FUCK TOPEKA!" was too much.

"GOD DAMN IT!!!" he roared. "Get me the chancellor. NOW! Call his direct dial first, and his cell phone if he doesn't answer the first time. This sort of shit has got to STOP!"

Billy did not understand the moods of the pro tem. But he had an energy that was unique in the statehouse, and it was invaluable to his boss, the Speaker. Using the phone on the pro tem's desk, Billy dialed the number, made sure it was ringing, then transferred the handset to Hampton. Then he closed his laptop and left Gerry Hampton alone with his phone call.

"Bob? Gerry." KU's Chancellor, Bob Barkett, knew who "Gerry" was. Gerald Hampton had attended every private meeting related to the budget for the University of Kansas and every budget hearing, too, even though the hearings had been run by the committee chair. It had been clear since February, just as it had been clear for several years now, that Gerald Hampton did not like KU. Getting past him was one of the hardest parts of Barkett's job as chancellor. Harder than any personnel decision, harder than any athletic department dilemma.

"Are you watching what *I'm* watching?" Barkett knew the question related to the news feeds about the protest that had moved past Strong Hall barely 30 minutes ago.

"Yes," said the chancellor, "sure am."

"Have you seen the SIGNS?!"

"Yes." Bob Barkett knew not to volunteer much when the Pro Tem was riled up.

"What kind of chickenshit children do you HAVE over there these days?! These signs are DISGUSTING! Does nobody over there appreciate that the Kansas Legislature PAYS for them to go to school?! They're all about accusations of 'privilege.' Don't they get it that THEY are the privileged ones? And that they owe the LEGISLATURE for their privilege? I mean, God dammit, Bob! What do you plan to DO about this?!"

Barkett was still quiet. In fact, the Legislature's share of KU's budget was a small fraction of what it once was, and what it ought to be. Now was not the right time for that discussion. But he decided he should say something, so he did. "What would you have me do, Gerry? So far as we know, this is a peaceful protest by people who are all of voting age. Doesn't that matter?"

Hampton's response was instantaneous. "Doesn't mean SHIT to me. Most of 'em don't even LIVE in Kansas. They can go home and vote for whoever they WANT! And as to what I would have you do, I'd have you stop it. Break it up. Send the children back to class in that high-priced kindergarten you run over there."

Bob Barkett took a deep breath. "This is a lawful, peaceful, public protest, Gerry. I can't 'stop it' any more than you can. These students have a constitutional right to be where they are and say what they're saying. I give you some of the signs are crude, and disrespectful, but it's also protected speech and assembly."

Hampton cut him off at "speech." "The LAST thing I need from you is a goddamn lecture on the First Amendment! Are you still looking at this? What do you see?"

"I see several thousand people surrounding a speaker, a number of them carrying signs you don't like."

"What I see is a bunch of children blocking a public street. Unless they have a parade permit, and I'll give you a hundred bucks they don't, that's a public safety violation, and that trumps your goddamn First Amendment. Now either YOU clean that up or I'll call John Daniels over at Kansas Highway Patrol Headquarters and arrange for 50 troopers who will clean it up for you. Word here is the protests are scheduled every afternoon at 2:00 o'clock. I'll be watching tomorrow; you better have some law enforcement out there to calm these folks down and keep 'em off the streets." And with that he hung up.

The chancellor sat there for a moment, staring at his cell phone. Then he called for Jill Swanson.

Jill set the Wednesday meeting for 6:30, which was the soonest Pat McGinnis could make it to Lawrence from the Med Center. The chancellor invited the chief of the campus police, KU's famous "Campus Cops," to join his leadership team at Strong Hall. But he had let him off the hook as soon as the chief told him his force had experienced so much turnover since the holidays he did not believe they were prepared to provide crowd control for thousands of young people. The chief did say he would be glad to invite either the Lawrence Police Department or the Douglas County Sheriff onto the campus. That would facilitate, and legitimize, their assistance to the university.

Barkett's call to the Lawrence Police Department was just as disappointing. The problem there was the forced turnover at the top that had occurred earlier in the week. In the opinion of the interim chief, which he asked the chancellor to keep confidential, that had left the department too distracted to deal effectively with any serious disturbance, on campus or otherwise. That left the Douglas County Sheriff.

Bob Barkett had met Curt Bennett only a few times, and never for much of a conversation. But he had his phone number, and he was down to his last box top. The young woman answering for the Sheriff's Department sounded like the other end of a 911 call. But she was pleasant, and once Barkett introduced himself she said she would put him right through. Curt Bennett answered only a few moments later.

"Curt, this is Bob Barkett, the chancellor at KU."

"Yes, chancellor, I know you. We met a year ago. How can we help the university?"

"I'm sure you know of this afternoon's protest and the speech at the law school."

"Yes," said the sheriff. "That's all anyone's talked about since it started. So far as I know, it has been entirely peaceful, which is great."

"Yes," said the chancellor. "But there will be another one tomorrow. It's scheduled for 2:00, and the way the protest leaders have performed so far I expect it to start at two o'clock sharp. Our understanding is the route will be the same—past Strong Hall and then down to the law school. But if they draw as many students tomorrow as they did today they will once again fill 15th Street between the engineering and law buildings, blocking traffic and creating a potential safety hazard. The university would like to provide some sort of law enforcement presence tomorrow. I think the protests will remain peaceful, but we need to manage the traffic next to the law school. Both the campus police and the City of Lawrence have deferred to your department, so I am calling to see whether you are open to helping us and whether you can join a meeting of my leadership team this evening to help us plan for tomorrow. 6:30; my office at Strong Hall. Can you do that?"

There was no hesitation in the Douglas County Sheriff: "Yes, sir," he said. "We can do that."

"That's terrific, Curt. Thank you. This isn't much notice for anyone, and it's an awkward time, so we'll be serving a light supper. Is there anything you can't eat?"

"Nope," Sheriff Bennett replied. "I'm good with anything you want to put down in front of me. See you this evening."

The meeting started precisely at 6:30. That's how the chancellor ran things. Everyone on the KU team was there on time. Curt Bennett was ten minutes early.

"I'll try not to make this a habit!" said the chancellor as he smiled at the still-upbeat team around him. Some of them chuckled as others pitted plastic knives and forks against the formidable chicken strips. While they had all been surprised by the protest, they were thrilled the student leaders had managed it so well and that it had gone off peacefully.

"We have a protest. But it went better than any of us might have hoped had we known about it in advance. That's a tribute to all of you and the job you do with our student leaders. Congratulations!

"We also have scrutiny. The Speaker Pro Tem of the Kansas House called this afternoon. I'll get into this in more detail in a minute, but it would be a serious understatement to describe him as 'mad as hell' about the signs the students were carrying this afternoon.

"Finally, we have a guest. By now you have probably met Curt Bennett, the Douglas County Sheriff, but I doubt you know much about him.

"Curt grew up in Lawrence, then served 20 years in the United States Navy, including more than 10 years as an officer with the Naval Intelligence Service, or NIS to those of you who have watched the TV series. When he retired he came back home, joined the sheriff's department, shot up the ranks, and was elected sheriff only a few years ago.

"Today, the Douglas County Sheriff's Department is one of the most modern, best-led, and most community-sensitive law enforcement agencies in the Midwest. Thanks to Curt's personal attention, it is also fully trained and fully equipped for crowd control.

"Unfortunately, our own police department is not capable of handling crowd control this week. The Lawrence Police Department recommended Curt and his department.

"I have asked Curt to join us this evening because I want the university to have experienced, trained officers providing crowd control during this protest. Curt can give us that. It was peaceful today; we want to be sure it stays peaceful tomorrow."

Curt Bennett said nothing, but he liked the chancellor's introduction.

"Why would we respond to a peaceful protest with the Sheriff's Department?!" The question came from an unexpected source—Pat McGinnis, the chancellor's closest friend on his leadership team. "No disrespect to you, Sheriff Bennett. But isn't a group of armed law enforcement officers the LAST thing we want to send in response to a peaceful protest? Doesn't that communicate a lack of trust in the students, not the confidence we want to communicate?"

"That's a fair question, Pat," said the chancellor. "And this gets to the point about scrutiny. Gerald Hampton, the Speaker Pro Tem of the Kansas House, did not call me this afternoon to congratulate us on a peaceful protest. As those of you who know him might expect, he is angry students are protesting the anti-DEI budget rider, of which he is the author. He is *furious* over the signs they are carrying. When I reminded him the students have a constitutional right to protest and carry signs he pointed out they were blocking a public street—15<sup>th</sup>—between the law school and engineering, which they were. He threatened to send the Highway Patrol to Lawrence tomorrow if we did not clear the street and monitor the protestors ourselves. I have known Gerry for years. He's hard on KU, and I don't think he's bluffing. If things did get out of hand tomorrow, and if we had ignored his insistence that we provide crowd control, somebody might get hurt. Beyond that, the publicity blow-back would be difficult, and the financial consequences for KU could be catastrophic.

"Asking the Sheriff's Department to participate in this is not my first choice. But Curt's people are well trained; both the university's police department and the City of Lawrence were glad to defer to their expertise in crowd control. I believe we can help the protest stay peaceful, and address these very real threats from Topeka, by deploying a restrained group of Curt's officers.

"What I wanted to do this evening was debrief you on today's protest, share my conversation with Gerry Hampton, introduce Curt, and then have as lengthy a discussion as you wish about tomorrow."

The next questions were addressed to Curt Bennett. The leadership team wanted to know exactly what sort of training the Sheriff's Department had provided, whether the training had been completed, whether the officers had done well with it, and how it was Curt knew *this* approach to protest management would be successful, especially in a university environment.

Curt had answers to all of their questions. The one they liked the best came in response to this question: "Sheriff, what do you teach your officers about the use of their baton?" Curt's "How *not* to use it." drew applause from at least half the people around the table.

Not an hour had gone by before the conversation had wound

down to the point the chancellor felt comfortable asking, "Does anyone else have anything for Curt?" No one did.

"So tomorrow, then," the chancellor continued, "do we all support Curt's deploying 30 officers, 15 on each side of 15th Street between engineering and the law school, to ensure the street is clear to traffic even during the protest?" Everyone supported the plan except for Pat McGinnis, who would have avoided any sort of law enforcement presence.

The chancellor thanked Pat for sharing his concerns. He thanked Curt Bennett for joining them and for providing the officers for tomorrow afternoon. He thanked the rest of his leadership team. Finally, he thanked Jill Swanson for doing such a fine job with the meal on such short notice.

As the sit-in had continued after the start of the protests, Farieh Bukhari was seated only a few steps from the chancellor when he adjourned the meeting. Like all of the students with her, she had seen the Sheriff when he arrived early. But the uniformed officer had an impact upon Farieh much different than any impact he might have had upon the others. Her thoughts went to Iran, and to Mehri, and to what would happen to her friends and the thousands of other students if these officers, as well, used violence. She could not allow that. She had led the students to this point. For the first time, what was happening here—a place far from Iran, a place she associated with safety—seemed enormous to Farieh, and dangerous, and she was responsible.

She got up, walked into the hallway that circled the rotunda, and pulled out her cell phone as she made her way down the stairs. But she walked out the north door, to the driveway behind Strong Hall. She did not want the hundreds of students gathered in front of the building to hear her.

"Rebecca?"

"Farieh. Hello! Things are going so well. You should have been with us this afternoon. Professor Zaidi was magnificent! No wonder you like his class so much. How are things with your buddy the chancellor?" Rebecca laughed at her own cleverness.

"He's not my *buddy*!"

"Okay, okay," replied Rebecca. "Sorry! What's the matter?"

"They're bringing in law enforcement tomorrow. The Sheriff's Department. They'll call it 'crowd control'; we'd call it 'riot gear.' Shields and batons—clubs! You *have* to alert the students, tell them to be careful, tell them to be safe. They won't want to listen to you. They think this is all a spring-day walk in the park. But it isn't. You *have* to make them listen. *Promise* me you'll do that!"

Rebecca did not know why Farieh was so worked up, but she clearly was. "I promise," she said. "But how do you think I should do that? How do I *make* them listen?"

Farieh replied immediately. "You always pause in front of Strong Hall. Tell them then. Tell them something has changed, something important. Tell them the Sheriff's Department will be waiting for them at the law school. Tell them the officers will have clubs, and that they simply can't do *anything* that might provoke the officers. We have been successful so far. We *have* to keep this peaceful. We'll *lose* if it's not! Tell them that.

"Far more important, someone could get hurt. Really, really hurt. This has to stay peaceful, no matter what!"

"Okay. Got it," said Rebecca. "I do understand, Farieh. I'll make sure the students do too."

They hung up. Farieh stood outside for a few moments. She needed to calm down before joining the sit-in on the second floor. She was the leader. She took a breath, blew it out, and turned toward the door.

# The Shot Seen Round the World

There was too much at stake for Farieh to stay with the sit-in so she joined the march as it reached Strong Hall. Rebecca did an excellent job telling the crowd about the Sheriff's officers and how to manage them. Farieh just hoped they were listening. It was warmer on Thursday; she was wearing a white tennis skirt.

Rebecca was in the lead, so Farieh waited until the middle of the crowd was passing her before stepping down from the curb to join them. She could exercise whatever control might be needed from there. She had barely cleared the Chi Omega fountain and turned the corner south toward the law school when she saw the students had again filled 15th Street between law and engineering, blocking traffic in both directions. Like the day before, no one seemed to mind. The students were loud but not unruly; the few drivers stopped by the crowd had gotten out of their vehicles and were watching from the sidewalks.

KU and the Sheriff's Department were not at liberty to allow a traffic stoppage that afternoon. Curt Bennett's 30 officers were just picking up their Plexiglas shields as Farieh passed beneath the pedestrian bridge that connected Slawson to Engineering. From lines on both sides of 15th Street, the officers stepped down from the curb in unison and moved slowly, carefully, into the crowd. But the students were packed together, it was inevitable someone would make contact with the shields, and soon a few students lost their balance and fell to the pavement. An instant later hundreds of students were scattering away from the officers, some of them running, most of them moving east. They overwhelmed the students in front of Slawson Hall, knocking several left and right as they rushed past.

Tripped and knocked off balance herself, Farieh fell hard and struck her knee against the rough curb in front of the Slawson Hall lobby. Her tennis skirt gave her no protection. The abrasion bloomed immediately, then bled all over her shin and sandal.

A photographer had been shooting the students when a sheriff's officer came even with Farieh and looked down at her through his mirrored sunglasses. He held his riot shield with his left hand. In his right was his baton, which he had forgotten to holster after using it to push his helmet back from his nose. He was concerned for her injury, and his instinctive gesture—reaching out to help the young woman on the curb—pushed the baton at her face.

The photograph captured an olive-skinned woman lying on the pavement, her blood streaming from a laceration somewhere. Startled by the baton, she had opened her mouth in what could have been a scream. It captured the approaching sheriff's officer, whose helmet and mirrored sunglasses and drawn club reminded of protests from the 1960s and the police violence that had met them. There were bold colors here: the black of the pavement, the crimson of Farieh's blood against the white of her skirt. But none of them could compete with the yellow of her head scarf.

The Kansas City Star employee who took the photograph checked her LCD screen. When she recognized what she had, she forwarded it through her editor to the AP wire. That took a minute. Al Jazeera needed only a minute more to flash it to the world.

# Press Conference

It had been more than a year since the chancellor had had a press conference. That one was called by the university to celebrate the Mississippi Street Gateway District, which combined a new football stadium, a new conference center, a new athletic dormitory, and hoped-for retail development into a $500 million project made possible by the stunning success of KU's current football coach. This one would be different.

KU had received the first requests for comment within minutes of Al Jazeera's posting the photograph of Farieh and her "assailant." The hundred requests that followed swamped the Office of Public Affairs and the Office of the Chancellor, which failed even to acknowledge them all, much less respond to them. By 5:15 p.m., Chancellor Bob Barkett realized he had a conflagration on his hands and that the only way to stop it was to carve a fire break on the far side. He huddled with the Vice Chancellor for Public Affairs, Jonathan Gribble, at 5:20, and by 5:30 the university announced there would be a press conference the next morning at 10:00 in Room 130, Budig Hall.

The building housed three large teaching theatres, collectively "Hoch Auditoria." At roughly 500 seats, Room 130 was the smallest of the three spaces. But the university believed it would accommodate the reporters and broadcasters and camera crews and others that might come to Lawrence the next day. The university had been wrong about several aspects of the DEI protests so far, and it would be wrong about this one too.

Jonathan Gribble left Strong Hall soon after the announcement, tasked with getting the room and the A-V gear set up, with communicating to the media what electrical and WI-FI and other service would be available to them the next morning, and with how many satellite trucks would be allowed to drive onto the main campus and park on Jayhawk Boulevard. The chancellor's assignment was to show up at 10:00 and have something to say. He would gladly have taken on the trucks and the building.

Bob Barkett was good in a crisis. He had dealt with multi-million-dollar cost overruns and job-site injuries, about falling academic rankings, and about firing a head coach. He could speak to all of these things. But he had never had to discuss why an Iranian coed in a head scarf had been beaten by a Douglas County Sheriff's officer whom he had personally invited onto the campus. He had just begun to consider that when Jill Swanson slipped into his office and put a note on his desk: "Curt Bennett is here to see you." Barkett looked up into the always-calming expression of his assistant and let out a sigh. "That's good, Jill. I was going to have to call him anyway. Please ask him to come in."

The Douglas County Sheriff came through the door and walked briskly toward the chancellor. Barkett had only begun to greet him when Bennett started in. "I've talked with the officer in the photograph. Rob Johnson. Been with us a long time; excellent record. He has no history of any kind of violence: none with anyone outside the department; not even a raised voice within the department. Everybody likes him.

"He came back to the office after the protest and knew nothing about the girl in the head scarf other than he tried to help her. When he saw the photograph that is still screaming across the internet he came to see me immediately!

"He talked with the girl—apparently it was right after the picture was taken. She told him she had tripped; he was concerned about her knee, which is where the blood was coming from. He used his field kit to dress the abrasion. He asked her permission first and she gave it to him. Then he told her where the student health center was, Watkins, and told her she should go there to have someone make sure the area was clean and the wound was as superficial as he thought it was. He even offered to go with her. But she knew where it was and said she could get there on her own. He says he wished her good luck, she thanked him, and he left.

"According to Johnson, that was it. She left; he assumes she went to Watkins. The crowd had disbursed by then. Nobody else was hurt.

"But the media is saying we abused the girl. Especially the foreign press."

"Johnson's version of this changes everything," said Barkett. "I didn't know about that."

Barkett read the Sheriff's face, which was more relaxed than it had been when he arrived. "Any chance I could meet with Johnson tonight?"

"He's outside, in my car. We drove on campus and parked where you do, in the parking facility behind Strong. I didn't want him walking through the sit-in to get here unless that's what you wanted."

"Good decision," said the chancellor, glad for the news about Johnson and for Curt Bennett's resourcefulness. "Why don't you drive him to the Outlook? It will take me 20 minutes—10 to make it through the students here and another 10 to walk home. You stay in the car in the parking facility until 15 minutes have gone by, then come over. There's a circle drive in front of the house, but don't park there. Park in back by the garage. I'll let you in the kitchen door. See you there."

It took Bob Barkett 20 minutes just to get down the stairs of Strong Hall and outside onto the sidewalk. Another 20 got him past the students who had filled Jayhawk Boulevard, past Watson and Fraser to his Lawrence residence, then through the kitchen to the back of the house. Bennett and his officer were still sitting in the Sheriff's SUV when the chancellor walked up to it and knocked on the window. "We're okay," he said to them, "come on in."

They walked through the kitchen into the small dining area.

Barkett gestured for them to take a seat and asked whether they wanted something to drink. "Water? Soft drink? I've got Pepsi and Diet Pepsi. And I may have some coffee left from lunch." Neither of the Sheriff's Department guests wanted anything.

The chancellor had liked Bennett from the moment he met him. But tomorrow morning he would have to tell hundreds of angry students, a turned-up and skeptical media audience, and likely a million other people watching on television and on streaming services what had happened between Officer Johnson and Farieh Bukhari. No matter how much he liked him, he wasn't willing to accept what his boss had told him about their encounter. He would interview Johnson himself.

It took 30 minutes. Johnson was tight at first. But as he sensed the chancellor was dealing with him in a straight-up way, he relaxed. His story was what Bennett had advertised, and it held up to the chancellor's questions.

Johnson told Bob Barkett he'd take that Diet Pepsi if it was still available, and as he drank the soft drink they all talked about spring football and whether KU might really win the Big 12 the next fall.

He was nearly finished with his drink when the chancellor got to the last item on his agenda. "Rob, I wanted to meet you and talk with you before I made this last request of you. I'd like you to be at the press conference tomorrow. It's important that the people there know what happened, and it's important that they have the chance to lay eyes on you when I tell them. It's the kind of story anyone would be proud to present, and I will be proud to present it. Look sharp: wear your uniform; have your sunglasses in your pocket; bring the same helmet you had on today. You're not going to wear the helmet and sunglasses, but I want you to have them.

"The photograph of you and the woman in the head scarf was not distorted; it wasn't photo-shopped. But it needed an explanation, and the press wasn't looking for one. It was provocative; that was enough."

The chancellor paused here. "What I'm going to say next relates to you only indirectly, Rob, but it's important. KU and Lawrence have seen real violence before, and you don't have to go back to the Civil War to find it. The Union burned here in the spring of 1970, when the university was in the middle of student protests against the Vietnam War. People remember that. The Kansas Legislature remembers it, for sure. That summer, two young men died. One, a Black man and community activist, was shot in the back of the head while running from the police. A few days later, a young white KU student was fleeing tear gas on the campus when he was shot by the police. In the eyes of many people there was no satisfactory explanation for either shooting at the time, and there has been none since.

"It's the not knowing that breeds the conspiracy theories; it's the not knowing that leads to contempt for law enforcement. And in 1970, not knowing why these two young men died fractured this community.

"We have the chance tomorrow to explain what really happened here. We're going to take it."

Both officers followed the chancellor to the back door and out into the paved area between the kitchen and the garage. The night was quiet; what light there was at the back of The Outlook came from the kitchen and from the scholarship hall to the north. Bob Barkett was shaking the officer's hand when he said, "You did your job today, Rob. Everyone has seen the photograph; tomorrow, they'll know the story that goes with it." He gripped his hand a little tighter. "I'm proud of how you handled it." Barkett turned to Curt Bennett next and thanked the Sheriff for bringing him over.

Bennett's response was brief: "It was important, chancellor. It will be really important tomorrow morning. Good luck."

As the officers got in the SUV the chancellor walked back into the kitchen. He felt better. But he had no idea how tomorrow might go.

Farieh Bukhari had read about the press conference only minutes before Rebecca's call jangled her cell phone. Rebecca had not talked with Farieh since that morning. Rebecca had led the students down the hill to the law school for the second day of the protests. She did not know Farieh had left Strong Hall to join them, and she did not know about the photograph until the protest was nearly finished. By then, Farieh had already gone to the walk-in clinic at Watkins. Because she had turned her phone off during the time she was with the examining nurse and had not turned it on again until she got back to her room at Miller, no one knew where she was.

"Farieh!!! Are you okay?! Where *are* you??? Did you go to Watkins? Did they treat you? The bleeding looked awful! Where did he hit you?"

Farieh heard most of Rebecca's questions and began to answer them: "Yes, I'm okay. I'm in my room at Miller. I did go to Watkins, and they did look at me. They said the bleeding had stopped and they changed my bandage and . . ."

Too excited not to, Rebecca cut in: "Have you seen the *picture*?!!"

Farieh had seen it. For a moment it had frightened even her! But the helmeted officer with the silvered sunglasses, the one who looked like he had just struck her with his baton, was the officer who had been kind to her, who had cleaned and bandaged her knee, and who had encouraged her to go to the very health center she had just come back from.

Rebecca was talking again before Farieh could respond. "You've got to be exhausted!

"Can you *believe* this?!! The internet is simply *on fire* with stories of the KU protest. We have been contacted by every TV station in Kansas City and Topeka and Wichita, and by dozens of others from around the country. *Everybody* wants to know about the press conference. Whether we will be there, whether they can talk with us beforehand, all that stuff. Did *you* know about the press conference?! The university has called it for 10:00 tomorrow morning—at Budig. The students are really *angry* and they're *all* coming. There will be cameras *everywhere*; they're going to broadcast it *live*! We've had a dozen calls from people who want to give us *money*!! This is just HUGE!!

"Lie down; get some rest. Gotta run—too many people to talk to!"

Farieh lowered the phone from her ear and saw a new text—from Richie Armstrong. He wanted to know how badly she had been hurt, and whether she had had medical treatment, and how she was feeling. Surprised, Farieh dashed off a quick response—"Feeling okay. Thanks very much for checking in."—and sent it before really thinking about it.

Richie was like every other KU student with a social media account; he could not have missed the photograph still bounding across the internet. But not every other KU person had reached out to her. Rebecca's call came after she got back to Miller, and Rebecca's primary focus seemed to be the publicity and what it meant for tomorrow. Texts from Wendy and Heather and the other women from Trinity Episcopal Church had arrived while she was being treated at Watkins. Helen Lochlear's text had reached her first, while she was still walking to Watkins, before she had even checked in at the student health center. But along with Richie's text, that was all.

The cool air moving across her shoulders was an unwelcome intrusion. Farieh looked up from her phone and noticed the window was open so she walked across the room to close it. She was staring through the panes of the upper sash when she noticed the three men walking out of the Outlook. There was no traffic in this remote corner of the campus. The only people about were the ones on the ground in front of her, and the breeze of the early evening carried their conversation across the lawn to the windowsill. While she did not know the Sheriff's officers, she knew the chancellor. As she listened to him compliment one of the officers, she guessed he was the one who had helped her that afternoon.

She pulled down the lower sash. Rebecca was right: she *was* tired. She sat on her bed, took off her boots, leaned back, and was asleep in seconds. It would be hours before Jamie returned to find her.

# Room 130 Budig Hall

The lines of students approaching Budig Hall at 7:45 a.m. were as thick as the basketball camping groups in the days before a big game. The ones who had taken seats around the large rectangular planter just north of the main doors were talking in low tones. Their bodies were taut, their backs facing the hundreds of red tulips in its center. Turgid in the cool, April morning, the tulips were also alert, seemingly impatient for the same press conference.

Jayhawk Boulevard was lined with the SUVs and satellite trucks of the Kansas City TV stations that had been arriving since 6:30. The mobile broadcast centers and portable power units had been parked on the sidewalk, and they ran from Budig all the way to Watson.

Bob Barkett was up early, too, walking to work as he did every morning. As he crossed the front of Watson toward his office in Strong Hall he noticed that the drivers and lighting personnel and generator technicians and broadcast coordinators hustling up and down the sidewalks were all in modern-day livery. Sneakers or the equivalent, jeans, same-color hoodies and jackets with the names of the stations displayed prominently front and back, and ball caps with logos on the front. Main campus lacked only large banners and broadly-striped fabric draped from the aluminum tent skeletons in front of Fraser and Flint to take on the look of a medieval tournament. Given the rivalry rife in today's broadcast news, the chancellor thought "tournament" was a particularly fine description for this particularly fine morning.

"What's the plan, Bob?" The question came from the Vice Chancellor for Public Affairs. Jonathan Gribble had been up since 5:00. Going over his lengthy checklist, but mostly worrying, he was glad to see Barkett walking through the door.

"I had an excellent meeting last night with the Sheriff's Officer who appears in the photograph. His name is Rob Johnson. The camera caught him just before he knelt to help Farieh, who had tripped over the curb next to Slawson and scraped her knee. That's where the blood came from. After asking her permission to help her, Johnson cleaned and field-dressed the abrasion and then told Farieh she should go to Watkins to have it looked at more carefully. He even offered to go with her! She thanked him, but she was able to go by herself. The photograph is entirely consistent with Johnson's recall. He never threatened her with his baton, and he sure as hell never hit her.

"I've confirmed the medical part of his story with the staff at Watkins. They said the knee had been field-dressed and the work was excellent. The bleeding had stopped, the wound looked good, and all they needed to do was change the bandage and give her some Tylenol. Farieh never complained about being hit with a baton, and there was no evidence of anything like that.

"That's our story at the press conference. The Sheriff's officer didn't hit the student, he helped her; and our university medical team backs him up.

"If we're asked about the protest, generally, we'll say we asked the Sheriff's Department to assist with traffic control because the streets had been completely blocked the first day. There was no plan to rush the students. We have video footage ready to support that. None of the Sheriff's officers ever ran at or threatened anyone. They had acrylic shields, and they held them in front of their bodies as they walked forward. Nobody ever swung one at a student.

"The only person who used a baton for anything was Rob Johnson. He had been jostled by the students running toward Slawson, his helmet was knocked forward onto his nose, and he used his baton to push it back. That was unfortunate, because that's what he was doing when saw the student in the head scarf. She needed help; and when he reached out to help her he still had his baton in his hand. That's the image in the photograph.

"This is a solid story; there is no evidence to the contrary. And Johnson's a solid guy. We're going to have him sit next to me in front of the auditorium. I think this will go well."

"Okay," said Gribble. "We've got a plan. I like it."

Barkett and Gribble had decided the chancellor would walk across Jayhawk Boulevard to Budig at 9:30—to "show the flag" to the students and to make himself available to Gribble and anyone else from KU who needed to talk with him in the moments before the press conference. That left him a full hour to work on something besides the protest, and he headed into his office to do just that.

When Bob Barkett crossed the street an hour later he was met by a thousand students. Placards were everywhere: "BIRMINGHAM COMES TO LAWRENCE!" and "ARE THE DOGS NEXT?!" Dozens more carried the Al Jazeera photograph. The students were working themselves up for the press conference, now only minutes away, and their shouted obscenities drowned out everything else. Ever the bridge-builder, the chancellor tried to make conversation with several of the groups; but he soon gave up and went inside.

Budig's lobby was also filled. There were fewer students here; there wasn't room for them. But they were just as angry and they were carrying the same placards. Barkett did not even try to make conversation this time. He pushed past them, heading for the A-V control area in the center of the three teaching auditoria. Jonathan Gribble was there.

"Seen the crowd in 130?"

"No," said the chancellor.

"Filled to the rafters," said Gribble. "Students are leaning against the walls. Every stair tread has kids sitting on it. If the fire marshal shows up, we're toast!"

Barkett looked into Room 130. The reserved area, the first

four rows, was filled with reporters and camera crews. Every row above them was crammed with students and placards.

"Good Lord!" The chancellor was speaking to himself this time, and quietly.

Gribble and Barkett walked maybe two steps into the well of Room 130. Ahead of them was the eight-foot-long table they had been told would be there. Its two chairs faced the audience and its two table mics were directly in front of the chairs. To the left and right were much smaller tables, each joined by a single chair, each supporting several wireless mics. "For the runners," volunteered Gribble. "They will bring a mic to the people in the audience who want to speak." Gribble stopped walking. "You ready?" Barkett nodded. "You will walk out first and greet the crowd. Officer Johnson will come out second. Good luck!" Gribble turned for the A-V control area. Alone in the large teaching amphitheater with the students, Bob Barkett did his best to relax as he walked to the table and took the seat on the right.

The crowd noise fell a few decibels as the students noticed the chancellor. But when Officer Johnson came out to join him, looking like he had just stepped out of the center of the Al Jazeera photograph, the crowd noise doubled. At least half of the students were standing now, many screaming at the men seated in front of them.

The chancellor began a short opening statement. But even with his microphone to help him his comments could not dent the jeers of the crowd.

Individual voices rose above the din. *"Tell us why you beat women students!"* rang out, followed by *"Why did you call the gestapo to a peaceful protest?"*

When the chancellor leaned back from the mic and simply sat there, the heckling slowed and then nearly stopped, permitting the chancellor once again to lean into his microphone.

"The university has made this time available to give *everyone* the chance to speak and ask questions. But 'everyone' includes the university; and this morning that's me, your chancellor. I've got only a few things to say, and one of them is this: No one beat anyone. What Officer Johnson and I want . . ."

At his mention of the Sheriff's deputy the students erupted again, and this time they would not quiet down. A troop of students marched into Room 130 from the lobby and paraded across the front of the chancellor's table. Then they then marched up and down the sloped stairways shouting. "HO HO, HEY HEY! DEI HAS GOT TO STAY!"

This first troop was still walking out when the second moved in. Their chant was different, and much louder: "KU DOESN'T CARE WHO STUDIES; KU BEATS ITS STUDENTS BLOODY!"

The second group angered Rob Johnson and the chancellor had to reach across and push hard on Johnson's arm to keep him in his seat.

Gribble had inched out of the A-V control area and was frantically giving Barkett the cut-throat sign from the wings: time to get out before someone got hurt. The chancellor hated the idea of giving up. But he understood what it was to lose control of a crowd, and he pushed his chair back away from the table.

A tall woman appeared out of nowhere and came to a stop in front of the same long table, her back to Johnson and the chancellor. She was wearing a yellow head scarf. One by one the students recognized her, and when they did, the room fell quiet.

Farieh Bukhari moved left and picked up a wireless microphone. Then she moved back to Officer Johnson, standing so close to him she could reach out and put her arm across his shoulder. And then she did just that.

"This man did not hurt me," she began. "He helped me! I was bleeding and he cleaned and bandaged my wound. I did not know where to go and he reminded me of our health center at Watkins. When I seemed confused about Watkins he offered to walk me there.

"We can be angry today; we SHOULD be angry today. But not with Officer Johnson, not with the Sheriff's Department, and not with the chancellor. We should be angry with the legislators in Topeka who are trying to destroy diversity on our campus!

"If you want to be angry, come back here this afternoon! We will meet right here—right in front of Budig Hall—at 3:00 p.m. You are all welcome!"

Farieh had not expected any particular reaction to her remarks, but she definitely did not expect the quiet that settled across nearly all of the nearly 700 students in Room 130. They had come to protest against physical violence. An off-campus officer had clubbed the young woman leading their protests. They had expected the victim of that violence to rally them against the university and its mercenaries.

Deborah Yancey—"I'm Deb Yancey!" to the people familiar with the conservative anchor from Chicago who looked like a supermodel and talked like a truck-stop waitress—stood up out of the silence, found a wireless mic for her left hand, pointed at Farieh with her right, and shouted her question: "How much did KU *pay you* to come here this morning and say that?"

Farieh was barely 20 years old. She did not flash anger and she did not blush embarrassment. Looking Yancey in the eye and with a voice as measured as Yancey's was not, Farieh spoke past the news queen to the students who were now on the edge of their seats.

"KU paid me nothing. Neither did the Sheriff's Department or anyone else. I came here this morning because I believe what Professor Zaidi said the first day of the protests. Our first responsibility is to tell the truth.

"No one beat me.

"No one threatened me.

"I *tripped* in the street next to Slawson—tripped over another student. I fell against the curb and I tore open the skin on my knee. I was just looking at it bleed and thinking how much it hurt when this Sheriff's deputy, his name is Johnson, knelt down and asked if he could help.

"I said he could. He used a spray to wash and clean my knee, then he bandaged it. I was unsteady for a moment so he encouraged me to go to Watkins; he even offered to take me there. But I knew the way and I knew I could get there on my own. I thanked him for his help and he left.

"That's the real story behind the photograph. That's what Professor Zaidi says I am supposed to tell you—the truth! The people at Watkins saw the bandage Officer Johnson put on my knee; they will tell you the same thing."

Farieh's eyes had been sweeping the front of the auditorium. She narrowed them now. She had been looking for Deborah Yancey like a Kansas rancher would look for someone who had stolen his dog, and she found her.

"You are a journalist, Ms. Yancey. Journalists are supposed to ask hard questions—so they can get to the truth. Hard questions do not offend me. But you did more than ask a hard question. You pointed your finger at me. You contorted your face into something hateful. And when you spoke you snarled at me. All of that was calculated. You have worked on that look; it was the look you wanted the camera to capture. I am sure you have used it hundreds of times.

"You are not interested in the truth. What you care about are your adoring audience and your ratings. When you could not deliver a story about police brutality you came after me. Did it even *cross your mind* I might be telling the truth?"

Farieh looked away from Yancey and once again took in the entire audience. "Does anyone else have a question for me?"

No one did.

Farieh took the several steps back to the small table where she had picked up her microphone. She had one more thing to say.

"Our protest is important. We will meet again this afternoon at 3:00, right outside Budig Hall. Then we will march to the law school. It is important that the governor veto this bill, and we need to let him know how we feel about it.

"You all know that *I* am a part of the protest." Finally accepting that Farieh had not been beaten, the students were warming to the comments she was making. A number of them applauded her at this point.

"It is my job to select the speaker for our gatherings at the law school," she continued. "I was busy yesterday afternoon…" More students joined in, interrupting with their laughter and their applause. "So I have not yet picked a speaker for this afternoon. But I have someone in mind."

The chancellor was still sitting at the long table next to Officer Johnson, and when Farieh Bukhari turned and smiled at him he knew he had no way out.

"Chancellor Barkett, if you are willing to join us we would be glad to hear from you."

Bob Barkett wasn't upset about being painted into a corner. Struck again by the young University Scholar and by her ability to command an audience, he was already chuckling at how she had done it. He smiled back at Farieh, gave her a thumbs up, and wondered what on earth he would say.

# The Way to Green Hall

The chancellor was across the street and back in his office by 11:00. He asked Jill to call what the *UDK* had labeled the "Disaster Response Team" and have them come to his office at noon.

Everyone was on time and Jill had again made a light lunch appear out of nowhere. Bob Barkett had already committed to showing up that afternoon at the law school. He wanted everyone's opinion about what he should say.

To the chancellor's surprise, only Jonathan Gribble had been present at the press conference. Pat McGinnis had watched it from Kansas City. Perhaps because none of the others had seen it, and seen the mood of the students, most of them were where they had been earlier—unwilling to confront the Legislature over the anti-DEI rider and assuming the protests would eventually run out of steam. But Bob Barkett was well past that. His impatience flashed as he told them he had a proposition for them to vote on.

"It's not May, but I want you to assume it is. Assume the Legislature has passed the budget bill and sent it to the governor. The legislative session is done. If the governor chooses to kill the anti-DEI rider he will do it by line-item veto; the rest of the budget, including all the money for KU, is safe.

"We've been asked to take a stand on this, to urge the governor to use his line-item veto.

"Under these assumptions, are you for it or against it?"

At least 20 seconds went by before anyone even cleared their throat. That was followed by 20 minutes of vigorous debate, the team members expressing themselves with far more volume than the small room required. Gribble had seen the crowd disperse out of Budig: the students were animated, but they were nothing like they had been inside. He was no longer afraid of the students, but he was afraid of the legislature. Even under the chancellor's hypothetical, KU would need money *next* year. "They may not be smart," he concluded condescendingly, "but they have long memories."

Pat McGinnis was participating by Zoom from the Med Center in Kansas City. Speaking as loudly as he could into his laptop he began. "I was against having the Sheriff's Department there, Bob. But we brought them in, and Gerald Hampton knows we did it because of him. The young woman leading the protests got hurt and got her picture taken and suddenly KU was the most oppressive place in America, a 21st-century Selma.

"We were moments away from a campus melt-down this morning when the same woman . . ."

McGinnis' emotions had crept up on him and he had to pause for a moment.

"She did not have to come to the press conference in the first place, by the way. She could have stayed away and let the students blow the roof off of Budig, and they *would* have!

"But she walked in and she calmed the waters. *How* did she do it? She told the truth. NONE of those students wanted to hear that from her, but she told it anyway. I wish I had guts like that.

"The issue for us is not whether it's May or not. It's not whether the Legislature has a long memory. We need to decide how to respond to Farieh Bukhari. Where is the *truth* here? And who's going to tell it?

"I know where I think it is. The truth is this anti-DEI rider is the opposite of what a university ought to stand for. We may be frightened for our financial future. But we can't be so frightened we don't call out oppression and duplicity when we see them.

"The best response we can make to the bravest act I've seen on this campus in years is to stand beside Farieh Bukhari and agree with her."

It was a while before anyone made any kind of a sound, and it was the chancellor who made it. "I told you at the beginning I wanted your opinions. Do we urge the governor to veto the rider or not? What do you say?" Barkett went around the table; everyone answered. With one exception, Jonathan Gribble, everyone was in favor of publicly opposing the rider.

"Okay," said the chancellor. "We've got a great communications team who could help with the message. And our lobbyists too. Anyone in this room could draft it. But if I can remember what Pat just said, that will be as eloquent a statement as the University of Kansas can make.

"Thanks to all of you for being here on such short notice."

Rebecca Seacrist was right on time that Friday afternoon, pulling up in front of Strong Hall at 2:00. The thousands of students walking with her filled Jayhawk Boulevard to Lippincott and all the way back to the Union. They were accompanied by the camera crews who had stayed around after the press conference and by at least two dozen reporters and photographers, all of them eager to see what surprises the afternoon might produce.

Bob Barkett walked out the front door of Strong Hall and down the sidewalk and made his way straight for Rebecca. His pace was brisk but he was smiling, and he extended his hand to her when he was still 10 feet away. Rebecca was not surprised to see him; she had been sitting in Budig when he gave Farieh his thumbs-up. But she had not expected him to be so friendly. When she took his hand he asked, "Do you march straight from here to Green Hall?"

"Yes," she said. "But the students may stop anywhere in between, and we have to be alert to that."

"Got it," said the chancellor. "Are you ready to go?"

With the chancellor at her side Rebecca was more than ready.

The two of them led off down the sidewalk toward Snow Hall and the Chi Omega Fountain.

It wasn't two minutes before most of the marchers knew the chancellor was walking with them, and what had started as a boisterous crowd became a spring gathering of young people gamboling toward the park-like lawn of the law school. Ahmed Zaidi was waiting for them there. So was his student from Tehran, Farieh Bukhari.

Farieh heard the students first; she was talking with Professor Zaidi and had her back to the oncoming marchers. She turned to see them and spotted Rebecca near the front and waved to her. It was when she saw the chancellor, to Rebecca's right and talking animatedly with the students between them, that she smiled. And then she laughed like she hadn't laughed since her pillow fight with her sister in Oxford.

The chancellor made it down the hill and across Bob Billings and up to the speaker's platform, where Farieh greeted him and thanked him for coming. She remembered leading him up the stairs and showing him the lectern and the microphone. She remembered his smile. She remembered moving down the stairs and taking her place beside Professor Zaidi.

After that, she remembered the shouts and cheers of the crowd and how quickly the chancellor's remarks had ended and how warmly he had been greeted by the students when he had stepped down from the platform. So much of it was a blur. And then he was standing in front of her.

The chancellor told her he had already called the governor on behalf of the university, asking him to veto the rider. He had made the call before he joined the march, said he wanted that "in his pocket" when he spoke to the students. He thought it would make his remarks "more powerful." With Professor Zaidi looking on, the chancellor thanked her for her courage. And then he was gone, swept toward the law school by reporters who were surprised by the stance the university had taken and who could not wait to talk with him about it.

Farieh's eyes followed the chancellor as he moved west to the crowd in front of Green Hall. When she looked straight ahead again Rebecca was right in front of her, screaming: "WE WON!!!"

They won in Topeka, too—at least the first round. Surprised by KU's position on the rider, but delighted, the governor was only too happy to use his line-item veto and strike it from the budget. The howls from the sponsors were immediate. The next morning, Gerald Hampton told the Topeka press corps the veto would be overridden in less than a week.

# Seeking Gerald Hamptom

Farieh had been studying Kansas legislative procedure since January. She knew the sponsors of the anti-DEI rider had one more shot at it—the override session. She texted her six companions and let them know they had more work to do.

"Watup?"

Head down in her notes, Heather had not noticed her best friend was already sitting at the table as she walked into Trinity's library from the parish hall. Gwendolyn Bernstein—"Gwen" to her parents, "Gwennie" in middle school, and finally "Wendy" by the time she graduated from Shawnee Mission East—was Heather's height and carried the same curly brown hair.

They had met their freshman year at Corbin Hall, KU's only residence hall exclusively for women. Though not her roommate, Wendy had drifted down the hall to Heather's room on a regular basis once it was clear Heather and her three roommates were way cool and way fun and smart as hell. Wendy would walk in, jump onto Heather's bed, crawl under the covers, get too hot, take off her socks, and fall asleep. When the rest of the young women had finished their conversation they would wake Wendy, then they'd all go out for pizza. The socks would stay behind. When rush came around that fall Heather had a drawer full of socks, and all five pledged the same sorority.

By the end of their freshman year Wendy had become more than a pledge sister to Heather. She became the sibling Heather never had, the best of besties. Their music preferences never coalesced and Heather's enthusiasm for sports never matched Wendy's. But on every other plane they were together.

They were especially all-in when it came to matters of diversity and inclusion, whether by race or faith or gender or sexual preference or national origin. They did not like what was happening in the Kansas Legislature, and they were excited when Farieh and Rebecca had asked them to become a part of a group to oppose it.

The group would meet tonight to consider the results of the research they had done into the backgrounds of the several legislators who had driven the anti-DEI rider in the Kansas House of Representatives. Rebecca had suggested the investigation into personal and family history to see whether there were stories that might be useful to shore up the veto. She had recommended that approach because there were Republican super majorities in both the House and Senate. Unless they could pick off several of the rider's supporters, the override would be successful.

Heather had taken Gerald Hampton, the Speaker Pro Tem, who had reported how "tickled" he was at the passage of the anti-DEI rider and who had convened a vitriolic press conference in Topeka to condemn the governor's line-item veto and to "Guarantee!" the Republican-dominated legislature would override it. It was her notes on the Pro Tem that Heather was looking at as she walked into the library.

"Wendy! Hi! Sorry to be so head-down. I think we have something on Hampton."

Heather walked farther into the small room, removed her backpack and put it in the corner, then pulled back a chair and sat across from Wendy as she placed her notes on the table.

"Hampton's family came from Poland—Gdansk. Their last name was 'Hanska.' They were Jewish. They had moved to Germany after World War I, settling in Berlin.

"The parents sent their oldest son to Warsaw in 1938 to protect him from the Nazis. Germany invaded Poland in 1939. In 1942, the Nazis arrested the family in Berlin and sent them to Auschwitz. None of them survived. The son, who was barely a teenager in

1938, became one of the famous Warsaw runners who would secretly leave the ghetto in the evening to acquire food and even guns for the people living there, then return just before morning.

"Somehow the son survived the war. He moved to the United States, changed his name to 'Peter Hampton,' and took a job in a steel mill in Gary, Indiana. He joined the Methodist Church, married, and had a family.

"The family stayed in the same area into the 1970s, when domestic steelmaking was declining in the face of cheaper, imported steel. That's when the family moved to Kansas City, Kansas. Peter Hampton took a job at the GM plant in Fairfax.

"Gerald Hampton grew up in Kansas City, Kansas, then went to college at Wichita State. He graduated in aeronautical engineering in 1990 and went to work for Boeing-Wichita, which later became Spirit Aviation. Like a lot of their employees, he lives outside of Wichita. In his case, it's a rural area south of Pratt, a county-seat town in the middle of the state. In 2016, he went on half-time with Spirit to run for the Kansas House. Hampton is smart, he ran a smart campaign, and he got elected. He has served in the Kansas House since, moving up to Speaker Pro Tem.

"The most interesting part is what Gerry Hampton was doing in college. He applied for the job at Boeing-Wichita in the fall of 1989; you can find the resume he used on the internet. In the summers before that he worked for a Western Kansas radio station, one whose messaging was anti-Semitic and racist. The station is no longer broadcasting. But it was notorious in the 1980s, an early voice of Holocaust denial. According to his resume, Hampton started as a runner. But he was promoted to an on-air position after his sophomore year, and he continued as a broadcaster until the summer after he graduated from WSU. He started with Boeing-Wichita that fall."

Wendy had been looking hard at Heather. "Don't be offended by this question," she said, "but it's important. You know there are a lot of Holocaust deniers. What evidence do you have that the family was sent to Auschwitz, and died there?"

"I know about the grandfather. He worked as part of a surveyor's team at Auschwitz and was accused of helping an escape attempt. To make an example of him, the Germans hung him in front of the other camp prisoners. The Germans kept those records. The Russians found them when they liberated the concentration camp in 1945, and they were used as evidence during the Nuremberg trials after the war ended. Jan Hanska, Gerald's grandfather, was hung at Auschwitz in 1944."

"Okay," said Wendy, "good. What ties Jan Hanska to Gerald, and to his father?"

"Gerald's father was born 'Piotr.' After the war, he came to the United States on board a ship that docked in New York City. He registered at Ellis Island in March of 1946, identifying himself and his parents. 'Piotr Hanska' listed his birthplace as 'Berlin, Germany' and his parents as 'Jan' and 'Zofia,' both 'deceased.'

"He must have been the one in a thousand who went through a formal name-change procedure, but he did. 'Piotr Hanska' became 'Peter Hampton' in Crown Point, Indiana, the county seat of Lake County, on November 1, 1946. Gary is in Lake County.

"I told you he joined the Methodist Church. He was married in Gary's Fifth Avenue United Methodist Church to Anne Stevenson in 1958. They had two girls. Then, according to the baptism records at the church, they had a son. He was born May 1, 1968. They named him 'Gerald.'"

Wendy stood up, walked around the table, gave her friend a hug, and said, "You should go to law school!"

# Birthday Kidnapping

G erry?"

The Speaker Pro Tem had been in a never-never land of alcohol-induced sleep and it took a long moment for him to realize his phone was ringing, to find it, and to recognize the voice on the line after he finally got it turned right-side up. "Tom?"

"Just right. It's Tom. I need your full attention for a few minutes. Can you find it?"

Tom Dennis, at the top of the state's top-tier of lobbyists, had known Gerald Hampton since he had first come to the Legislature in 2017. It wasn't every day the Kansas House picked up a freshman representative with an aeronautical engineering degree. Dennis had been the first to see the potential in him, and he had cultivated Hampton carefully. In turn, Hampton quickly recognized Dennis was a player. In the several election cycles since they had formed a close relationship, one that was critical to Hampton and that was as close to a friendship as Dennis would permit himself with an elected official he was paid to influence on behalf of his clients. Since Norman Gaar, the Capitol had not had a consensus "smartest guy in the building." But Tom Dennis was on everybody's short list.

Gradually returning to the land of the conscious, Gerald Hampton ran his eyes across the top of his phone. "Goddamit, Tom! It's 7:15 in the morning. Why does my wakeup call come from you?!"

"Because someone needs to get ahold of you before you wander into your palatial office this morning and get ambushed by a dozen of your best media buddies carrying microphones and cameras. It's obvious you haven't seen the *Capital-Journal*. Would you like to know what it says?"

Tom Dennis had his full attention now, and Gerry's reply was more moderate: "Sure."

"It says your father is Jewish—a Holocaust survivor. And it says you're a racist."

Hampton's reaction was as loud as it was immediate: "Racist! Jewish father! What is THIS about? And why is this *bullshit* all over the paper?"

"That's what we need to find out," said Dennis. "That's why you've got me for your wakeup call. Did you know your father was Jewish? Did you ever work for a Western Kansas radio station whose programming was anti-Black and anti-Jew?"

"God Damn!" replied the Speaker Pro Tem. "I was a kid when I had that radio gig. That was nearly 40 years ago."

"Do you have a Jewish father?"

"How would I know?! I grew up in the Methodist Church— sang in the goddamn choir! I thought my father was from Indiana. I barely knew him. He was an asshole."

"Okay," said Dennis, his thoughts expanding well past his reply.

"So now what?" asked the wide-awake Speaker Pro Tem.

"Where's Mary?" Tom Dennis had asked about Gerry Hampton's wife, for whom "long-suffering" was no cliché. But they had what Dennis would describe as an "effective" marriage. Mary, God love her, adored the guy who decided to supplement a career designing winglets for passenger jets by becoming a superstar in Kansas politics.

"On the ranch, I assume. She hates Topeka. You know that."

"Right," said Dennis, smiling to himself. He had met Mary Hampton only twice. But she was friendly, and she knew the wheat from the chaff, and he really liked her. "I do."

There was a pause, then a playful question: "Who's got a birthday coming up?"

"I do, asshole. This Saturday. Thought *you* of all people would have remembered!"

The trademark sarcastic sparkle having returned to the Pro Tem's voice, Tom Dennis felt he could make some progress. "I did, and it's perfect. Let's get Mary to kidnap you! Today; this morning. Take you out of town for a few days.

"It's Thursday. There's nothing of any consequence going on at the Capitol. Between now and next week we can check out the radio station and figure out who your father was. You and Mary can come back next Tuesday. By the time the press finds you we'll have some answers for their questions."

"How is Mary going to *kidnap* me when she is puttering around in her flowers 200 miles away and I'm hung over in a hotel room in Topeka?!"

"I'll handle that," said Dennis, the plan having already formed. "It's really not that complicated. It's 7:30 now. I want you showered and dressed and packed for a short trip to a low-key resort and sitting in the front seat of your car by 8:30. You still drive that old beater of a red Mustang?"

"Damn right!" said the pro tem.

"Good. It will be easier for the Uber driver to find you. There will be an Uber pulling up in the parking lot next to you at 8:30. You still drinking at the Capitol Plaza but staying someplace cheaper?"

"Of course," said Hampton. "My constituents love it that I stay at the Hilton Garden Inn. Nobody cares whose bar I'm in before I go to bed."

"Hilton Garden Inn, it is. Be in your car at 8:30. And stay out of the lobby! Take the stairs down to the back door of the hotel, the one that opens to the parking lot. Go straight to your car, get in, and close the door. Don't turn it on; just sit there. The Uber driver will find you and take you to the Wichita airport. Don't worry about the cost; I'll cover it. Mary will meet you there.

"Where would Mary take you?"

"How the hell should I know?!" Hampton's reply was curt;

but then he spoke again. "Sorry, Tom. I am finally getting it, but it was a long night. She always wanted to go to Taos."

"Taos is great. It's away from here. It's not Santa Fe, which is way more visible; that's a plus. And there's enough to do there for three or four days. You'll have a great time.

"Your job is to get into your Mustang, transfer to the Uber at 8:30, and stay off your phone on the way to Wichita. We'll handle everything else with Mary—the air, the ground travel, and the hotel in Taos."

Again a pause, then Tom Dennis wrapped it up: "I know this is sudden, Gerry. But you are really out on a ledge right now. You are the anti-DEI poster child for Kansas, and you just can't greet the press with a racist job history and no clue about your own family. We'll have the answers for you by the time you and Mary get on the plane to come home. Okay?"

It wasn't okay. But Gerry Hampton knew he was out on a ledge, and he knew the one guy in Topeka capable of pulling him off of it was trying his best to do so. "Yeah," he said, "I'll get cleaned up. And Tom—thanks."

Tom Dennis called Monday morning, but not so early as he had a week ago. "Gerry?"

Hampton was already awake; had already had breakfast, in fact. "That's me," Hampton mugged. "Taos is great, Tom. Livin' the life!"

"I'm glad it worked out, Gerry," said Hampton. "But things up here are not working out so well."

"What's the problem? Did I actually *have* a Jewish father?"

"That's what it looks like, Gerry. Not only that, he was a hero of the Polish resistance. Incredible stories about what he did to keep people fed and to slip guns into the Warsaw Ghetto in the early hours of the morning."

Hampton continued, "So what? I didn't know about him. That can't be a crime. If he was a hero during the war, why can't we spin that to my advantage?"

"If it weren't for the Western Kansas radio station, we could try that. But someone found recordings of the broadcasts made by the station during the time you were working there as part of the on-air talent. They made transcripts of the recordings and gave them to the *Capital-Journal*. The paper included excerpts in its Sunday feature on the override session. I know that was decades ago, Gerry. But the language is pretty raw."

"But it doesn't sound like the paper's saying *I* said those things. I wasn't the *only* person working there; how are they going to pin it on me?"

"According to the *Capital-Journal*, there were only two on-air broadcasters doing shows when the recordings were made. The paper identified both of them; one of them was you.

"I went to the paper this morning and asked if they had the recordings, along with the transcripts. They did. And when I asked whether I could listen to them they just handed them to me, along with a turntable, amp, and speakers. I played one of the recordings. Your voice is a lot younger of course, but it's you, Gerry."

Gerry said nothing for a long while. "Everybody loves a fighter, Tom. Why can't we fight this? Tell people I was a kid, needed the job, that sort of stuff?"

Tom Dennis needed to get Hampton on track, but he needed to do it delicately. "If you had made what someone might call 'a youthful mistake' and had replaced it with a track record of welcoming minorities—Blacks, gays, Jews, etc., there'd be a chance for that. But you've spent the last four months attacking DEI; and your language has not always been that careful. Your co-sponsors and the hardliners don't care about that, but the party moderates do. They like the woke fight; they'll take a public stand against reverse discrimination and so on. But they won't take a public stand against people of color and Jews. Holocaust denial didn't sell in Kansas in the 1980s, and it doesn't sell here now.

"You get to make this decision, Gerry. But I have looked at it pretty carefully, and I believe you'll put your career on the line if you decide to fight."

Gerald Hampton asked a slow, careful question: "What would you do, Tom?"

"I'd stay in Taos. Let this burn down, then let me throw water on it."

"Who else can carry the override action if I'm out? Phil? Pat?"

"Phil was awarded a highway job in Northwest Kansas as a minority contractor when he had no minority workers on his payroll. Looks like someone in the office fabricated the application."

"What about Pat?"

"This is his first year in the House. He believes in the rider, and he jumped at the sponsorship because of the publicity. But he's never been in this kind of spotlight before, and it never occurred to him the spotlight might spill over onto his family. Both of his kids are in college, but not in Kansas. The boy is a freshman at Colgate. Came out as gay almost as soon as he stepped on the campus last fall. The daughter is a sophomore at the University of Colorado. She's co-chair of the student ACLU chapter there. Both of them pounded their dad about the rider after you held your press conference on the override. Pat caved; publicly withdrew his support for it."

"Then who's gonna handle the override session?"

"It's dead, Gerry. If you let this go, let it all blow over, you can still be the pro tem next year. If not, you're dead too."

One of the things Tom Dennis liked about Gerald Hampton was his base-line practicality. If there was a chance to win something, you wanted Gerry on your side. He'd fight harder than anybody. But if there was no chance, he would be one of the first to see it.

"We like it down here in Taos, Tom. Please extend us another couple of days in the La Fonda, and let me hear from you when it's safe to come back."

# The Bottleneck

Granger, Jamie's favorite garage band from her high school time in La Grange, Illinois, had gotten serious about their music and had started touring. When Jamie found out they were playing at The Bottleneck on Friday night she bought six tickets herself, figuring she'd have no trouble finding takers. It was Friday; she had one left. When she got back to Miller in the early afternoon she found Farieh lying back on her bed, relaxed, staring at the ceiling.

"How's KU's answer to Rosa Parks?"

Farieh grinned at the ceiling before turning toward her roommate. "That was a week ago, Jamie! Everyone's forgotten about it by now."

"Not me, O great victorious one! And now that the override effort has collapsed, you really did win! Diversity is safe in Lawrence for at least another year."

Jamie pulled the sixth ticket from the front pocket of her jeans and placed it on Farieh's bed like an offering.

Farieh had to sit up to look at it. "What's 'The Bottleneck'?"

"It's a bar. Downtown. A favorite stop for bands touring through the Midwest. A bunch of us from Miller are going tonight to hear my old high school boyfriend. He can't carry a tune in a backpack, but he's a lights-out drummer. The gang he runs with—"Granger"—was popular in high school; and they're up to over 100,000 followers on Twitter. "YOU need to celebrate! You're coming with us!"

Farieh reached for the ticket.

Lawrence's founders from The Massachusetts Emigrant Aid Society named its main drag to honor the state they came from. The streets running parallel to what the locals call "Mass" were named for other states, more or less in the order of their admission to the Union. New Hampshire, the street immediately east of Massachusetts, had always struggled to find its commercial footing. For decades, the street's most beautiful building was home to the Reuter Organ Company, whose management loved the building and its location and whose artisan-employees loved them even more. But the prospect of building fine pipe organs into the future required at least the hope of economic success, so management at last packed up the bending brakes and table saws and moved them to the country.

The *Lawrence Journal-World* had once occupied a splendid brick building on the other side of New Hampshire. But print media had suffered in recent years, and economics forced its move, as well. To an economy slice of a North Lawrence strip mall.

The middle and south ends of New Hampshire had fared differently. Tall buildings for apartments and condos, a new Marriott, and the creative programming of the Lawrence Arts Center were the anchors. There was also a city-owned parking garage. Sited a block from the Court House, which did not need the capacity, it stands across the street from a grateful Arts Center, which did.

The Bottleneck, on the west side of New Hampshire, sits just north of Eighth Street and across the street from the condos. "Home to cold beer and live music since 1985," its low roofline, occasionally-painted exterior, and broken sidewalks look like they did forty years ago. But on a weekend night in the spring or summer The Bottleneck and its 500 patrons welcome a rock group as well as any bar in the country. That's why Granger wanted to play there.

Jamie and Farieh and the four other women from Miller were in the front row a full half hour before Granger took the stage.

Having worn her head scarf unfailingly during the protests, Farieh had put it on this evening without thinking about it.

So excited to be a part of the band's first trip to Lawrence, Jamie nearly swallowed her old boyfriend's face with her first kiss. Then she embarrassedly introduced him—"Chris"—to Farieh and the others before Chris returned the favor. Chris' love tap was unmistakable to the hundreds of others who didn't get it; and the women from Miller were seated in front, where they rode out the set like royalty.

Farieh did not recognize the music, and she would have had to lie to say she liked it. But being in a place that was hot and crowded and loud with that kind of energy was the celebration she needed. They stayed past Granger's show, nattering with the band for maybe 20 minutes, and left when the band broke for their bus. As Jamie had stayed behind with Chris it was Kelsey who took the lead, moving everybody south toward Eighth Street.

"Anybody want ice cream?!" she yelled. Everybody did, so they continued south on New Hampshire. They walked past the condos and the apartment buildings, past the Marriott and the Arts Center at Ninth Street, and past Maceli's in the ten hundred block before finally reaching the court house. That's where they turned right toward Silas & Maddy's, Lawrence's top-shelf ice cream parlor, just across Mass on the southwest corner.

Farieh's group was moving west into the intersection when a twosome moved through the angled door of the ice cream shop and started in their direction. The young man in the lead was wearing a ball cap. When he saw Farieh he turned to his friend and spoke in a voice loud enough to carry all four corners:

"Well lookee here! We got ourselves a for-real camel jockey walkin' right at us. And a gal to boot! Hey, there, little lady. Y'all must be a long way from home! That right?"

Farieh had stepped off the curb first. Hearing every word, she stopped in the crosswalk so suddenly that Kelsey, who had been talking with the three trailing friends, walked right into her. That brought Kelsey's head around, and soon all five of the young women were blocking the north-bound lanes of traffic.

The young man who was speaking paid no attention to the cars and the pickups backing up south of the intersection, or to the traffic that was stopping north of it. His buddy no more than two paces behind him, the man with the ball cap continued into the intersection until he was barely six feet away from his target. But his proximity made no difference to the sound of his voice; he was still shouting at Farieh as he glared at her: "Hey! I asked you a *question*, little miss rag-head. You got an *answer*?!"

Farieh had been called out several times her freshman year, but none of them bothered her. It was usually a lone male walking toward her late in the afternoon, the comment nearly inaudible because the speaker swallowed it. Being called out in the middle of a downtown intersection was new. *Silly, too,* she thought. *And here? In front of the ice cream shop?!*

As her friends retreated to the east curb, Farieh stared at the skinny young man in front of her. Her father had covered muggings with all three girls when their family had moved to London, and she remembered his instructions: Don't move; avoid eye contact; speak softly; give them what they want. Avoiding eye contact was the last thing on her mind tonight. Farieh's eyes were alive with anger. Had they been her super power her antagonist would have been a cinder on the pavement.

This wasn't a mugger. This was a bully. Farieh had dealt with bullies. You confronted bullies.

She moved forward, never unlocking her eyes from his. As she came close enough to touch him a dozen conversational responses flashed past, and she chose one: *Why are you bothered by my head scarf? It is a symbol of our faith—did you know that?* But before she could turn the thought into words another person had jumped into the crosswalk, distracting the young man who had taunted her.

Richie Armstrong and his roommate had just finished their

waffle cones and were almost through the same angled door and onto the sidewalk when Richie saw Farieh. When the "Hey!" and the "You got an answer?!" registered with him he ran into the crosswalk, shouting back at Farieh's tormentor: "Hey, *yourself*, asshole! Leave her *alone*!"

The guy with the ball cap was maybe 25 years old, 5'10" and 130-140 pounds. He wore a plain, gray sweatshirt over blue jeans and rough work boots. Richie's sudden appearance and height got ball cap's attention, and as he turned toward Richie he pulled a knife out of the leather scabbard on his hip. The intersection was brightly lighted and Richie had no trouble seeing the arm movement, the scabbard, and the blade. Instinctively, he leaned into a ready stance and waited.

Bobby Hinshaw had spent his evening at a different bar, across the river at the original Johnny's Tavern. Johnny's was a comfortable place for him to be any night of the week. Because he was not really hungry he had helped himself to only a pair of Johnny's famous double cheeseburgers and a couple of beers. But he was always interested in an ice cream cone—chocolate chip. He had crossed the river and driven down Massachusetts and was parking his F-250 doolie just south of the ice cream shop when the rednecks started in.

He couldn't miss the commotion as he got out of his truck and stepped into the street. And he had no trouble recognizing the young woman in the middle of the intersection. Her protest photograph had been all over the internet the last two days.

She was "Farieh." She hadn't said much as they had rolled north to K-10 that winter morning back in February. But she had told him her name, and she had repeated another: "Richie." Saying it had seemed to calm her down. When Bobby had asked who Richie was, Farieh said only, "He's a very nice boy, a basketball player." Bobby figured the tall kid who had come to Farieh's defense with nothing to call on but his good looks had to be him.

As he got closer to the intersection Farieh looked the same.

The yellow head scarf was new, but she was still pretty.

When Bobby got to the crosswalk, he spoke to the taller of the two young men who were staring at each other across a space not big enough for a pool table: "You must be Richie."

Not willing to turn away from the knife, Richie sputtered, "Right! Who are *you*?!"

"I'm Bobby—Bobby Hinshaw. Ever been in a knife fight before?"

"No," said Richie.

"'S'what I thought," said Bobby. "Helps if you bring a knife. Here," he went on, "you're holdin' nuthin'; hold my jacket." And with that Bobby handed him a leather jacket that would have fit Mark Mangino. As he did so he eased past the Kansas basketball star, taking Richie's spot in front of the guy with the ball cap. Bobby's arrival changed the dynamics of the confrontation, and ball cap started moving his knife back and forth in a slow, flat figure eight.

Bobby reached behind his back with his left hand, pulled an 18-inch chain off his belt, and palmed the grip with his right hand. Custom-carved of oak but so sweat-stained it looked like old ebony, the grip had bright cutlery rivets that held one end of the chain securely between its top and bottom. Bobby was huge, nearly as tall as Richie and well over 300 pounds. But the grip fit him, and the forged links of the chain would have pulled a tractor out of a bar ditch.

"You boys like pickin' on girls?" asked Bobby, his eyes locked onto the two twenty-somethings in front of him. Bobby's head never moved, but his eyes rotated slightly toward the young man who was not yet holding a knife. "You got a knife? Jump in; play with your buddy. Not—best move back a little." The second man moved all the way to the curb, then backed up onto the sidewalk.

Bobby rotated his eyes to the guy in front of him. "Knives are great for cuttin' up deer and elk after you shoot 'em so you can carry the meat outta the woods, and for workin' a ribeye down to size after grillin' so you can eat it. But they're not much of a combat weapon. Hard to get close enough to the other dude to use it. Ever watch *Indiana Jones*? That'll tell yuh. Prob'ly not I guess. You're not old enough. Here, lemme show yuh."

Bobby's arm movement was so fast it could have been a muscle spasm. But it snapped the chain up into ball cap's forearm and sent the knife flying into the intersection behind him. Both the radius and ulna now broken, ball cap's right arm drooped toward the sidewalk as a scream tore out of his mouth.

The screaming didn't bother Bobby, who just kept talking. "'Less you're way better left-handed than y'are right, and half crazy to boot, I'm guessin' we're done." Bobby nodded left toward the intersection, still looking at the young man wailing in front of him. "Leave the knife."

This time Bobby nodded right. "Ah'l bet that's your truck right in front of mine. Stars 'n bars on the back window? That right? You boys best get in it and get the hell outta here."

Nobody moved.

"Now'd be good," said Bobby, raising his eyebrows over eyes that had never left the guy in the crosswalk.

The one who was not hurt walked to his friend, put his arm around him, and walked him toward his pickup. Bobby watched them until they had both got in and the truck had pulled away from the curb and into the street, heading south. Everyone else watched them too.

Figuring it was time for him to go, Bobby turned away from the intersection to the sidewalk in front of the ice cream shop. On the way south to his own pickup he thought about chocolate chip ice cream. He could get a cone tomorrow night. He opened the door, tossed the chain over to the passenger side, and stepped up into the crew cab pushing the "START" button as he slid into the driver's seat. As the big Ford came to life Bobby checked his side mirror. Richie and the girls had just cleared the intersection.

Straight down Massachusetts ahead of him there was nothing for a couple blocks, so he made a slow U-turn in front of the Douglas County Courthouse and straightened out toward 11th Street. Bobby lived in North Lawrence; Massachusetts Street would take him straight across the bridge and home.

Farieh and Richie had made it to the sidewalk in front of Silas & Maddy's. Richie had his back to the door and was staring at Farieh like she had just stepped out of a space ship. Farieh was holding Richie's hands. But when she saw the big Ford's movement reflected off the glass of the ice cream parlor and Bobby's face looking at her out the driver's side window, Farieh spun her head around and yelled at him:

"Bobby Hinshaw! Thank you!"

Bobby Hinshaw knew a couple things about the young woman in the yellow head scarf. One: she had a powerful tendency to get herself into trouble. And two: if she ever needed help again, he'd be first in line.

He touched his hand to the brim of his cap and drove on.

# You Can See Salina From Here

Farieh was alone as she walked through Marvin Grove. The campanile was west and up the hill but she had turned south out of the Spencer Museum's parking lot instead. There was shade here all the way to Memorial Drive, the curving street that separated the Museum's sibling, the Spencer Research Library, from the Campanile. Shade was what she wanted right now. It was May, and the option was bright sun at the end of a 90-degree afternoon. *How can it be May? A whole year gone and I'm not only stuck on a guy, I'm stuck on the same guy as a year ago!*

*No,* she thought, *that's not fair. It's not fair to me and it's not fair to the others. I did get stuck on a guy. But I got past Steven. And along the way to now I worked on something important. It took months of organization, and a protest, and a press conference to get here. But we made it.*

Farieh had never slowed as she moved out of the grove, but her stride looked more confident now. *I was never stuck on Richie Armstrong, and I'm not stuck on him now. But Silas & Maddy's happened. Richie was there, he did something exceptional, and he did it for me. I need to acknowledge that. I want to acknowledge that.*

*But how? A thank-you note?* It seemed absurd for Farieh even to acknowledge the option.

*Should I text him? 'Richie? Sorry I never returned your calls from last year. That was really nice of you, risking your life and all out in front of Silas & Maddy's.'* A few more steps. *Totally stupid,* she thought.

She had climbed out of Marvin Grove and had to turn left or right or go back downhill into the sycamores. It would be light for several hours. Jayhawk Boulevard was nearly empty at 6:00, and she didn't care about eating, so she took the sidewalk uphill along the east side of Bailey, turning west along Jayhawk Boulevard. Continuing past Strong Hall, she treated herself to a smile as she remembered how the sit-in had entered the Chancellor's Office like an apparition.

Farieh continued to smile as she remembered Bobby's wading into the downtown confrontation at Silas & Maddy's, and how he had teased Richie about his lack of knife-fighting experience and had used him as a coat rack to get him out of harm's way.

But Richie had stayed until it was over. She remembered how she had felt then. She was grateful to Bobby. But she was so pleased to be with Richie, and to be holding his hands.

The moment collapsed when he asked to walk her home. She told him she was "with friends." And in that careless remark she rejected not only his company but the most important gesture anyone had ever made toward her. Richie withdrew his hands, and then all of him, turning a reddened face away from her as he jogged west on 11th Street to join his teammate.

Farieh had felt awful about it as soon as the words passed her lips, helpless as she watched him move away.

She had walked around the Chi Omega fountain and was headed south, downhill. The protest flashed across her eyes: the first afternoon, the speech at the law school. She could hear Professor Zaidi's voice rising above the thousands of students: "The most important responsibility is to tell the truth."

*When it comes to Richie Armstrong,* she asked herself, *what is the truth?* She didn't know.

A day later, back at Miller Hall, Farieh still did not know where "the truth" lay in their relationship. But she had made a decision about it. She had texted Richie and had invited him to join her at the Union at 7:00 that evening. She was five minutes early. Her head scarf was back in her room.

Her eyes picked him up as he came through the main entrance

from Jayhawk Boulevard, and she waved to catch his attention as he walked toward her table next to the coffee bar on the main floor. He was bigger! Having not kept up with the nearly-constant flow of news about him during the basketball season, Farieh did not know Richie had gained 15 pounds and was half an inch taller than he had been as a freshman. At the end of his sophomore season KU had listed him as 6'7" and 220.

Farieh had been so caught up in the confrontation at Silas & Maddy's she had paid little attention to how Richie looked. He had appeared out of nowhere, and then Bobby Hinshaw took over. She had been with him on the sidewalk for a moment afterward, but then she was distracted by Bobby's departure. And then Richie had asked to walk her home, and she had foolishly said, "No." And then he was gone. The Richie Armstrong standing in front of her now was no longer a boy from Salina. He was a powerfully-built young man.

"Wary" had not been part of Richie's emotional repertoire a year ago, but he was using it now. He would have stood across the table for an hour had she not gotten up and pulled out a chair for him and asked him to sit down.

Farieh had already drunk half of her tea; Richie had not yet bought a drink. "Can I get you a coffee?" she asked. "Do you still like lattes?"

That Farieh had remembered what he liked to drink was a little thing to her. But as Richie smiled at it, the hard set of his shoulders relaxed. "Yes," he said, "I still like them. I should have ordered one. But I saw you, and then I was here at your table. I'll get it. I'll be right back."

As Richie moved toward the coffee bar Farieh watched his back move beneath the fabric of a polo that was at least a size too small for him. He returned with his latte and sat down without any urging on her part. But he said nothing, just took tentative sips and looked at her.

*He is just gorgeous!* she thought to herself.

*And he wants to be here. There is a part of us he remembers, a part that makes him happy. But he has no confidence in it. He does not know what to say, or what to do, or where this might go. But he hasn't left yet. I'm just going to have to lead.*

"We used to take walks. I thought we might take one this evening. Is that okay with you?"

A year ago, Richie's "Sure!" would have followed instantly. There was a moment this time before he said, "We could do that."

It was Farieh's turn to smile. She had wanted that answer more than she realized.

Remembering his impatience of a year ago in this same spot, and willing to tease him with it this evening, Farieh stood up. "Let's go!" she said. As she expected, Richie's first thought was for the latte, barely touched in front of him. What raced across his face was not frustration, and certainly not anger. But surprise was there—a boyish, *You mean NOW?! But I just sat down!* kind of reaction that made Farieh smile again.

She pushed in her chair and headed for the southeast corner of the Union, where the door opened onto Ascher Plaza. She reached the door first and held it to watch Richie walk out into the warm spring evening she had been hoping for when she sent her invitation.

That Richie was quiet as they walked south across the front of Dyche Hall was fine. She had planned the rest of the evening; it was the getting him to this point she had not been able to count on.

They were crossing the street toward Danforth Chapel when Farieh asked the first of her questions.

"Did you know Persian weddings have a thousand flowers?"

Danforth Chapel had flummoxed Richie on one of their earliest walks, and he was not about to discuss weddings tonight, no matter now exotic their setting.

Farieh led them along the east side of Fraser, then up the steps toward its lobby. She had checked to be sure the building would be open for classes that evening. Farieh walked directly to the small elevator on the south wall, pushing the button for "7," the top floor. Richie followed her into the car then turned to face the doors closing in front of him. Even though the trip was familiar—it was the same one Richie had planned himself just a year ago, neither said a word.

When the doors opened on the seventh floor Farieh exited first and turned south for the conference room in the southwest corner. She had been there earlier that day to wedge the door open and to pull up the blinds at the west-side windows. They walked into a room flooded with light from a sun still riding above the trees and buildings of Jayhawk Boulevard. But on ridge lines miles to the west the same sun was sinking into the canopies of different trees; and soon Farieh and Richie could look west without hiding their eyes from its glare.

There were three windows in the west wall. Farieh stood in front of the middle one. To her right, in front of his own window, Richie was no more than four inches away. Needing almost no movement to close that distance she closed it, her right side snug against his chest, her head against his shoulder.

They had been here a year ago, in precisely this place and position. A year ago, Farieh had felt the tension form as she had moved against him then relax as she had stayed. She remembered his heart beating, just as it was beating now. She remembered his face and how he had stared straight ahead, so handsome in the light and the shadow. But Richie never looked at her a year ago, and Farieh had at last moved away.

Farieh asked her second question: "Did you know that if it's not cloudy and you look hard enough, you can see Salina?"

Richie said nothing. But his heart beat faster, just like a year ago. And this year he moved, turning his body away from the sun so he could look down at the face that was turned to his. His expression was puzzled, and his open mouth seemed to confirm his confusion.

Farieh posed her third question to herself: *What is the truth of my relationship with Richie Armstrong?*

She did not know the answer. But Richie could walk her home whenever he wanted.

She stretched up to meet him, covering his open mouth with her own.

# Acknowledgments

Thanks first to my wife, Dru, whose excellence in combing through the drafts of *Farieh* and sorting the tangles I had left is matched only by her patience with me and my love for her.

Thanks to Julie Schonhoff, whose technical skills once again bridged the distance from where I started to professional drafts ready for the editor.

Thea Rademacher, who leads Flint Hills Publishing, supported *Farieh* in the midst of a blizzard of new projects, always treating me as though mine was her only one. Thanks to her and her entire team, especially Amy Albright and Nicole Lopez.

Nathan Fredrickson, my editor, brought so much more than a keen eye. He understands people, especially young people. He recognizes even strong characters have doubts about life. He understands outcomes are not so important as the working toward them, and the choices made along the way.

Louis Copt painted the cover, capturing Farieh's spirit as well as her image.

I was fortunate to have talented people read the drafts and share their reactions. Thanks to David Brown, Ted Everingham, Lara FitzSimmons, Clenece Hills, Phil McKnight, Patty Statham, Kathy Stover, and Matt Wiltanger.

As he did with *Wheat Fields*, Matt Biscan helped with structure and character development and a dozen other things. Most important, he helped when things bogged down and what needed help was not the writing but the writer.

For *Farieh* and for *Wheat Fields*, thanks to the person who inspired Helen Lochlear—Mary Klayder. Perhaps KU's finest teacher of English literature, and certainly one of the most popular, Mary has introduced generations of students to the authors who excited Farieh Bukhari. She has helped lead the honors program;

she has personally led at least a thousand students to Costa Rica, England, and Scotland. Perhaps more brilliantly than anything else, she stays in touch with her students, who love her for it.

# About the Author

Bill Sampson served as a Judge Advocate with the United States Navy before returning to Kansas for private practice. After a legal career trying and managing cases, teaching, and leading professional organizations throughout the country, he retired from the courtroom and now lives in Lawrence with his wife, Dru. Their three children and seven grandchildren live in Philadelphia, San Francisco, and Moscow, Idaho. In 2023, he published his first novel, *Wheat Fields.*

www.billsampson.us